SACRIFICE MOON

"Daniel Jackson is a formidable warrior," Teal'c conceded. "I did not know he had such strength and speed."

"He usually doesn't," Jack said. "Just part of the fun on Adventure Planet." He leaned at a better angle against the ruined wall, the better to prop his head up and give his neck muscles a much-needed rest. "Look. If he's right, this thing may have delayed onset, so we need to watch each other just as much as we watch them, right? Stay alert for any signs of... weird behavior."

"Such as a tendency to violence." Teal'c was quiet for a minute or so, then asked, "How will we then recognize a difference?"

"Teal'c! Was that a joke?"

"I do not believe it was, O'Neill."

Jack snorted and cut his eyes toward Daniel. Yep, the man was napping, head down. Too bad. He'd have liked to have had a witness to that; it had to be a landmark occasion.

"Do you believe we will survive this?" Teal'c asked.

"Hell yes. This is just another Goa'uld. We've kicked their bony butts before. There wasn't enough of Ra left to fill one of those canopic jars Daniel likes so much. By the time we finish here, Teal'c, this goddess is going to wish she'd never heard of Earth."

"I do not believe she has heard of Earth."

"Figure of speech."

STARGÅTE
SG·1™

SACRIFICE MOON

JULIE FORTUNE

FANDEMONIUM BOOKS

An original publication of Fandemonium Ltd, produced under license from MGM Consumer Products.

Fandemonium Books
PO Box 795A
Surbiton
Surrey KT5 8YB
United Kingdom
Visit our website: www.stargatenovels.com

STARGÅTE
SG·1™

METRO-GOLDWYN-MAYER Presents
RICHARD DEAN ANDERSON
in
STARGATE SG-1™
AMANDA TAPPING   CHRISTOPHER JUDGE   DON S. DAVIS
and MICHAEL SHANKS as Daniel Jackson
Executive Producers ROBERT C. COOPER   MICHAEL GREENBURG   RICHARD DEAN ANDERSON
Developed for Television by BRAD WRIGHT & JONATHAN GLASSNER

reprinted 2005

WWW.MGM.COM

ISBN: 0-9547343-1-9
Printed in the United Kingdom by Bookmarque Ltd, Croydon, Surrey

DEDICATION

To JoMadge, without whom this book wouldn't be possible.
Literally.

And to all of my fellow Stargate fans...
hope I got it right, guys.

THANKS

To the staff of the Starbucks in Irving, for caffeine,
moral support, and opening at 5:30 a.m.

Patient editorial assistance provided by Major William Leaf, US
Army, ret., Jackie Leaf, JoMadge, and P.N. Elrod.

Joe Bonamassa, Eric Czar, and Kenny Kramme.
Blues Deluxe saved me.
Go buy it. www.jbonamassa.com

And to the nice folks at Fandemonium, who gave me
the opportunity to play in their sandbox.
(But I'm keeping the action figures.)

CHAPTER I – HOME
σπίτι

"Well, that's…" Dr. Daniel Jackson's eyebrows worked up and down, then settled into a straight line frown. "…Interesting."

Which was one word for it, Colonel Jack O'Neill acknowledged, just not the one he'd have chosen. *Screwy* would have been better. Or, better yet, *weird.* SG-1 gazed – with varying degrees of repulsion or reverence – on the tableaux laid out in front of them. *We have to keep moving,* Jack thought. *Otherwise, they'll pick us off one by one.*

"Captain?" he asked, never taking his eyes off of the danger. Couldn't be too careful, at moments like these.

Captain Samantha Carter, whose brainiac tendencies he was only beginning to fully appreciate, didn't take the hint to move down the serving line. She cocked her shag-cut blonde head to one side, and looked completely fascinated. "It *could* be an alien life form."

"Ya think? Nothing on Earth is that color naturally… Teal'c, trust me, don't touch that." Teal'c, clueless, was reaching for the spoon and scooping some of the lime-green semi-solid substance – allegedly part of a balanced, nutritious breakfast – into a bowl. And putting it on his breakfast tray. "Look, I know you're brave, but really. Nothing to prove, here."

Across the chow line – or, as Jack had started to think of it, the skirmish line – Airman Collins, whose turn it was to take the abuse and serve up cheer with a side order of breakfast, was downright scowling. Jack gave him a brightly false, thin smile and ladled some oatmeal into his own bowl. Oatmeal was safe. Usually.

SG-1 was, ominously, the only human presence in the vast, hostile commissary environment. The only ones not actively at duty stations, anyway. And privately, Jack was starting to wonder if the chefs hidden away in the back really deserved the classification of *human.* He assumed there *were* chefs. It was possible there was alien technology involved.

"This food resembles *rak'tal* from my home world," Teal'c said. Daniel was doing coffee and eggs. Carter wisely stuck with hermetically sealed yogurt and some strawberries that only looked vaguely suspicious and finally took the hint – reinforced by Jack slamming his tray against hers in a bumper-car strategy – to move on from the danger of the glowing-green glop.

Which was lucky. Jack was sure he'd seen something in there move.

Teal'c was holding up the line again. The big guy – *man*, he was big, the sheer physical presence of him would be enough to make most alien life forms hold up their tentacles and surrender – was bent slightly forward, inspecting the mixed fruit with a slight frown grooving the skin around his gleaming gold forehead thing. He directed a slightly deeper frown at Airman Collins, who looked intimidated. Teal'c finally retrieved a bowl full of nuclear-colored cubes and moved on.

Jack wondered if the shaved head thing was a fashion statement. Most of the other Jaffa he'd seen (shot) hadn't favored the chrome-dome look. *Have to ask him that sometime.*

But given the frown, probably not right now. "So. Good stuff, *rak'tal*?" he asked Teal'c.

"No."

"But you got it anyway."

"Do you not form attachments to campaign food, O'Neill?"

"Look, I admit, sometimes I get a craving for a good MRE…"

Teal'c looked blank, which might or might not indicate that he failed to understand.

"Meals, Ready to Eat," Daniel supplied, reaching over Teal'c for silverware. "Excuse me. Also known as Meals Rejected by Everyone."

"Who told you that?" Carter asked, amused.

"Major Kawalsky."

As soon as Daniel said it, there was that second of silence, that shadow that slid like an oil slick over Jack's soul. Charlie Kawalsky had been dead just four days. His had been one more in an endless series of memorial services Jack had attended, buttoned up in dress blues. It had also been the first one at which he'd refused to give a eulogy. He couldn't talk about Kawalsky. Not without remembering how he'd given the order to close the Stargate and shave off half of Kawalsky's skull.

Daniel either felt the tension or was off in his usual Daniel-place, because he went on with his voice pitched in the Sahara-dry range. "Jack, for the love of God, tell me those aren't limes next to the pancakes."

"Goes with the tequila syrup," Jack responded. Carter groaned. He poured whatever coffee that Daniel hadn't already appropriated, and took point, heading for his favorite table. Well, newly favorite. It was all pretty new around here. Still smelled of cleaning products and fresh paint, or maybe that was *rak'tal*. He settled down in a chair and began doctoring his oatmeal to his satisfaction. "Remind me to tell the General that we need to kidnap a real chef for this facility."

Daniel settled in the chair across from him, Carter at his elbow. Teal'c took Jack's left, settling into the plastic chair carefully – he still wasn't quite convinced, Jack thought, that Earth furniture wasn't going to collapse. Too used to the big-ass overdone stuff the Goa'uld liked.

Teal'c spooned the green goop resembling *rak'tal* into his mouth, chewed contemplatively, and announced, "It is not unpleasant."

"Sure, that's what you say *now,* just wait until they come up with the ever-popular goulash…"

"I have served in many places worse than this facility. Why would someone not wish to give service here?"

Oh. Right. Teal'c wasn't talking about the green stuff.

"It's just that here on Earth, people have a lot more freedom to choose where they want to work. And live," Daniel said. Always the lecturer. Hadn't changed a bit. Jack dusted his oatmeal with sugar. "Serving here in this command is probably not the hottest job in the world, for – well – people who aren't – "

"Crazy?" Jack offered. "Bug-eyed nuts? Clinically – "

"Actually," Sam Carter cut in as she peeled back the lid on her yogurt, "General Hammond told me he's had to turn away volunteers for almost every position."

Jack gestured at Teal'c's rapidly disappearing bowl of goop. "And yet, with the *rak'tal*."

"Sir, have you ever met canteen food you liked?"

"Beside the point, Captain, and I didn't notice you signing up for the green alien goo from beyond."

She surrendered the conversational field. Teal'c finished the bowl, got up and went back for seconds. Daniel watched him, a forkful of eggs halfway to his mouth, and said, "He's fitting in, don't you think?"

"Better than you," Jack said cheerfully. When Daniel blinked behind his glasses, hurt, he amended it to, "Okay, the first time. You remember. Ferretti had fun making your life hell, as I recall."

Carter watched with bright eyes. She was always alert for any tidbits of information between them about that first mission on Abydos. She'd read all the reports, Jack knew, but those probably didn't include the less than enthusiastic welcome Kawalsky and Ferretti had given a long-haired, four-eyed, sneezing geek who didn't know one end of an MP5 from the other. Daniel had been along on sufferance, and at the time Jack hadn't given a crap because he hadn't expected to survive the trip himself. And hadn't wanted to.

Something about this oatmeal just didn't smell right. Maybe it was the limes by the pancakes. Lime contamination.

"I don't think anybody around here will be kicking sand in Teal'c's face. Including Ferretti." Daniel said, and scooted over as Teal'c eased back in at the table. It wasn't so much the Jaffa's admittedly impressive physical mass as the even larger bowl of goop, judging by the way Daniel leaned away from it. "Ah, how *is* Ferretti, by the way?"

"Doing okay, according to Doc Warner. Couple of weeks in the infirmary, then some rehab. Practically a flesh wound." Granted, Jack's definition of "flesh wound" was more flexible than most, but he thought Ferretti would appreciate a lack of public concern. "Something wrong with your eggs, Daniel?"

"Still not used to home cooking, I guess." The man *did* look green around the gills. "I'm okay."

"Ah, the famous *I'm okay*. Get thee to the infirmary, let Doc Warner poke at you a while. That'll make you feel better."

Daniel pushed his tray back and focused on his coffee. "What time's the briefing?"

"Fourteen hundred."

"I forget, what is that in civilian time?"

"Two o'clock, Dr. Jackson," Carter supplied.

"You really don't have to keep calling me doctor. Not even my students did that, if they survived the first boring lecture. Daniel's just fine." He sent her a rare smile – rare these days, after having his wife Sha're taken from him, and pretty much everything else he had to care about. Jack had forgotten what kind of wattage Daniel had, when he turned it on. Even Carter, who he suspected was notoriously thick about these things, seemed to get a jolt.

"Daniel," she amended. "Right. You taught?"

"In my field, you can't exactly avoid it."

"Hey, we have something in common. I lecture every year at the Air Force Academy…"

Jack sat, watching the two of them chatting, like friends, remembering how long it had taken him to warm up to Daniel – admittedly, that had been his own problem, his head hadn't exactly been in a good place – and seeing Teal'c calmly accept his place next to them. Not speaking, but somehow participating anyway. Something in his body language, and those surprisingly gentle dark eyes.

This might actually work, he thought, and felt something that had been clenched like a fist inside of him – since he'd seen Charlie Kawalsky die – slowly relax.

It took time to build a team. Time, and trust, and respect.

He sipped coffee and was content to listen.

At fourteen hundred on the dot, Jack appeared at the top of the stairs in the briefing room. He surveyed the room, turned to Sergeant Siler, coming up the stairs behind him, and said, "Pay up." He wiggled his fingers for emphasis.

Siler looked over his shoulder, sighed, and took twenty dollars out of his wallet. Jack snatched it away.

Captain Carter, sitting alone at the conference table, watched with a frown buckling her forehead. "What was that?" she asked as he took a chair next to her at the big mahogany conference table. The leather sighed patiently under his weight.

"Well, Siler bet me that I'd be the first one here. I bet him that *you'd* be the first one here."

"Why me?"

"Because Teal'c will follow me – " And there, right on cue, was the heavy tread of Teal'c's steps on the treads, heading up. "And somebody's going to have to install an alarm clock in Daniel's ass to remind him of briefings, especially if he's reading, and I don't mean anything fascinating, I'm talking cereal boxes, here."

He kept it light, but he couldn't honestly tell if Sam Carter was one of those stick-up-her-butt officers who disapproved of gambling, along with dancing and drinking and smiling in public. Good to get it out in the open if she was. He could deal with it, but he wanted a little warning.

She looked at him for a few seconds, then said, without a flicker of her blank expression, "Twenty bucks says Daniel will be here in less than two minutes."

"Oh, I don't want to take your money, Captain." He gave her an evil smile. Hers was nearly a match.

"Well, I'd like to take yours. Two minutes." She tapped her watch.

"Five, and that's only if we page him."

"Done." She opened the fancy leather binders set out on the table and looked at the EYES ONLY red-striped folder inside. "P3X-595 sounds like a very interesting place, don't you think?"

"I hear it's nice this time of year."

"Actually, sir, from the axial tilt of the planet in relation to its star it's probably – "

He held up a hand. "Captain Carter, tell me: am I going to care about what you're about to say?"

She looked thrown, but only for a second. He was used to Daniel, who just kept talking. Nice to know his second in command actually *listened*. "Depends on how much you like hot weather, sir. It could be as hot as Abydos. We'll know more when the MALP data is fully analyzed."

Jack checked his watch. Forty-five seconds left on Carter's bet, which would put him up forty dollars in five minutes. Not bad, for a Monday.

Teal'c settled into a chair next to Carter, and he offered them a restrained, dignified nod. Jack responded with an absent "Hey," since he was focused on the seconds counting down. He raised a cautionary finger. Carter was checking her own watch too, brow starting to furrow in concern.

And then Jack heard a fast thump of boots on the stairs, and Daniel's disheveled head poked up over the railing. He had an arm full of books. "Am I late?" he asked breathlessly.

Carter should *not* look that smug. Not if she knew what was good for her. "Not at all, doctor."

Jack sent Daniel a mean, murderous look, which slid off without effect, since Daniel was juggling a notepad, a coffee cup, and some thick leather-bound books as he approached the table. "Daniel?"

"Jack?" He looked up over the tops of his glasses, blue eyes caffeine-bright.

"*Why* are you on time?"

Daniel held up his wrist. Strapped to it was a brand new Air Force-issue watch, complete with alarm features. "Captain Carter set the reminder function… ?"

Jack turned to look at Carter. Her hand was out. Fingers wiggling significantly.

He sighed, dug Siler's twenty out of his pocket, and turned it over just as the door at the end of the room opened and Major General George Hammond stepped through. Big, balding, approaching retirement, he should have looked grandfatherly and missed it by a mile. Something about the eyes, which were as sharp and assessing as any drill sergeant's. Scuttlebutt in the halls said that Hammond's bullshit detector was legendary, and Jack had personal cause to know it was true. Hammond had certainly called *his* bluff the first time they'd met, with a dead-eyed threat to blow the crap out of Daniel and everybody left on Abydos.

If it *had* been a bluff. Truthfully, Jack couldn't quite tell.

He and Carter came to their feet until Hammond was seated. Daniel looked conflicted, as if he was wondering what the protocol was for a civilian; Teal'c rose a second later and offered a respectful inclination of his head. Daniel, remaining seated, settled for a nod.

Hammond nodded back, confirming Daniel's choice, and then swept the rest of SG-1 with a look. "Be seated, people. We've got a lot of ground to cover." His gaze fell on the twenty-dollar bill in Carter's hand. "Offering me a tip, Captain?"

"No sir. Sorry sir." She hastily stuffed it in a convenient BDU pocket.

Jack hid a smile and settled back in his chair, folded his hands over his unopened folder, and gave the General his best attentive expression.

"I trust everyone has reviewed the briefing materials."

Nods all around, except for Jack, who tried to keep the attentive look while shooting Carter a significant glance.

"There were materials?" he murmured. Daniel silently slid a memo down the table to him. "Oh. *Those* materials."

Hammond skewered him with a stare, decided not to press the issue, and continued. "*As you know*, the MALP data on P3X-595 shows a very warm Earthlike atmosphere, much like what we found on Abydos and Chulak, but with a higher humidity level. Dr. Jackson, go ahead with your briefing."

"Of course." Daniel slid out of his seat and pressed a control to dim the lights, then another to bring up a video still image. It was distorted and static-tattered, but clearly showed some kind of wide landing, with the steps leading down that seemed to be a design feature of just about every Stargate. "As you can see, this is… um… I guess the word would be unexpected…"

What made this one different were the *people*.

Lots of 'em. Crowding around the MALP, looking curious. They were wearing what looked like…

"Togas?" Jack said, eyebrows raised. "Wait, didn't we just do the Rome thing back on Chulak?"

"I don't think each planet will necessarily have a different cultural derivation, and actually, those aren't togas, Jack, they're tunics or chitons, probably of Greek origin… notice the draping of the – "

"Greek?" Jack interrupted.

Daniel, undaunted, took it up right where he'd been. "Notice the draping of – "

"Daniel." Jack made it a flat two-syllable roadblock; Daniel's explanation crashed into silence. For a second, Jack was sorry, but only for a second. "Okay, fine, great threads. So what are we looking at?"

Daniel took it for the olive branch it was. "Well… they're friendly. Or at least we don't see any weapons in evidence here. Also, look at the range of people pictured. Young, old, even children. And I don't see anyone who looks like a Jaffa, do you?"

"There are none present in this image," Teal'c said definitively.

"In fact, there's nobody with *any* kind of marking to suggest that this is a Goa'uld stronghold. No Jaffa, no – " Daniel tapped his forehead. "Tattooing, not even any jewelry depicting Egyptian symbols, which seems to be pretty standard among the Goa'uld, so far as we've seen to date."

"The other thing is that nobody seems alarmed at the presence of the MALP," Carter pointed out. "They just look curious."

"Exactly, Captain – Doctor – which is a very interesting point," Daniel nodded enthusiastically. "We'd assume if the Goa'uld *weren't* present that there would be nobody coming through their Stargate, but it looks like a pretty busy place, judging from the number of people we're seeing from the video. Either the Stargate is in a high traffic area, or…"

"What's our objective, General?" Jack asked. "They look like nice folks, snappy dressers, but if there's no Goa'uld, what's the tactical mission?"

"This is only your second scheduled mission through the Stargate, Colonel," Hammond said. "I don't know what the tactical mission might be. We're on a fact-finding brief at this point. Our mandate from the President is to perform reconnaissance, assess any threats that may exist, and make peaceful contact with these people. If the Goa'uld *aren't* present on this world, it's possible these people might have found a way to eliminate them, or at least deter them."

"And they're obviously operating at a pretty high cultural level," Daniel jumped in. "If what I see here is representative, it's a prosperous, living history of ancient Greek society. We can't possibly *not* explore this place, regardless of what kind of technology exists here. And we can offer them some kind of trade, build peaceful relations…"

Oh, great, Jack thought. *Now it's some kind of U.N. mission. Those always work so well.* He turned to Teal'c. "This place look familiar to you?"

Teal'c was studying the picture closely. "It is difficult to be certain. Apophis rules many worlds. This has some resemblance to one he visited, though rarely."

"But there would have been Jaffa on duty at the Stargate, if Apophis ruled the planet, right?" Carter asked. Teal'c nodded. "Then this might not be his world at all."

Daniel looked solemn. "But if it *is* his world, then maybe they have some idea where Sha're and Skaara might have been taken. Jack, we can't take the chance. We have to at least investigate the possibility."

Hammond folded his thick hands together and leaned forward, elbows on the table. It occurred to Jack – late – that this was the first time he'd seen the General out of his full dress kit. The short-sleeved look suited him, made him look more hands-on, less consciously intimidating.

Not less authoritative, though.

"Colonel?" Hammond asked, focused on him. Jack was starting to get a feel for Hammond's command style, and it mostly added up to *choose the best people and trust the hell out of them.* And probably *kick their collective asses when they screw up.*

He could live with that.

Jack nodded. "Guess we're a go, sir."

"Go it is." Hammond shut his folder. "SG-1, see the Quartermaster for your gear. Captain Carter, what's the next full daylight window on this world?"

"The MALP's been there long enough to take some readings. By our calculations, it's before dawn there now, sir. Any time before twenty-one hundred should put us in for a daylight arrival."

"Let's make it a departure at seventeen hundred. I'll get the orders drawn up." Hammond stood. Jack, Carter and Teal'c rose with him; Daniel, already standing, settled for another cautious nod. "Dismissed, people."

Jack picked up the memo that Daniel had left on the table as Hammond closed the door of his ready room. "Oh, Daniel?"

Daniel was already gathering up books, coffee cup, pens, leather binder, folder… he paused in the act of juggling. "Yes?"

"Funny thing, but this memo has my name on it."

"Well... yes... I was supposed to give it to you. Nobody knows where your office is. Including me, by the way."

"Good. Let's keep it that way." Jack flicked the memo across the table with a fingernail toward Carter, who fielded it and put it in her own folder. "Captain, as my second in command, you're the keeper of the paperwork. And, next time a little pre-mission briefing, okay?"

"Absolutely, Colonel."

Was that a smile? Nah.

Couldn't be.

Based on Hammond's seventeen-hundred departure time, they had three hours to kill.

Jack chivvied his team into the Quartermaster's office, without so much as a restroom break. Ultra-secret, high-tech, save-the-world kind of stuff as this program might be, he knew damn good and well that Quartermasters offices around the world ran at exactly the same speed... slowly.

Four standard SG field packs, two MP5s, three Beretta sidearms, and one staff weapon later, they'd wasted nearly two hours, between the inventorying, packing, unpacking, repacking, and forms. There were *always* forms. Even Daniel had been spooked by the amount of paper being generated.

Which left them an hour. Carter, who'd taken on the role of Daniel's keeper, helped him set his alarm for departure time, which in typical military fashion she specified as t-minus ten minutes. *To be early is to be on time, to be on time is to be late.* Waiting was a sacred meditation.

Jack had dispensed with that years ago. He showed up on the dot, every time, but knowing Daniel, having a ten-minute window of opportunity probably wasn't a bad idea. Still wouldn't keep him from being late, but it would keep him from holding things up too much.

Funny, how well he seemed to know Daniel, considering they'd spent all of a couple of days together, more than a year ago. But they'd been highly concentrated days, full of the kind of stresses that either tore people apart or forged them together for life. He could tell that Carter felt disadvantaged by that, but she'd adjust; in this line of work, they'd all get a chance to build those bonds. The trouble was, it would probably come at one hell of a price. It usually did.

After a relaxing hour of target shooting in the base range, he cleaned his weapons and got everything ready, and strolled into the Embarkation Room at exactly seventeen-hundred hours, to find the team – even Daniel – already assembled.

"Sir," Carter said. She looked tense and a little flushed. Adrenaline pumping.

Jack nodded to her, to Teal'c, and fastened a weather eye on Daniel, who looked keen as a new recruit. "Got your Kleenex?" he asked.

"Even better," he said. "Prescription allergy pills." Then, inevitably, an uncertain look. "And, ah, tissues. For backup."

"Good plan." Jack turned to look up at the control room, where General Hammond stood at a loose parade rest, staring out. "Radio test."

They each confirmed their radio reliability, and he made a *crank it up* gesture at the little guy in the glasses, the one seated at the console next to Hammond. *Need to find out his name,* he reminded himself. *Probably a good guy to know, considering he has his finger on the button to close that iris thing and smash us into little particles so small even Carter couldn't measure them...*

Then he settled in to watch the Stargate begin to dial.

Something awesome about that, watching the massive bulky thing fire up, the inner ring begin to grind its way around. Chevrons locked, each in turn, with heavy metallic *chunks*. This close to it, he felt a surge of electricity sweep over him, not exactly static, not exactly anything he'd felt anywhere outside of this room. His skin shivered into gooseflesh.

When Chevron Six encoded, the room started to shake. He rode the turbulence with practiced ease, watched the seventh symbol lock in.

Plasma boiled toward them in a furious explosion, reaching nearly twenty feet straight out, and then collapsed back to form the glittering, liquid-silk entrance to the rest of the universe.

"Wow," Carter breathed. "Just doesn't get old."

"Nope." Jack adjusted his hat. "Carter, take point, move out of the line of fire when you arrive. Daniel, you're next. Teal'c, behind me."

At his nod, Carter strode up the incline of the ramp, heading for another world.

CHAPTER 2 – JOURNEY
ταξίδι

It was like falling, just for an instant, into a sea of stars that blazed and froze and tore him apart and put him back together, and then he was falling as gravity took hold and rolled him painfully, two or three feet.

Jack landed flat on his back, staring up at a *really* bright white sun, and heard Daniel sneeze, hard, two times.

A black shadow occluded the sun, and Carter reached down and hauled him to his feet, then gave the same assistance to Daniel, who was blowing into a tissue nearby. Teal'c was up, hell, he'd probably never even gone down.

They were the center of attention.

You could have heard a pin drop. The scrape of their boots on stone sounded ridiculously loud, because nobody else was moving. There were more people than probably even Daniel had been expecting – at least thirty or forty in the near vicinity of the team on the landing, and another hundred or so in the large open square below the steps.

Jack's first tactical instinct kicked in, scanning for threats, and came up with nothing. No weapons in evidence, nobody making hostile moves.

Kind of a nice surprise, actually.

The people had on a wide variety of colors and styles – long tunics, short ones, in blues and greens and golds and prints like tartans; some looked like silk, some like cotton. Gold trim. Sandals. Nice hair.

Civilized sort of place.

Everyone was standing in neat little carefully roped lines, under canvas canopies. There were desks set up in rows in front of the lines, too, fancy curlicued things with backless stools for chairs and men perched on them who were writing on what looked like sheets of pale paper.

People had *bags*. Carrying bags, with handles. Some even had wheels. There was a pallet full of bags stacked nearby, with a large sign on it in symbols that seemed to be – and this was just a guess on Jack's part, because he'd seen enough fraternity shirts in his day – Greek.

"Oh my God," Daniel said numbly. "Do you see this? This is… incredible!"

Jack turned and looked for the MALP. The bulky robot was parked over on the side, labeled with another sign, tucked in a corral full of battered-looking luggage.

"Daniel," he said slowly, "Tell me what that sign says."

"Lost and found," Daniel translated.

They all stood in silence and contemplated the strangeness.

After a few seconds, the natives started talking. Loudly. Mostly commenting to each other, pointing, but some getting argumentative with the – staff? – sitting behind the desks. One of the functionaries got off his chair and ran up the steps, looking anxious and harried; he had ink-stained fingers, and his toga – tunic? – was yellowed and frayed at the hems. Knobby knees. Definitely a working-class man.

Jack backed off from the frenzied gestures and resisted the impulse to swing the MP5 into a firing line. "Daniel? Little help?"

Daniel was focused intently on the man's fast-firing speech. He made the universal gesture for *slower*, looking uncomprehending, and the man took a deep breath and evidently started over. Annoyed. How exactly had SG-1 gone from the locals bowing and scraping and hailing them as gods to some bureaucrat being *annoyed* at their arrival? Jack felt robbed.

"I was right, it's a derivation of Ancient Greek. Ah… he says we're off schedule," Daniel interpreted. "There aren't supposed to be any incoming travelers right now. This is the departure hour."

They all stared in silence at the lines of people, the bags, the paperwork. One guy getting searched by a burly-looking man in a dark tunic, who confiscated what looked like a belt knife.

The lost luggage corral.

"It's an airport," Jack said, resigned. "We're at a freakin' airport."

"All we need are the vending machines," Daniel agreed, and then pointed to a vendor at a cart handing out drinks and paper-wrapped snacks.

"Okay, now that's just *weird*."

Their harried bureaucrat upped the volume on his complaints. Daniel focused on him again. "He's asking us to get off the, ah, I guess for want of a better word it would be *runway*," Daniel said. "Apparently, we're holding up the scheduled departures."

The guy was making furiously animated shooing gestures. Jack led the way down the steps, then followed the air-shoves off to the left. Behind them, a group of people queued up near the DHD, chattering and staring at SG-1's strange gear.

Dark-tunic guys ahoy. Ah. Airport security. Figured. One of them flexed his muscles, but next to Teal'c he was nothing to write home about. Not that Jack hoped it would come to hand-to-hand, because if it did, well, there was Daniel.

One of them made an unmistakable *give it over* kind of gesture, and pointed to Jack's MP5.

"They're not touching my weapons," Jack said pleasantly. "Might want to tell him that before we get into the shouting and hitting part of diplomacy."

Daniel was deep into his *Hi, we're peaceful explorers* speech, which he seemed to reel out with practiced ease. *Prepped it before we came, eh?* He could well imagine Daniel standing in front of the mirror, trying out non-threatening expressions. Well, fine, that was his job. Jack's was to look dangerous, though probably not as dangerous as Teal'c, who had that frozen cold distance thing down pat. Probably had a class in it at Apophis University.

Carter was... fascinated. Looking everywhere at once, taking in more than Jack would probably ever see if he spent a week with a camera. Hammond had warned him she was way smarter than him, and he was strongly reminded of it in the cogent way she surveyed the layout of the place. He decided to take advantage of it, at least. "Captain Carter? Thoughts?"

She could barely tear her eyes away from her appraisal. "Apart from their understandable confusion, I don't see anybody panicking, sir. They're used to visitors here, though we're out of the ordinary. Dr. Jackson would be able to say for sure, but it sounded to me like a number of languages being spoken out there, which means a very multi-cultural sort of place." She paused. "Have you ever seen *any-*

thing like this before?"

"In my vast experience? No. Which means, oh, exactly zero, Carter. I've been to *Abydos*. Even Daniel will tell you it wasn't the crossroads of the universe."

"Sir, I just can't see this kind of industry springing up under Goa'uld rule. They strike me as anti-trade, unless it's to their benefit. And this isn't exactly slave labor. It's more like…" She nodded at a family of five clustered nearby in one of the lines. Baby in arms, three-year-old squalling and clutching at Mom's skirts, Dad looking harried, an older boy trying to appear haughtily disinterested. "This sounds crazy, sir, but that looks like vacation, sir. Holiday travel. Something like that."

"I'm still adjusting to the fact that they have a *lost and found*."

"Sir, these people look, well, normal."

He couldn't dispute that. The more he looked past the costumes – and truthfully, they weren't as wild as all that, he'd seen stranger things walking around Times Square – the more he saw people who might not have been out of place back home in blue jeans and sneakers, kicking their heels at LaGuardia or LAX. A few were sitting on their baggage, reading scrolls or sipping drinks.

Drinks… he followed the lines and saw a building off to the side. With a built-in counter. And high, three-legged stools with patrons firmly in place. More tables and chairs inside, in the shade.

Of course. What was an airport without a bar? The resilience of the human spirit never failed to amaze him. You plunk a few people down in alien terrain, give them nothing to do, and within a few weeks, one of them would master home brewing…

"Jack!" Daniel was back, glowing with enthusiasm. "This is Iestos, he's, well, I guess you'd call him a ticket agent. I've explained to him we came through the Stargate."

"And?"

"And he gave me a list of three planets we could have come from! Delphi, Sikyon, Mycenae – Jack, they're names of ancient Greek city-states! This is incredible – apparently each of these worlds has trade routes through the Stargate to this place and – "

"Vacation travel, yeah, we got that." Daniel's enthusiasm was contagious. Jack had a hard time keeping his necessary pessimism intact.

"You made him understand we didn't just get separated from our tour group, right?"

"He understands that we're from a world outside of their normal routes – it's called the Helos Confederacy, apparently – and the name of this world is Chalcis, by the way." Daniel took a deep breath and visibly calmed himself. "He's sending a message to his superiors. We're supposed to wait."

The dark-tunic guys – who didn't need Security badges to identify them, the body language was unmistakable – were looking nervous about all the talking and gesturing. Jack tried a friendly smile. None of them smiled back. "So? We wait?"

"Yes."

Jack let a brief silence go by. "Right here? In the sun? 'Cause it's going to get toasty."

"Well…" Daniel looked around and focused on the building. "There's a place to wait in the shade over there."

"That's some kind of tavern, Daniel."

"Oh." Daniel's eyebrows went up. "And…?"

For the life of him, Jack couldn't think of a single reason not to do it. He turned to the security guys and said, "Right. We'll… be in the bar."

Two important things to learn about offworld bars.

One, money was important. Daniel had managed to trade some kind of jewelry he'd brought along – for the sake of history, Jack hoped it wasn't beads – for a round of local brew. Jack had specified nonalcoholic, but Daniel wasn't sure the concept had translated. Teal'c unhesitatingly tasted his, and said gravely, "This contains intoxicating substances."

"Right. Stick to canteens." He gazed at Teal'c for a few seconds. "But it's safe, right? Not poisonous or anything?"

"I do not believe so. My symbiote would react if the drink contained anything harmful."

That did it. Jack frankly couldn't resist a sip – not every day you run across alien daiquiris – and was surprised at the taste that exploded on his tongue. Heavy, silky, fruity, sweet, with a nice brisk slap at the end for freshness. "Not bad," he said. Might try it on the way back, especially if they ended up stuck in the departure line for, oh, hours. Take a sample of it back for the lab geeks. Might have some medicinal purposes.

Oh, the heavy duty of exploring the galaxy...

Daniel was examining his glass too – not the drink, the glass. Turning it around in his hands like some kind of precious artifact – which, Jack realized, it probably was, from an archaeologist's point of view.

"It's hand blown," Daniel announced. "Not very well made, but – "

"It's a bar glass." Carter finished his sentence. "It stands to reason they'd make them sturdy rather than decorative."

Which made Daniel's face light up. "Well, you'd think so, but some of the cups we unearthed at digs around Athens really showed a very high level of sophistication in manufacturing techniques, not to mention style. The sand here must have a completely different composition – most glass from this period on Earth is green, maybe yellow, but this is more iridescent... of course you get iridescence with age and oxidation, but --"

"Kids," Jack said. "Take it outside if you're gonna geek out. Teal'c and I are trying to maintain our dignity."

He could have sworn the Jaffa smiled. Or quivered a lip, at least.

Daniel looked offended. "*Geek out*? Jack, we're here to observe, record, learn – "

"Like I said. Geek out." He didn't mean it; it was part of their established patter, and it helped keep everybody from tensing up. Including Daniel.

Daniel probably would have continued the verbal duel, but he was interrupted by the approach of a large band of well-dressed, well-scrubbed men in long robes.

"So, they're not togas?" Jack muttered. "Look kinda like togas."

"Tunics. Actually, they're chitons, Jack. Oh, or peplos, and that guy with a cloak, that's a himation,"

"Chitons. Isn't that insect skin...?"

"That's chitinous."

"Oh, sure, and there isn't a connection... ?"

Daniel just stared back, thrown. Jack gave him a thin smile and stood up to greet the newcomers.

Daniel recovered and blurted out the standard universal translator greeting, *we come in peace* or *peaceful explorers* or *take me to your leader*. He needn't have bothered. It was pretty obvious that the guy Jack was facing *was* the leader, or at least high level enough to make decisions.

He was tall, broad-shouldered, a little older than Jack's age, apparently; thick silver-gray hair, worn in long curls, fastened here and there with gold pins and clips. Dark eyes. Jack didn't normally meet a lot of men in eye makeup, but he'd hit a run of them recently... Apophis, Teal'c, now this guy, who had dramatic sweeps of eye liner and something shiny on his lids.

He was wearing that summer-weight wool, like some of the others out there waiting in line; apparently, he wanted to be a man of the people. Only his wool was high quality, the clasp pins on his tunic were intricately worked gold with ram's heads, and he had that sleek, tailored look of somebody accustomed to the finer things in life.

His name, Daniel supplied, was Acton.

"Pleased to meet you," Jack said, and extended his hand. Acton reached out and did a wrist-to-wrist grip. The guy had an orator's deep, plummy voice, as well as the authoritative body language, but it was just noise to Jack. He sent Daniel an inquiring look.

"He says they're honored to have us as guests."

"So this is going well."

"Seems to be."

Jack extricated himself from the man's grip, smiled and nodded. Heads bobbed in the delegation behind Acton. Everybody looked cautiously pleased.

Daniel listened to another fast burst of syllables, then offered, "They want to give us hospitality at – I'm guessing the word means lodge. Or maybe hotel."

"So long as it's not prison, hey, not turning it down."

Daniel didn't need to translate the *after-you* gestures the delegation was making. They were all trying their damnedest to look friendly about it, too, except for Acton, who stayed dignified, and two extremely cold-eyed guys in the back that Jack had pegged for some kind of internal security. Or maybe their breakfast had been served up by a really bad mess line, too.

Outside of the tavern, Jack slid on his sunglasses against the fierce glare, much to Acton's interest; he handed them over at Acton's curious gesture, and watched the guy slide them on and look around. There was a great deal of outcry from the lackeys that Jack hardly needed Daniel to translate – he knew the sound of sucking up when he heard it. *Oh, sir, those are you! They make you look so august and imposing!* Acton brushed it off, well accustomed to having his butt kissed, and handed the glasses back to Jack with an appreciative smile. Jack silently gestured for him to keep them, and took another pair out of a handy pocket on his tac vest.

Acton looked pleased as punch as he slid on the shades.

"I think you've discovered a huge trade opportunity, sir," Carter said, poker-faced under her own sunglasses and cap. "We export Ray-Bans to alien worlds."

"That and chocolate bars, Captain. Okay, let's move out, kids, before our cool wears off."

He followed Acton's lead, heading out. As he did, the local Stargate behind them belched out plasma and settled into a waiting blue circle. A neat line of travelers began walking through – parents, children, old folks. Chattering like the trip was nothing to speak of. Like they'd all done it before.

Daniel was right. This was interesting.

Jack just hoped it wouldn't, like the Chinese curse suggested, be *too* interesting.

It was a long way to wherever they were going. For one thing, the Stargate seemed to be outside of town proper; when they emerged from the big gray stone walls that enclosed the courtyard, Jack saw lots of scrub-covered hills rolling down toward a glittering blue sea, and – up a long slope – a city. A *big* one. It straggled halfway down the hill, in stepped terraces of gleaming white buildings. A pale road snaked toward it, jammed with pedestrians and a few slow-moving carts.

"Unbelievable," Daniel murmured, stopping next to Jack's shoulder. He pointed at a massive, majestic temple, complete with big white columns, sitting on the crest of the hill. "Jack, that's an Acropolis."

"Like Athens."

"… Only this one's intact and functioning. Probably the seat of the city's religious center. God, just *look* at it! Jack, we'll be able to see how things are arranged inside – the exact placement of the altars and statues…"

"Fabulous. So, we walk?" Jack said.

Carter nodded toward the shade at the back of the wall. "I hate to say it, but… do you think those could be taxis?"

Next to another sign labeled in Greek, there were lines of horses, carts and what looked like chariots, and a bunch of guys idling in the dirt, throwing the local equivalent of dice. Acton's people sprang into action, shouting, and the taxi drivers – Jack wished she hadn't said that, now he couldn't get it out of his head – crowded around, gesturing urgently at their vehicles and spouting torrents of words that could only be testimonials to how comfortable, fast and affordable they were. Acton gave a couple of sharp, barking orders, and it got sorted. Acton's sporty-looking personal conveyance rolled up, taking the Head Cheese and three lucky suckers-up; the keen-eyed security guys Jack had noted got their own ride all to themselves. It looked fast and anonymous, and the charioteer had scars on top of his scars, a squashed nose, and banks of swords and daggers built into his – what would you call that? Dashboard?

Jack and Carter ended up in one taxi, Daniel and Teal'c in another, crammed in with the remainder of Acton's retainers. Their driver, who smelled like garlic and good old-fashioned sweat, snapped the reins and the horses clopped calmly up the hill toward the city.

The sun beat down mercilessly, and Jack adjusted his cap to give maximum coverage as he held to the metal railing for stability. Carter had been right: it was going to get hot. Over in the other cart – chariot – whatever, Daniel was chattering to the driver and translating for Teal'c's benefit. Whether or not Teal'c was interested. The Jaffa looked alert and relaxed, staff weapon braced next to his feet. He wasn't holding the rail. Jack tried letting go, but the next hard jolt nearly sent him off the back of the vehicle.

Must have been a Jaffa thing.

"Sir," Carter said, and pointed. "Think that's a cemetery?"

Sure looked like one. Small marble cenotaphs scattered along the roadside, many with little bundles of dried flowers lying in front of the closed doors of miniature marble buildings. A few statues; Jack couldn't tell if they were meant to be guardian gods, or memorials of real people. Real people, he thought. One in particular, of a woman seated on a bench, holding a child in her arms... there were fresh flowers next to that one, fluttering pale petals in the ocean breeze.

"Better watch Daniel," Jack finally said. "Make sure he doesn't dive off to explore."

Sure enough, from the other cart, Daniel was leaning over the rail, making a photographic record of their progress and looking dangerously frustrated at not getting a closer peek. He had a brief conversation with Teal'c, which Jack imagined went something like, *I think I'll get off and look around,* and Teal'c saying, *Then I will have to hurt you, Daniel Jackson,* because Daniel ended up staying on the chariot and looking disappointed as the cenotaphs receded in the distance.

Soon enough, they were approaching the city walls.

Big city walls. Jack craned his neck, looking up, and decided the granite blocks must have stretched about fifty feet into the air. Some buckling, here and there, but not enough to weaken the defenses; it looked pretty damn formidable. It'd take some serious firepower to bring this place down, bombing runs by B1B Lancers, maybe. Which he was pretty sure wouldn't fit through the Stargate in the first place. The security had Abydos beat all to hell.

A huge set of wooden gates, reinforced with iron strips, stood open, and traffic passed freely in and out. A couple of Acton's retainers hopped down as they slowed and ran ahead to shout and shove a path through the crush of people and carts gathered inside the walls, and pretty soon, they were passing into the sunlight again and the city proper.

Under the merciless blue sky and hot golden sun, the city gleamed. Mostly white, but here and there Jack saw pale pink, blue, green, even a splash of red trim on a window. Flowers in boxes, graceful-looking pines and evergreens planted in rows to provide much-needed shade. Lots of billowing canvas-like awnings. The street was paved with interlocking stones, and the horses' hooves took on a hollow clop as they moved forward. Along the streets, houses rose two or three stories on either side.

"Jack!" Daniel was waving at him from the other cart, and pointed at a building ahead. "It's a stoa! Markets!"

Which meant zero to Jack, until they got close to the open-sided, colonnaded building to see the tables set up, loaded with fruits, vegetables, fabrics, jewelry, glassware, cloth, and a hundred things Jack didn't immediately recognize. Flea market. Huh. Who knew the Greeks invented that, too, along with democracy and pita bread?

Daniel continued to gesture and name things, but Jack let it slide away; he was busy examining the place in terms of tactical advantage. Which, to be honest, wasn't much. They had pretty good stonework, and some nice jewelry, but weapons didn't seem much advanced beyond sharp pointy things to stick in other people. If there was technology here, it was well-concealed.

They rolled to a halt in front of a vast open area, like a town square, with a huge spraying fountain in the center. Lines of women with jugs, getting water while they chatted; kids playing and splashing each other, brown as nuts. Jack and Carter jumped off the taxi and turned toward Daniel, who was heading toward them with his face lit up in wonder.

"This is the agora," he said, still locked in uncontrollable lecture mode. He spread his hands and turned in a complete circle. "God, Jack, I can't believe it, just *look* at it! It's like Athens reborn... the stoa, the statues. I think that's a fountain house over there – "

"Daniel." Jack put a hand on his shoulder. "I'm not seeing anything related to the Goa'uld here. Are you?"

Daniel shut his mouth with a snap, and some of the intellectual fever cooled in his eyes. Jack was almost sorry for that. "No," he said, in a more moderate voice. "I haven't seen anything yet."

"Nor have I," Teal'c contributed, coming to join them. "If the Goa'uld had come here recently, there would be signs. These statues would be of the System Lords, and the inscriptions would be invoking the power of the gods."

Jack felt his eyebrows twitch. "You can *read* the inscriptions, Teal'c?"

"I can."

"You, ah, didn't want to mention this?"

Teal'c looked, very faintly, surprised. "Can you not also read the inscriptions, O'Neill?"

"Pretend I can't. Just tell me in the future if you've got something, okay?"

"I will do so."

"So, do they say anything we need to know?" His eyes flicked toward Daniel, including him in the question. Mistake. Naturally, Teal'c and Daniel started talking over each other.

"I do not believe there is anything of significance to the – "

"Most of the inscriptions are histories about the founders of the city and the laws they – "

Jack held up a hand. "So, no, then. Captain Carter?"

"Sir."

"Stay alert."

Like she hadn't been already. She gave him a brief, warm smile. "Yes sir."

Right about then, one of Acton's retainers bowed stiffly toward them and launched into an explanation that Daniel interpreted to mean *follow me*. Which, Jack had already assumed.

They crossed the big open square. Leader and Head Cheese that Acton was, nobody talked to him, but plenty of townsfolk, including some of the women, drifted over to mutter questions to his retainers.

"The gossip mill's running," Jack said. Daniel nodded. "Hope they're telling everybody what good friends we're going to be."

"Actually, they're saying we seem to be lost. They're making themselves out to be generous and charitable to some pretty dumb strangers."

"Whatever works. Makes you wonder if it's an election year… You'll let me know if they say we're on our way to getting our heads removed, right?"

"Right." Daniel's tone was only a little ironic. "I *think* I get the priorities."

According to Daniel, the building they entered was called the bouleterion; it was where Acton had his offices, and the town council did their business. Built a little like the massive Acropolis farther up the hill, it was majestic but small, with some grubbiness around the corners of the polished marble and some chips out of the steps. A couple of guys in short tunics were scrubbing at stains with thick brushes, paying no attention to the higher-ups who stood around trying to look important. No armed guards looming, which boded well for the general stability of the government; Jack exchanged nods with some startled functionaries as they were led into a large atrium with a garden in the center, where some people were obviously sitting down to a lunch they carried in striped cloth bags.

SG-1 was shown into a big open room with padded benches, black and white tiles on the floor, and an absolutely stunning mosaic running all along the walls. All four sides. Daniel immediately went to the far right, next to the door, and began studying it, putting his video camera to use.

Acton's retainers, talking excitedly, left them to their own devices.

"So there's no king here, right?" Jack asked.

"What?" Daniel was barely listening.

"No king...?"

"Athens was the cradle of democracy, Jack. It's possible they might have one, but everything I've seen points to an Athenian society. Oh, except the women," Daniel added, as an afterthought.

"What about the women?" Carter asked. "They looked pretty normal to me."

"Exactly... yes, for the kind of society we're used to in the modern Western world back home. What I mean is, they're walking around outside, unescorted. Greeks were pretty conservative about that kind of thing. Women were absolute rulers in their own homes, but outside – well, they didn't go outside that much. Men ran the world." He shrugged. "This seems to be more like a Roman system, socially. Lots of freedom... Wow, look at that." His attention was arrested by the mosaic. He bent closer, practically putting his nose on it.

Carter was interested, and came closer. "Wow, what?"

"This is *unbelievable*. It must have taken years to complete – matching the colors – the technique is more advanced than anything we've uncovered in digs on Earth in the period, it's more like the work being done in Byzantium nearly a thousand years later..."

Jack wasn't about to get up and go join the gawk patrol. He sat, stretched his booted feet out at a comfortable angle and said, "It tells a story, right?" Because there was a Stargate, and blood, and people dying, and Jack was intensely interested in that part.

Daniel nodded. "Yes, definitely."

"Fact or fiction?"

Daniel finished his filming, and backed off to sit down next to him. Carter was crouched down, examining a section that showed men and women running in terror, wide-eyed, their hair streaming loose behind them, as others chased behind. The woman in the foreground looked almost insane with fear, clutching a baby in her arms as she ran. The city, in that section, was on fire.

"Can't tell," Daniel admitted. "In the beginning, it looks like a prosperous city, maybe this one... certainly Greek. Then there's some kind of event – see, the Stargate activating – and then..."

He stopped, got up, and went to examine a section of the wall. He reached out and touched it, smoothed his fingers slowly over the tile, and then stepped back, frowning.

"Daniel?"

"That's strange. It's been changed," Daniel said. "Somebody revised this. There's a section missing. They tried hard to match it, but they couldn't quite do it."

The section was a close-up of flowers, trees, peaceful streets.

"How can you tell?"

"The colors are different," Daniel replied absently. "And look, the pieces are larger, a little clumsy... whoever did this wasn't as accomplished as the one who completed the mosaic in the first place. Maybe a repair... no, it doesn't make sense. They removed part of the story."

"Revisionist history," Carter said. "Funny they only took out the one part. The rest of it looks pretty dire."

"But they took out the part that tells us what caused it," Daniel said. "See... peaceful city, then the Stargate activates... then peaceful city again... then the first trouble. A fire. The city fathers meeting, more fires, maybe riots... "

He stopped, frowning even deeper. *Careful, Daniel, your face will freeze like that,* Jack thought, but he followed the archaeologist's stare to the specific portion of the mosaic, and felt a familiar shiver race down his spine.

"Teal'c," Daniel said, and got very close to the image. "Take a look."

He pointed at the single tiny figure, almost hidden in the chaos of the smoke, fire, and fallen bodies of the dead.

Teal'c bent over to look, then straightened so suddenly Jack practically heard the snap.

"Jaffa," he said. "The Goa'uld were here, once."

Carter joined them at the wall. "But we knew that, right? These people must originally have been brought here by the Goa'uld. Maybe this is a record of them being relocated to this planet. Or, maybe it's a record of their native city on Earth."

"Maybe," Daniel said doubtfully. He went back to the part of the wall where the restoration had been done, dragging fingertips over the tile as if he could read the secrets underneath. "But then why change it?"

Jack swept the rest of the wall with a long look. Fire, destruction, riots... people dying... and then, at the end of the wall, a crumbled, deserted place, with the Stargate serene and quiet. The light was different on that section.

Moonlight.

It should have looked peaceful, but it didn't. Trouble lurking right around the corner, right off the edge of the picture, waiting to pounce.

It occurred to him what was bugging him about that particular section of wall. "I don't think that's a record of these folks being taken from Earth," he said, and got up to walk over to it and touch his fingers to the moon.

Then the *other* moon.

The doors at the far end opened with a sudden metallic *chunk*, and Jack turned fast to face them. Two fancy-dressed men stood there, and one of them offered some explanation with a polite smile, spreading his hands wide.

"Time to go?" Jack guessed. Daniel nodded and hitched his pack together, carefully storing the video camera, and SG-1 followed their guides into the next room.

Acton must have had one hell of a staff, because Jack thought General Hammond himself, with all of the resources of the SGC, might have had trouble pulling together a full meeting like this on a few minutes' notice. There were at least a dozen important-looking guys sitting behind a table, looking grave and composed, and fresh flowers in vases scattered around the room. These were the city fathers, Jack presumed; they had the sleek, well-fed look of men in control of their lives. Acton – still incongruously wearing the sunglasses – was standing at his place in the center of the table, and he gestured gracefully at four straight-backed chairs that had been placed in front.

The place was large, with windows opening onto gardens on one side, a sea view on the other. The twittering of birds and the steady dull pulse of the surf was the only sound. Besides the thump of the door shutting behind SG-1.

Jack resisted the urge to look behind him, pasted on a smile, and inclined his head to Acton. Who inclined right back. "Daniel? All right to sit down?"

"Ah… your guess is as good as mine."

What the hell, his knee had a twinge anyway. As soon as they sat, Acton settled as well, looking satisfied. Apparently, the first hurdle had gone well.

Some servant-type guys in short togas – *chitons* – circulated, filling glass goblets for the council, and offering some to SG-1; Jack conferred briefly with Daniel and decided they'd better accept and sip. Turned out to be wine, thin and vinegary. Jack drank as much as he figured was polite, then set it aside. A servitor whisked the glass away.

Without orders, Daniel launched into a variation on the *hello we're peaceful explorers* speech again, which Jack was content to allow. He was watching Acton, who was watching *him*. No fool, this guy, despite the eye shadow and fancy curls. A cold political mind behind all that pampering.

Acton had something to say, after Daniel was finished. It took a while.

"He says that they're pleased to receive a delegation from another world," Daniel said. "Ah, it sounds like he thinks we're applying to join the Helos Confederacy or something."

"He's posturing for his guys," Jack read. "Making us look like we're paying him court."

"So what do I say?"

"Change the subject. Ask him if he knows about the Goa'uld."

Daniel engaged in some lively discussion, so lively he seemed to forget about translation until Jack waved his hand for his attention. The town council was joining in, whispering to each other, asking Acton questions. While Acton answered, Daniel said, "He says they don't know anything about the Goa'uld, except as distant legends. From the beginning of the city. He's probably not lying; we haven't seen any sign of the Goa'uld around here."

"Except in the mosaic," Carter reminded him.

"Except in the *revised* mosaic," Jack said. "Not too sure I'm buying the party line on this one." He was reading Acton's body language, what there was of it. That was proving difficult. Different cultures, different rules. But he *thought* the man looked guarded.

The town council had continued to babble amongst itself, and now Acton spoke again.

"He wants to hear about our world," Daniel said. "Jack...?"

"Sure," Jack said. "Medical advances, food, trade, what nice folks we are. That kind of stuff. Let's keep this on the U.N. peace-and-love level. I'm not ready to get married just yet."

Daniel set about painting a picture of Earth that, while true, wasn't entirely complete, and Jack sat back and watched Acton. This guy had some battle scars. Not *just* a politician. There were walls around this city for a reason. If they'd been ceremonial, they'd have been a whole lot shorter, not to mention thinner. This place had been built for defense, and that meant there were people dying to get inside.

Jack thought back to the airport, the civilized, polite curiosity, and wondered if Chalcis might be the top of the food chain, in terms of cultural and economic power. If the other Helos Confederacy planets weren't so well off, maybe there had been reason to fortify some time in the past. Or, hell, last week. Or maybe there had been an army of Jaffa coming out of that Stargate, set so conveniently outside of the city walls, once upon a time.... In the murals, the Stargate had been *inside* of a town, and the town had been destroyed. Maybe these people had learned something from that.

The rest of the diplomacy consisted of smiling and nodding, and was pretty much as boring as Jack expected for the rest of the afternoon.

CHAPTER 3 – FRIENDS
φιλία

By the time they were finished with the Town Council, it was dark outside, and the birds had gotten tired of twittering. Acton's boys escorted them from the bouleterion across the wide, open town square, to what must have been one of their finer hotels – considering they had an airport, it wasn't too surprising there were hotels, too – and set them up with four separate rooms, second floor. Jack was surprised to find that the concept of beds translated perfectly well – no weird-looking contraptions, no alien slabs. Feather mattresses on wooden platforms with carved sturdy legs. Bundles of fabric for pillows. Some kind of white fluffy wool rugs on the floor. Bathrooms were in a building out back, but there were chamberpots provided in the rooms.

Note to self, Jack thought. *Tell SGC to screen planets for indoor plumbing.*

He ducked back out into the hall, where the rest of the team was still talking quietly. "First scheduled contact with the SGC is at 0800," he said. "Everybody ready at 0700 to move out. Let's get some rest."

"We're all going in the morning?" Daniel asked, hesitating in the act of opening his door. "Just to send a message through? Isn't at a little, ah, excessive?"

"No, we're all *going*," Jack said. "As in, outta here. Back to the SGC."

"But – "

"No, Daniel."

"There's so much to learn – "

"Maybe so, but there's nothing to learn about the Goa'uld, that's pretty clear. We're an exploratory team. We've explored. Let somebody else do the follow-up."

Carter must have sided with Daniel; he caught the frown and the narrowing of her eyes before she turned away to her own room. What was it about scientists? Sure, these seemed like okay folks, there were some cool buildings and nice statues, probably a million things to putter around with – but they weren't in the business of funding academic research-they were on a mission to find alien technology and fight the Goa'uld. *And find Sha're and Skaara.* So far, they hadn't asked around about that. That might have been why Daniel looked mutinous. Well, that and the unavoidable fascination with learning stuff nobody could possibly use.

Jack shut and locked the door, tested the feather bed, and sat thinking for a while before he thumbed on the radio in the tac vest he hadn't yet removed.

"Daniel," he said, and waited for the response.

"Yes, Jack." Daniel sounded resigned.

"Listen… there were still some people downstairs in the lobby. If you get a chance, show Sha're's picture around. It's worth a try."

Silence, for a few hissing seconds, and then Daniel's quiet reply. "Thanks."

It wasn't much, but it was something.

Jack took off the tac vest and hat, set the MP5 next to the bed and the M9 actually on it, next to him, and stretched out still wearing his full kit.

Sleep failed to come.

He listened to the soft thud of Daniel's boots moving down the hall, down the stairs, and thought about the wisdom of sending him off on his own, even just downstairs. But Daniel wasn't some wet-behind-the-ears recruit, he was – in his own way – a seasoned field agent, and hell, he was armed and knew when to yell for help, if it came to that.

But Jack still couldn't sleep, waiting for the inevitable crisis to blow up, for the shouting and shooting to start. *Should've gone with him. Daniel has a history of landing himself in trouble.* And after about thirty minutes of fruitlessly trying to convince himself that he was being paranoid, he got up and strapped on the firepower again.

He'd only taken two steps down the hall when Carter's door opened. No surprise to find that she hadn't disarmed, either.

"Trouble?" she asked tensely. He shook his head.

"Oh. Sorry. I mean, good."

"Daniel went downstairs a while ago. I'm just taking a look around."

She started to step out and shut her door. He shook his head and motioned her back inside. "Nah, Captain, you stay here. Rest. No need for both of us to be cranky tomorrow."

She looked unconvinced, but he gave her the silent command stare, and she just as silently obeyed. Her door clicked shut, but he was under no illusions she'd follow the part of his orders that talked about resting; she'd be sitting tensely all night, waiting for the other boot to drop.

On the whole, he was finding he preferred camping out and living rough on these expeditions. Civilization made him nervous, and besides, he hated to waste a good feather bed.

Combat boots weren't really made for stealth, but Jack had a lot of practice; he eased down the hollow steps slowly, listening for any hint of trouble. Before he was out of the shadows, he realized a couple of things simultaneously: one, there wasn't any trouble, and two, he'd just walked in on something private.

It hadn't occurred to him to wonder why Teal'c hadn't come out along with Carter, but it was obvious now: Teal'c had the jump on all of them in the stealthy exit category. He was already downstairs, and sitting by the low-burning fire with Daniel. Over at the other end, a couple of sleepy-looking bartenders polished glasses and yawned pointedly, trying to emphasize some after-closing-time message.

Not that Daniel and Teal'c were likely to pay any attention.

Daniel was saying, in a low tense voice, "Tell me how it's done." His head was down, shoulders hunched, as if he was protecting himself against a blow.

Teal'c looked as uncomfortable as Jack had ever seen him. "I do not think it would help you to know," he said, and the context clicked into place for Jack with an almost gut-wrenching snap. He should have known better than to think that Daniel had let that particular pain go; he'd never really stopped digging at it, and never would, until he knew it all. No matter how much it hurt.

He wanted to know about Sha're. About how she became a Goa'uld.

Daniel confirmed it by saying, "Whatever you tell me, it can't be worse than what runs through my head, believe me. I'd rather know than just guess."

"I have made a full report of this to General Hammond and Colonel O'Neill – "

"Teal'c! They're not going to tell me this, and *I need to know!*" Daniel sounded almost desperate, and Jack heard the sharp intake of his breath as he calmed himself down. "Please. I just – need this. You were there, right? You saw it. Just tell me how the Goa'uld take over a host."

It was too late to retreat back up the stairs; no way could he be *that* stealthy. Jack eased the strain in his left knee carefully, trying not to wake a creak out of the wooden boards, and watched as Teal'c thought it over.

And then the Jaffa slowly bowed his head. "As you wish," he said. "The Goa'uld leaves the safety of its Jaffa's pouch and enters the host through the back of the neck. Once inside, it establishes control of the host within a matter of moments."

"But some hosts resist."

"Few." Teal'c glanced up, then away. "Those who do are subjected to extreme pain. I have never seen one succeed in keeping a Goa'uld at bay for long."

"But Sha're…"

"Your wife resisted," Teal'c said, low and quiet. "She was very strong."

"Was there much pain? Teal'c, did she – did she – "

"I do not know." That was a lie, and Jack could feel it all the way across the room. Daniel, closer, had to know it too.

"Did she scream? Teal'c?"

"Daniel Jackson, it cannot help you to know." Teal'c's voice was overwhelmingly compassionate. "But – I must tell you this. As First Prime of Apophis, it was my duty to select potential hosts for him. The choice was mine – who to take, who to keep, who to discard."

Daniel slowly raised his head, and his glasses caught random flares of firelight. "I don't understand." But he did, Jack saw it in the growing tension in his shoulders. Sometimes the body knew better than the mind what was coming.

"I was with Apophis when he took your wife on Abydos."

I should stop this, Jack thought. *Put on my best cheerful idiot face and ask them what they're talking about. Daniel won't pursue this in front of me.* But that would just prolong the pain, and leave Teal'c to have to cauterize the wounds later. This conversation had to happen sometime, and it would only hurt worse when there was more trust to betray.

Daniel was shaking his head impatiently. "I knew that. I don't blame you for that."

"There is more. On Chulak, I was given the responsibility of selecting a woman to be the host for Apophis' queen. The woman of the Tau'ri I selected was unacceptable, and Apophis killed her. I was told to choose another... "

Daniel looked sick, and his blue eyes had gone very wide. "No. It wasn't – let's not go into this, okay?"

"It was my choice. I chose the fairest, the one with the most spirit... I chose your wife. Had I not – "

"Stop! Just... stop!" Daniel sounded on the edge of desperation. "You can't tell me this. I knew she suffered, that's not – that's not new – but I can't hear that it was just – God, I can't hear that it was *you*." He stood up and wrapped his arms around his chest. "Dammit, just *stop*."

Teal'c stood too, facing him, golden serpent emblem glittering and flashing in the firelight. "No. I am the one who brought your wife to Apophis. I witnessed her humiliated and stripped, and I did nothing. I heard her screams and pleas, and I did *nothing*. I have no right to your trust. You should know this."

Daniel stared at him for a few long seconds, face gone white and still. His eyes were glittering with pain, or tears, or both.

"Daniel Jackson – "

Daniel turned away, heading for the stairs and Jack's safe, anonymous shadows. Too late for him to go back up the steps. Busted. He tried to think of something to say, but the truth was, there was nothing he could say. *Sorry* just didn't cut it when you'd eavesdropped on something that personal.

Luckily, he didn't have to trot out the lame-ass excuses. Daniel wheeled around after a few steps and went back at Teal'c, fists clenched hard at his sides.

"Listen to me," he said. His voice was shaking, barely under control. "What you did – you had no choice, you were just as much a slave to Apophis as she was. *I* had a choice. *I* left Sha're alone by the Stargate. I was so eager to run off with Jack and Captain Carter, to be the *expert*, to... to show off! I didn't even think what could happen, and I should have, I know better than *anyone* what could come through the Stargate. God, I don't blame you. I can't."

The Jaffa stood absolutely still, unspeaking.

"Teal'c, I don't want..." He had to stop and swallow hard. "I don't want your guilt. I want your *help*. I want you to swear that you'll help me find her, and save her, and make her what she was before this happened. You owe that to her, not to me."

Teal'c's eyes glittered, softened, and he put his open hand over his heart. "I will carry your words with me, Daniel Jackson. And I will earn your trust."

"You don't have to earn it. You already have it." Daniel, with a visible effort, smiled. "You saved my life, all the lives of those people back on Chulak. We're in this together now." He offered his hand. "Friends?"

Teal'c gravely shook his hand, up and down. "Yes, Daniel Jackson. Friends." He switched it to a clasp of forearms. "And brothers."

Something passed across Daniel's face, something Jack thought he understood... Daniel had been alone, most of his life. Orphaned, passed around from one artificial family to another, never had anyone to call his own before Sha're. Being called a brother was a powerful thing.

After a warm, awkward pause, Daniel asked, "Want to, ah, help me ask some questions? Around town?"

"I will assist you," Teal'c nodded.

Jack let out a long-held breath as the two of them walked out of the door, into the dark street, and he finally turned around and went back to bed.

Sleep was still a long time coming, but at least he had one less thing to worry about.

His watch – set to local time – read about 4 a.m. when he heard footsteps coming back, and a very small knock on the door. Jack got up and opened it, found Daniel standing outside, looking tired and discouraged and dusty.

He gestured him inside and shut the door.

"Nothing," Daniel said, before Jack even asked. "I showed Sha're's picture, described Apophis, Skaara, the Jaffa... Teal'c even came with me as a visual aid. If these people know anything, they're good liars. By the way, wine shops stay open all night around here. In case you're interested."

"Anything else?"

Daniel combed his shaggy hair back from his face. "Maybe. Seems the mosaic on the wall might have referred to a fifth planet in the Helos Confederacy, only everybody seems to agree it doesn't exist anymore."

"Blown up?"

"I'd have to get Dr. Carter's opinion on that, but I think planets don't usually blow up, outside of the movies. No, I think they made it disappear. Off limits. Forbidden... something bad happened there, and they want to forget about it, at least in terms of it actually having happened."

Jack sat down on the bed. "Goa'uld?"

"Maybe. *Something* came through the Stargate there, anyway. And a lot of people died. I couldn't get anybody to tell me how many, but it must have been thousands."

"Any talk about how they defeated it?"

"That's just it," Daniel said. He took off his glasses and rubbed his eyes impatiently, as if getting tired was a disappointment. "I don't think they *did* defeat it. I think they treated it like an infection, and sealed it off. Removed it from their Gate addresses. See no evil, hear no evil..."

"... get killed by the evil you're ignoring," Jack finished sourly. "I'm liking this less the more I hear."

"It's possible this fifth world is where the Goa'uld have their stronghold. It could be the place Apophis went when he escaped Chulak."

It was a very long shot. As much as Jack hated that skinny, glowing-eyed bastard and wanted to rip him in half, he wasn't going to drag an untested team into an unknown, obviously hostile situation on the strength of one of Daniel's wild-ass guesses.

Well. Not yet, anyway. It'd be nice to come back from their maiden voyage without smoking holes in their new BDUs.

"We'll go back," he said. "Report to General Hammond, grab some coffee, catch some sleep. You didn't get a Gate address for Planet It-Is-Forbidden, right?"

Daniel shook his head mutely.

"Then it might be a moot point. We couldn't get there if we wanted to."

"I could keep trying. Somebody has to know something."

"T-minus three hours to departure," Jack said. "You're worn out. Get some rest, Daniel."

Daniel gave him that level, unflinching stare Jack remembered so well from Abydos. "Was that an order?"

"Would you listen if it was?"

Daniel blinked. "Maybe."

Well, that was new. Jack shrugged, leaving it up to him, and as Daniel turned to go, said, "Keep the radio on, will ya?"

Daniel's footsteps didn't turn toward his room. Jack listened to them thumping back down the stairs, and went to the window to look out. Moonlight bathed the town. Here and there, lanterns glowed and flickered, and shadows moved around the streets. Three moons floated in the sky, one large and pale blue, one small and pure, bright white, one a kind of squashed orange.

He remembered the mosaic, the final stillness of a ruined city, and the moonlight shining down. *Should've ordered him to bed,* he thought. *The more he wants to know, the less they're going to want to tell him. And this is a big place to search if he goes missing.*

But in the morning, at 0700 sharp, Daniel was back, eyes vague with weariness, and everything seemed perfectly normal.

Daniel's barhopping hadn't yielded a whole lot of information, it appeared. As SG-1 had breakfast in the hotel common room – trestle tables and benches, a lot of bright chattering people in colorful robes and lace-up sandals, all of whom stared covertly – Daniel described chatting up the locals. The more or less sober ones, anyway. He and Teal'c hadn't been on their own after all; at least two of Acton's quiet security detail had trailed them all night.

Carter in particular listened to Daniel's story of a fifth, lost world intently. "And they didn't give you any details about what came through the Stargate to cause the disaster?" she asked, and took a neat bite of flatbread loaded with sliced olives. She'd politely refused the lamb and rice wrapped in grape leaves, which Jack thought actually tasted pretty fine. "Seems like it had to have been something pretty frightening. Like a Goa'uld war party."

"I didn't get the sense it was something that... well, that simple," Daniel replied. He was wolfing down some kind of porridge that Jack wouldn't have tried for money... but then, Daniel wasn't exactly squeamish about new foods. "Not *just* a Goa'uld war party, if that was part of it. It seemed like they were afraid of something worse than that. These people understand war, I think they've had struggles among their planets from time to time. You saw the walls..."

"Wondered about that," Jack said. He tried the flatbread. Not bad. Maybe they should hijack the cooks and take them back to the SGC commissary.

"Yeah, well, even this planet's got its own political divisions. Seems like there are several different city-states that all want control of the Stargate. This city – it's called Aclythos – has been in charge of it for about fifty years, after the last war. But there's a couple of other cities within a day's travel that use it, too, and have to pay for the privilege. Apparently, travel through the Stargate is free for the local citizens, but not for everybody else."

"So it's not a planetary government?" Carter asked.

"No. We'll probably only find a planetary government where the Goa'uld have an active presence, or did. These worlds seem to have been seeded by the Goa'uld, but they never got back around to asserting a claim. So... tribal politics as usual. The slaves broke up into city-states, patterned a life after the one they'd had back home."

Teal'c said, "Yet this other unnamed world may still be under Goa'uld control."

Jack looked around one more time – the calm diners, the ripple of conversations going on, smiles and laughter. Busy servitors, looking harassed and palming coins for tips. Chefs shouting to each other in back rooms. Like the airport, it looked a lot like home, if you switched out the wardrobe. And if the Goa'uld had a foothold on one of these planets, it was only a matter of time before they came calling here on Chalcis, too, burning and destroying.

And after that, just a couple of steps on to Earth.

"Let's get moving," Jack said, and tugged his hat into place.

It was the general rule in the field; when the commander was done eating, the team was done, too. Carter left her flatbread and olives; Teal'c immediately abandoned his plate of fruit. Daniel scooped up two hasty mouthfuls of his porridge, then a third while standing, and was the last to leave the table.

Two guys in dark tunics got up from a seat in the corner of the room and followed SG-1 out. Jack noted them, exchanged looks with Carter and Teal'c and nodded slightly toward their new friends. "Teal'c. Watch our six."

Culture shock. Teal'c looked at him with a blankly inquiring look, one eyebrow threatening to shoot up. Daniel looked just as clueless. "There are not six of us, O'Neill," Teal'c said. He managed to say it as if he wasn't calling his CO a lunatic. Probably how he'd survived Apophis all these years.

Carter smothered a grin. "Guys," she said, and described a clock with her hands. "Twelve o'clock is in front, six o'clock is behind. Watch our six means – "

"Behinds," Jack finished in exasperation. "Watch our behinds."

"Ah, Jack, you do know our watches are digital now…"

He sighed. "Shut up, Daniel."

Outside, the big square – the agora – was again bustling with people moving, only this time the flow was all in one direction. Toward the Acropolis at the crown of the hill.

"Jack?" Daniel pointed. "Think we should have a look?" He took a couple of steps in that direction. Almost immediately, their dark-tunic-wearing minders looked worried. One of them scurried off fast, probably for backup; the other came up to Daniel and stepped in his way.

"Not a linguist, but I'm guessing that means no," Jack said. "Invitation only up at the temple."

"Maybe that means we should go," Carter put in.

"Or shouldn't," Daniel said. "Maybe it's a religious taboo. No foreigners allowed."

Jack didn't like that idea. "And maybe these fine folks have been yanking our chain. Let's find out."

He stepped forward, and sure enough, the security guy wasn't quite sure how much force he was allowed to use. Or, Jack thought, having been on *that* side of the problem a time or two, whether he had enough authority to stop them no matter what. Jack pushed past him, walking across the courtyard through the misting breeze of the fountain.

"Maybe it's a morning religious observance?" Carter asked. "Sunrise service?"

"Well… maybe." Daniel didn't sound convinced, and Jack could see why; this crowd didn't have the bored, comfortable look of people coming to church. Lots of people, tightly clustered. Parents and children alike, everybody very quiet.

"Funeral?" Jack guessed.

"Something serious," Daniel replied. "Sacrificial rites? I don't know. The Greeks weren't known for anything too extreme in their rituals, except for Tauris – Euripides wrote about human sacrifice in honor of Artemis in Tauris. She was their patron deity."

"Who's the patron deity in these parts?" Better safe than sorry…

Daniel gestured at a massive, gorgeously carved marble statue of a dignified man, seated on a throne marked with seashells and sea creatures. Surprisingly, it was painted – the robes were saffron, the flowing hair black. Dark eyes that seemed to follow everybody who walked by. He was shown holding a trident.

"Poseidon," Daniel said. "God of the sea."

"And Artemis is…?"

"Goddess of the hunt and the moon. Sister of Apollo, god of the sun and medicine. She's also an aspect of the triple-faced goddess: Artemis, Hera, Hecate. Maiden, mother, crone."

Moon. Moonlight. A shattered city in still white light.

Over at the Acropolis, a priest draped in white with a cloth over his head held up a scroll and showed it to the assembled crowd. Jack stopped, watching, as the man unrolled it and read something out.

"What's he saying?"

"Hard to catch." Daniel stepped forward, as if an extra foot or so might make the difference. "Sounds like… something about paying tribute… and the safety of the city. Maybe a draft for the local militia."

The priest handed over the scroll to an attendant and was brought a huge silver bowl on a tripod, and a silver baton. Another priest tipped a bag full of tiles into the bowl.

The silver baton was put to use stirring the tiles.

"Daniel?"

"I'm not sure. Lottery?"

"I'm guessing it's not Powerball."

Jack put his hand on the butt of his MP5, reading the tension in the crowd. They were very, very quiet as a tile was drawn and held up to be read.

The priest said something. One word.

"I don't know," Daniel said before Jack could ask. "A name, maybe. A clan? A family?"

A sigh went through the crowd. Most of them turned to go, hurrying away, clutching the hands of their children.

A small knot of people stayed, clinging together.

"Sir," Carter said quietly. "We really should get going, if we want to stay on schedule."

Jack watched for a few seconds more. The knot of people left made some kind of group decision. An old man kissed the foreheads of two adults, a man and a woman, and knelt to embrace his grandkids.

Then he went up the steps to the temple.

"No human sacrifice, huh?" he said. "Right."

He'd be *really* happy to get out of here, feather beds or not.

The walk back to the Stargate took longer than expected, because Daniel kept stopping to take video and rubbings of inscriptions, until Jack's temper flared and he flatly ordered him to stay on the road and keep up. Carter wasn't looking too approving of Daniel's distraction, either. Her eyes stayed focused on the slowly-approaching bulk of the Stargate airport, except when they moved for fast glances behind, at the security detail trailing them.

"Sir?" She moved up next to him and fell in with his loose-limbed stride. "Are you sure they're going to let us leave?"

"Oh, pretty sure that they won't be able to stop us," Jack said. "Not with the weapons we've seen so far. But I don't think it'll come to that. These folks seem like the diplomacy-first types. Probably they'll just fuss a little and want us to wait for the official kiss-off. By the time they get their act together, we'll be back home."

Daniel cleared his throat. "Shouldn't we – "

"No, Daniel."

"You don't know what I was going to say."

"And yet... still no."

The airport wasn't exactly bustling early in the morning. Even the taxi stand was empty. Jack led the way through the big gates – which were open – into an empty expanse of courtyard. The bar where they'd sipped alien daiquiris was shuttered and locked. The desks all stood unoccupied. The only sound was the flapping of canvas in the breeze, and the distant heartbeat of the sea.

The Stargate sat silent in the morning light, looking like a particularly impressive piece of round alien sculpture in the middle of all of these sharp right angles.

Despite the lack of travelers, there was plenty of security on duty, Jack noticed. Twenty or more. They were standing at the steps of the 'gate, armed with spears.

"O'Neill," Teal'c said. "It appears that those who followed us have summoned assistance."

How? No radios on any of these guys... Jack gave up wondering, because it didn't matter. The fact was that the security detail behind them had swelled to five. When added to the uniformed guys standing in front of the Stargate, that presented bad odds if you didn't want to mow people down with automatic weapons, which would kind of spoil the generally positive diplomatic tone they'd achieved.

"Jack," Daniel murmured, and jerked his chin toward a doorway in the wall that was opening near the Stargate. The door was painted jet black, and the ones coming out of it were in black, too – head to toe, covered in veils that drifted in the morning breeze. Very ceremonial stuff. The first one out carried some kind of smoking brazier on a chain. The second one carried flowers.

He was reminded, again, of funerals.

"Sir, maybe all this isn't for us," Carter said. "Maybe the extra security's for these people."

"Who are…?"

Nobody on SG-1 answered Jack's question. They all paused, watching, as the procession came to a stop at the foot of the steps and the Dial Home Device.

One of them unveiled and began punching an address into the machine.

"Daniel? Symbols?" Jack kept his voice soft, but the crack of command in it made Daniel jump and fumble with his pack. He got the video camera and held it out to the side, trying for a good angle. Chevrons lit up on the Stargate as the address locked in.

The one dialing hit the red ball on the DHD, and the Stargate activated, plasma boiling like water. When it settled into a shimmering pool, the veiled travelers began to walk up the steps. One or two faltered and had to be helped along by their fellows. The armed security detail didn't move, until one ripped off her veil and backed away. She turned to run, but spears clashed in front of her, forming a glittering fence.

"She's just a kid," Carter blurted in alarm. "Sir – "

"We don't know what's going on, Carter," he said flatly. "Hold your position."

He didn't like it, *really* didn't like it. The girl was crying. One of the others took off his veil and came back down a couple of steps to take her by the shoulders, then embrace her. A man old enough to be her father, maybe. He put her veil back on and adjusted it, then his own, and led her by the hand up the steps.

"No bags," Daniel said softly.

"What?"

"They're not carrying any bags. No packs, no food… nothing. This isn't travel. They don't expect to need anything, where they're going."

One by one, they disappeared through the wormhole. The man led the girl through, still holding her hand tightly.

The one who'd dialed the gate, and the few left standing at the foot of the steps, removed their veils and dark robes as the wormhole disengaged with a snap and a flare.

Familiar faces underneath. "Acton," Daniel murmured. "And the rest of the town council... um... Jack...?"

The town council was turning in their direction. Acton's finger pointed at them.

"Think our diplomatic card's been pulled," Jack said. "Right. Time to go."

He led the way toward the Stargate, MP5 held at the ready across his chest, warm and lethal. Acton wasn't pointing at them any more, but his expression had gone dark and rigid.

"Tell him thanks for the hospitality, but we're due back home."

There was some back and forth, fluid syllables that sounded, on Acton's part, more than a little angry. Daniel gave it right back, short terse responses, and Jack watched his eyes begin to glitter.

"Apparently," Daniel finally said, in a flat, tense aside, "we shouldn't have seen that. Some kind of religious taboo."

So this wasn't going so well. Perversely, he felt himself relax. At least things were back to normal – trouble.

"Just dial the gate, Daniel," Jack said, and stepped in to face off with Acton. He'd been right, this guy wasn't just your average glad-handing politician. Acton had that dead-eyed stare of a man who'd fought and killed, and he didn't blink when Jack engaged him in a silent battle of wills.

Behind them, Daniel moved toward the DHD. One of the guards got in front of it, blocking his path. Jack brought his MP5 up in an unmistakably threatening way and pointed it right at Acton's chest.

"Go around him," he said flatly.

"Jack, he may not understand..."

"Oh, he understands," Jack said. Acton's eyes were burning with fury. "Just dial."

Daniel eased around the guard and began entering symbols. Each solid *chunk* of the sequence eased just a tiny bit of tension in Jack's spine.

They were going to get out of this after all, and leave it for Hammond to fix whatever diplomatic valve they blew. Good in theory....

... until it all went to hell.

"Colonel O'Neill!" Teal'c yelled, a full-throated cry of warning, and the Jaffa's staff weapon fired with a shockingly loud burst. Whether they'd been looking for a fight or not, they were in one now; Jack instantly shifted his grip on the MP5 and slammed the butt around to connect with Acton's head. Acton went flying. *Dammit, we're outnumbered, I don't want to kill these people...*

He spun to assess the situation, just as Teal'c took a step back, firing over the heads of advancing security guards. Something happened Jack couldn't actually see; Teal'c went down in a haze of crawling blue sparks. Daniel stopped dialing and ducked for cover. Captain Carter leaped like a panther to Teal'c's side and let loose a rattling burst of auto fire – still aiming over the heads of the massing guards. Jack did the same, covering their six, and backed up to grab Daniel by the back of the shirt and drag him upright. "Dial!" he barked.

Daniel gave him a white-faced, anxious look and slapped a symbol with more than necessary force. There were five lit up so far. Two more...

Something hit Jack in the back, hard, and spread over him in a red convulsing haze. He heard Daniel yell his name, and then he was down with no sense of impact. The stone was hot under his cheek, but he couldn't move. Paralyzed. *Dammit.* A hit to the spine?

Daniel went for his holstered Beretta. Too slow. Clumsy. Needed more training...

Not that it would have helped. They swarmed him like ants and brought him down on the ground, next to Jack.

Jack had an ant's-eye view of sandals trampling past him. Acton was talking in a sharp, angry voice to the rest of the town council. *That's it, talk it over,* he thought. The paralysis was temporary. Had to be temporary. He'd get movement back, and then he'd kick some bony Greek ass, no question about it. The stone felt warm and gritty under his cheek, and he saw a trickle of blood flow past his left eye. His own? Carter's? Teal'c's? It was just a trickle, not a flood, but it was very, very red.

The argument ended with some flat pronouncement from Acton. *Dammit, Daniel, I need to know what's happening, a little translation would be good...* Of course, Daniel must have thought he was unconscious. From time to time he heard Daniel's voice rising and falling, spiked with anger but unnaturally even, as if he was making a huge effort to be reasonable when all he wanted was to strangle somebody with their own guts.

One of the guards stepped in at a curt word from Acton, and, by the sound of it, slammed the heavy metal-clad butt of his spear against Daniel's face.

That ended the conversation.

Jack listened to the percussive sound of symbols being entered into the DHD. Seven symbols. Then the explosion of the wormhole forming.

The sun, warm and golden, beat down on his back like a giant hand, holding him still. He saw movement from the corner of his eye; black drifting veils brushed the stone next to him, and then somebody was tugging Jack's numbed body up by the collar of his BDU shirt.

Acton. He had something in his hands... a round silver mesh circle with a white stone in front. He touched the stone, and the circle opened.

He wrapped it around Jack's neck and fitted it together. Some kind of words that sounded formal. *No, thanks, it really doesn't go with my outfit,* Jack's brain babbled, at the same time the practical side of him was firing off questions about what this was, what it did, and why the *hell* hadn't he shot this damn bastard when he'd had the chance...

He felt the silver collar click together, and something cold shot through his body. The mesh constricted like a living thing, tight against his throat. He wanted to gag, but couldn't even do that.

Acton looked briefly into his eyes, and for a second Jack thought he saw something that might have been pity. Then Acton stepped back and ceremoniously covered his eyes with his hands, in a not-seeing gesture. The floor lunged up at Jack as the guys holding him dropped him. Rustles and clicks told him that the same ritual was being repeated with Daniel, Carter and Teal'c. Daniel was the only one able to resist, but that didn't seem to make any difference.

Apparently, everybody who visited Chalcis got a free Goa'uld souvenir...

Hard hands grabbed Jacks arms, flipped him over, and towed him painfully up the steps. All he could see were the foreshortened faces of two security guards, looking pissed off at the effort of lugging him, and the harsh golden sun staring down.

Then the shimmer of the Stargate.

Then nothing.

CHAPTER 4 – DESCENT
κάθοδος

The next thing Jack knew, he was in pain. Yep. Pain. Lots of it. Sharp spikes all up and down his body, an ankle that felt like it might as well have been chopped off with a dull axe, and a throbbing headache.

He tried to sit up, but something was holding him down. Daniel's hand, flat against his chest.

Jack opened his eyes, blinked, and brought the world into focus. First, a dim, dusty kind of sunlight, the wrong color, shading toward blue. Second, a cold dry wind loaded with sand that stung his exposed skin and made him involuntarily squint against it.

Third, the look on Daniel's face, which was somewhere between terror and relief.

"Jack?"

"Daniel?" He looked pointedly at the hand pushing him flat.

Daniel removed it and slumped back into a sitting position. He looked battered, but intact. The bruise turning purple along his cheek and forehead was going to be a real beauty. "I don't think you should sit up yet. You took a hell of a hit."

"Yeah, yeah." Jack not only sat up, he kept going. Daniel made ineffective *don't-do-that* motions as Jack rolled to his feet – creaky, infinitely slow, but still mobile. He got vertical with a sense of grim triumph, which eroded some when he tried to put his weight on his gimpy left ankle. *Crap.* Felt like somebody had taken a hammer and shattered his bones into ground glass. "Carter? Teal'c?"

"Here, sir," Carter said from behind him. She was sitting down, leaning against what looked like a ruined stone wall. Pale as milk, with a drying smear of blood on her cheek. "We're both fine, sir. Teal'c's having a look around."

Not a bad idea. Jack followed suit with a quick comprehensive scan of the immediate area. One big circular Stargate, and steps they'd probably tumbled down, which would account for all the bruises and sprains. One DHD, sitting off to the side.

His gaze swept it, stopped, and came back to contemplate it further.

"Captain Carter?"

"Sir?"

"I'm no scientist, but shouldn't we be, oh, dialing out of here? Right *now*?"

Carter didn't move. Her voice was weary. "Yes sir. It looks like somebody removed some of the control mechanism, probably a crystal of some kind. It's not broken, just disabled. I had a look around, but if the missing part's here, it's hidden. Without it, the Stargate won't dial."

"Peachy," Jack said. He kept going on the visual survey. Not a lot to see – they were in some kind of an open courtyard, like the airport concourse back on Chalcis, only this one was destroyed. Tiles broken and buckled, walls tumbling into heaps, wind dragging grit around in aimless drifts. "Daniel, what the hell just happened?"

"I don't know." The younger man sounded discouraged, not to mention tired and depressed. "Jack, I'm sorry, I had no idea they were going to attack us. Acton told his people to deal with us. But I thought he meant dealing as in *trading* with us, not – "

"Daniel, you really need to take a class in political doublespeak. Could come in handy if we ever get out of this alive." He tried putting his full weight on his ankle and couldn't control a full-body flinch at the immediate wave of protest. The ankle folded.

"Sir?" Carter was immediately at his side. "How bad is it?"

"I'm fine, Carter." He shook off her support and tried to focus on something else besides the sickening throbs of pain. His neck itched. When he tried to scratch it, his fingers banged into slick silver mesh, and memory flooded back. Silver mesh around his throat, some kind of white stone at the front. A sensation of choking. *Doesn't go with my outfit.* He got his fingers under the silver mesh and pulled. He tried pressing on the stone, the way he'd seen Acton do. Nothing. "Okay, somebody want to fill me in about the jewelry?" Because now that he looked, they all had them. Identical matching accessories.

"We can't get them off," Daniel said. "We've been trying."

"Oh, there's always a way."

"Okay," Daniel amended blandly. "There's no way without taking our heads off, which is, forgive me for saying so, a little counterproductive."

"They went *on*. They'll come – " Jack's fingers stretched and strained, and the mesh seemed to constrict around his throat like a living thing. He choked. " – *off*."

"Sir, maybe you should rest for a minute," Carter said.

Actually, his knees were feeling a little unstable. He grunted, hobbled a couple of steps and put his weight against the wall Carter had used for a backrest. It didn't feel too strong, but it would do. Jack slid down and stretched out his leg with a suppressed hiss.

"Jack?" Daniel's eyebrows had drawn tight together. "No offense, but you don't exactly *look* fine."

"Never been better. Captain? How are your first aid skills?"

"Depends on if it's sprained, broken or needs amputation, sir." Not that Carter looked to be any prize herself in the health sweepstakes; he kept sweeping her with looks, trying to see where the blood on her face had come from. No visible wounds. She crouched at his side with the kit and manipulated his ankle with ruthless disregard for the sounds of protest he made. Daniel stood watching, arms crossed, frowning tensely.

"Not broken, sir," she finally said. "You should probably keep the boot on, otherwise the swelling's going to be worse. Best I can do is anti-inflammatories and pain pills, and you should try to stay off of it."

"Which is, oh, not gonna happen, Captain." She was digging through the kit. "Just the anti-inflammatories. I'll dope up once we're back home."

"Yes, sir." She passed them over, along with her canteen. He downed them and passed the water back. "We have enough food for a couple of weeks, but we're going to need fresh water within the next two days. So far, there's no sign of life around here, no vegetation, no nothing. Just ruins, sir."

"Um…" Daniel shifted his weight anxiously. "That's not… exactly true. I found footprints over there, in the sand. I think they're from the people we saw being sent through the Stargate earlier. I don't think we're – "

He was cut off by the thick metallic sound of the Stargate activating. One chevron lit up, then two. Jack motioned for Carter to help him up, and the three of them retreated to the relative cover of the sagging wall.

Jack reached for the radio on his tac vest and clicked it on. "Teal'c."

"I am here," Teal'c's voice came through his earpiece. "I have located some temporary shelter, O'Neill."

"Great. Get back here on the double."

Three chevrons. Five. Seven.

Ka-whoosh. The plasma flume swept out, then snapped back to stasis.

Daniel's head was exposed to whatever fire might be coming out of the Gate; Jack grabbed his collar and yanked him down, pulled the M9 pistol from Daniel's holster and pressed it into his hands, and gave him an imperative finger-to-lips signal for silence when he opened his mouth.

Then he peeked over the wall, squinting against the blowing grit, and saw two people step out of the Stargate, hand in hand. Nobody carrying staff weapons, or anything that looked like trouble – dressed in those flowing black robes again, with black veils over their faces. They were terrified, clinging together for support. They stumbled down the stairs and huddled together, whipped by the gritty wind, as others followed them out. Jack counted as they emerged – ten in all. The wormhole bubble snapped, and as one, all of them turned to stare at it. Somebody cried out, and two dashed back up the steps as if they could dive back through the empty circle.

One tall figure dragged the black veil from his head. An older man, bearded, with his curling shoulder-length gray hair worked with beads and shells. Fierce as a hawk.

"You dishonor us!" he snapped, and grabbed two of the most panicked of the party, shaking them hard. They calmed down immediately. "Would you have the others see us in such fear? Have you no pride? You carry the honor of your people! Unveil yourselves. Let the gods see you."

One by one, they did, dragging the black veils off of their heads. Apart from Grandpa Preacher, they were all young. Some were barely more than kids. Six men, four women. No packs, no food, no weapons.

Each had a thick silver mesh collar around their throat, white stones in front, just like SG-1.

"He says' – " Daniel began.

"I heard him," Jack interrupted, and only then did it hit him that he *had* understood what the old man had said. As if the man had been speaking modern English.

Huh.

He looked to Daniel for an explanation...

...only to find Teal'c crouched next to him. He hadn't even heard the Jaffa approach. Damn, the man could give shadows a lesson in stealth.

Daniel, on the other hand, hadn't relied on stealth, just quickness. Jack threw out a hand - too late - and then Daniel was around the wall and approaching the new arrivals, hands held passively at his sides.

Great. Jack braced his elbows on the wall and sighted his MP5 on Grandpa Preacher, heard the dry metal rattle as Carter followed suit a bare half-second later.

Carter groaned softly. "Does he *always* do this?" she asked.

"Yep. Remember Chulak?"

She sent him a wide blue-eyed look. "Should I go after him, Colonel?"

"No. No, he may be crazy, but he knows what he's doing. Hold your position." Teal'c's warm body was next to Jack's, standing tall, his staff weapon held in firing position at shoulder height. "Teal'c. We've got it covered."

Teal'c slowly lowered his weapon and grounded the butt in the sand. He looked impassive, except for his eyes, intensely focused.

"Big guy?" Jack tugged on the man's BDU shirt. "You want to present a big easy target, join the Marines. In the Air Force, we duck."

The Jaffa reluctantly bent his knees.

"Hello," Daniel was saying, in his warmest voice. Hands relaxed at his sides. "Hi. My name is Daniel Jackson, I'm part of a group called SG-1, don't be afraid, we're not your enemies – "

After the first instinctive recoil, the newcomers hesitantly stepped forward, gathering around him, spoiling any possible line of fire. Even Grandpa Preacher, though frowning and crossing his arms over his chest, looked interested. He stepped forward into the center of the little knot of people and said, "You are not of Helos."

"Well, no, we're not. We're peaceful explorers – "

"You are sent as tribute from another world?"

"Tribute? Ah… "

"You wear the mark of Artemis. Do your people worship her?"

"No, I wouldn't exactly say *worship*…" Daniel was struggling. "Forgive me, but I think it's very strange that we understand each other. That we're speaking the same language."

Grandpa evidently had no idea what he was talking about. "You speak our language well enough."

"Okay, but see, you seem to be speaking *mine*…"

There ensued a tennis match of an argument about who was speaking what, which the other nine members of Grandpa's party watched with bright-eyed interest.

"Sir?" Carter asked. She hadn't moved, hadn't taken her focus off of Daniel's six. Iron concentration. Jack approved. "I could be wrong, but they don't seem all that dangerous."

"Yeah, getting that." He hesitated another second, then straightened up and took the MP5 to a neutral position, sliding the selector switch into safe mode. "Let's join the party, Captain. Teal'c, come with."

Jack limped out from behind cover, Carter and Teal'c at his shoulders, and a few of the newcomers shrieked and ran away. Daniel chattered on, earnestly trying to convince the rest of them there wasn't any danger. Grandpa Preacher wasn't one of those who panicked, Jack noticed. Neither did a young man, maybe 18, max, who pushed a younger girl behind him and stood his ground.

"Jack," Daniel greeted him, as brightly as if he hadn't just disobeyed, oh, just about every order Jack had given him. "This is Alsiros…" Grandpa Preacher. "And this is Pylades, and his sister Iphigenia." The 18-year-old and the younger girl. She was already peeking out from behind her brother, cute as a button, probably about sweet sixteen. Both had long brown hair, curling in glossy ringlets; both had big brown eyes and fine, delicate bone structure. On Pylades, it looked noble and refined, and subtly morphed into innocent beauty in Iphigenia.

Pylades gave SG-1 a stiff nod, clearly wary. He didn't let his sister come near them.

Daniel gestured vaguely at the rest of the milling black-robed people. "Sorry, didn't meet the rest yet."

"We'll do name tags. What's the story?" Jack rested his hands lightly on his MP5, watching Alsiros's deep-set eyes. Not trusting, either. He had the special glow of the fanatic to him.

"We were just getting to that. I'm still trying to figure out how he understands me... Alsiros? You understand my friend?"

"He speaks Greek." Alsiros sounded out of patience with the whole thing. "Why should I not understand him? Do you think I am so feeble?"

Daniel turned to Carter, face alight. She looked just as fascinated. "This is incredible," she said. "If he's speaking Greek but we hear it as English..."

"...then the Stargate must be translating for us."

"That doesn't make sense. It didn't work for us before."

"Yeah, but look, we used *our* Stargate to get to Chalcis – "

"-- and *their* Stargate to get here," Carter finished, enthusiasm bubbling up. Her blues eyes took on that mad-scientist shine, as if it was contagious. Maybe Daniel was a carrier. "They had a DHD. We don't back home, we cobbled the system together by trial and error. Maybe there's something in the DHDs that translates languages – "

" – yes! Software, some kind of part, I don't know, but *something's* doing this." Daniel was almost jittering with excitement. "Captain – Doctor – do you know what this means? We can – "

" – understand alien cultures, even the ones with root languages that may not be familiar to us," Carter said. They both grinned like schoolkids left in charge of the candy store. "We just have to analyze it and retrofit the – "

Jack rolled his eyes and said, in infinite careful patience, "Kids? Let's stick to the program. I'm sure these fine folks," *not to mention me*, "have better things to do than listen to technobabble."

Daniel took offense. "It's not technobabble, Jack, we're talking about a breakthrough that could change – "

"Life as we know it, yadda yadda, I'm more interested in finding out *how to get off this rock*." The suppressed fury in his voice had a bracing effect. Some of the glow faded out of Daniel's eyes, and Carter looked positively chastened. "Now. Gran – Alsiros here said something about tribute. What's that mean?"

Daniel cleared his throat. "Well, it's actually kind of fascinating. You remember the story of the Minotaur?"

"Um... Ugly monster. Maze."

"It's a little more complicated than that, but yes. The important thing is that the Greeks sent a regular tribute of victims to Crete for the Minotaur, who was a divine mixture of man and beast and ate human flesh." Daniel indicated the black robed men and women. "Well, so far as I can tell, there's no Minotaur, but Colonel Jack O'Neill, meet the tribute from Sikyon. The people we saw come through before we were – um – "

"Sandbagged?" Jack contributed sourly.

" – before we were sent through the Stargate were the tribute from Chalcis. I assume there must be groups from Mycenae and Delphi here, or on the way."

"Because...?"

"Obviously, there's someone or something here that they want to appease, the same way the ancient Greeks wanted to appease the Cretan monster."

Oh, that was a happy thought, and yep, it had Goa'uld written all over it. And Daniel's enthusiasm for it made Jack's guts clench up. *Don't think you really want to make friends with the monster, Danny boy.* Although, hopefully, a couple of high-velocity rounds in the monster's ass might make it a little less hungry.

Alsiros had had enough. He pulled himself up to a stiff, unbending height, looked down his nose at Jack, and said, "We will leave now to make our way to the temple."

"Temple?" Daniel turned to him immediately. "Where?"

"It lies at center of the Great City." Alsiros frowned at him, the way he'd frown at a puppy puddling the carpet. "Were you given no instruction?"

"No, we were sent – well, without instructions. Which are...?"

Jack let Daniel keep up the conversation, content to watch over the rest of Alsiros's party. Nothing special there. They all looked scared, but mostly determined; the youngest one, the girl – Iphigenia – clung to her brother's arm with both hands, big brown eyes sneaking nervous glances at Jack from time to time.

The brother didn't seem to approve. He turned to her, whispered something, and she looked down, cheeks burning.

"The sun is setting." Alsiros interrupted the flow of Daniel's questions to point at the faded bluish disk sliding down behind the horizon. "We may not waste any more time with your foolishness. I will tell you what you need to know in order to give honor to your people." He looked as if they should have been grateful. "You must make your way to the temple, and Artemis will judge your bravery. Your heart will be weighed before the eyes of the goddess, and you will join the Divine Hunt."

"Okay, hold on… hunt?" Jack asked. "What kind of hunt? And that heart-weighing, that's not literal, right?"

Alsiros shook his head impatiently and stalked away. The kid, Pylades, spoke up. "The Divine Hunt," he said. "Our sacrifice keeps our people safe. If we are judged worthy, we'll join her company and serve her in the temple. Otherwise…" He gave Iphigenia a glance and kept whatever he'd been about to say to himself. "The goddess knows a pure heart. I hope to see you in the temple."

He followed Alsiros, who was already striding through the rubble and heading for one of the two sagging doorways. The rest of the black-robed group straggled after, talking excitedly.

"Well, that was the end of a beautiful friendship," Jack said. "What now?"

"I guess we find the Temple of Artemis," Daniel shrugged. "Listen, won't the SGC have some kind of protocol when we don't check in?"

"Oh yeah."

"Which is…?"

"They'll open the wormhole to send a message through to us." Jack squinted at the sun. "If we miss more than two contacts, they send SG-2 in after us. Major Dixon's in command while Ferretti's still in rehab."

"They'll look on Chalcis first," Carter said.

Jack nodded. "Acton's bunch will have a real nice story. They saw us to the gate, waved bye, don't know what the heck could have happened. Unless SG-2's *real* motivated to thump an answer out of somebody, we can't count on rescue showing up here any time soon....Options?"

"Sir, the temple's the only landmark we have so far. If that's the center of this place, maybe that's where we find the missing piece to the DHD," Carter put in. "Shouldn't we follow them? Alsiros seems to know where they're going."

"His type always do. Teal'c. Get up high, take a look. We need a lay of the land."

Teal'c nodded, handed his staff weapon to Carter and lunged up the tallest pile of rubble, then vaulted up again onto the nearest standing wall, athletic and graceful as a cat. The top of the wall was narrow, but he balanced like an acrobat, rock-steady, and turned in a slow circle.

Jack shaded his eyes against the dying glare of the sun. The wind must have been pushing hard at Teal'c, but the Jaffa didn't seem bothered. "See anything?"

"Yes," Teal'c said. His voice sounded odd. "The city stretches for many miles. It is vast and ancient. Much of it is in ruins."

"Any sign of a temple?"

"I cannot say. There appear to be some large intact buildings in that direction." He pointed. "But the streets are narrow, and many are blocked. It is a difficult path."

"Guess Alsiros was right," Jack said. "Probably good to get a head start, then, if there's some Goa'uld time limit to this thing. And he never answered me about the heart-weighing issue. Anybody else bothered about that?"

Teal'c jumped. Just... jumped, right down from a height of about twenty feet or so, easy as if he'd been jumping off a foot-high step. He landed with flexed knees, straightened, and extended his hand to Carter. She smiled and handed over his weapon.

"Well, I don't know," Jack said, straight-faced. "You stuck the landing, but the Russian judge only gave it a three. ...Daniel, Alsiros seemed a little hairy about the sun going down. Any idea why?"

"Well, it's getting colder. It'd be nice to find some shelter." Daniel rubbed his hands together, then clasped them under his armpits.

Teal'c spoke up. "I located a defensible position when scouting, O'Neill."

"Lead the way." They all looked at him. "What?"

"Sir... not that I'm doubting you, but are you sure you're in shape to make any kind of a hike right now?" Carter asked.

He tested his ankle and found the pain level about a six on the Jack O'Neill Scale of Debilitation, which meant he could soldier on effectively. He'd hit an eight once, when he'd blown out his knee the first time on the parachute drop. Came close to a nine in a Baghdad prison. He figured by the time he hit a true ten, he'd be dead anyway.

"I'll be fine," he said.

They all exchanged looks.

"What?"

"Nothing, sir," Carter murmured.

He followed Teal'c across the confines of the courtyard, trying hard not to limp. Familiarity with pain bred contempt, so it got easier as he went along. It looked like there had originally been several exits from the courtyard where the Stargate sat, but with the walls collapsing it was more or less open ground with random cover.

More walls at sharp right angles outside of it, these still standing and at least two stories tall. They were completely enclosed, looked like, except for two narrow alleyways, one to (he checked the compass on his watch) east and one to west. Presuming he could read an alien planet's magnetic field the same way as back home. *Ought to ask Carter.*

And yet... no.

"The shelter I located is in this direction. Also, I believe these streets are unblocked for much of the way." Teal'c pointed. Opposite from Alsiros's tracks. Jack made a move-out gesture.

Even though Teal'c kept the pace slow and easy for the sake of Jack's ankle, it was tough. Carter kept hovering behind him, clearly worried, which left Daniel at the rear; Jack glanced behind, and sure enough, Daniel was lagging fifty feet back, busy looking at the walls, rubbing his hand over them with an interested expression.

"Captain, this is why he doesn't hold down the rear. Oh, Daniel?" he called back.

"Yeah, just a minute."

Jack rolled his eyes and nodded Carter toward him; she went to round him up. Daniel immediately tried to enlist her to his side. "Captain – Doctor – take a look at this. What do you think? These reliefs – "

"Not now, Dr. Jackson." Carter's voice was brisk and professional.

"But the reliefs… it's just that the material of these walls doesn't match what – "

"Daniel." A little more steel under the friendliness. It brought Daniel up short. "Time and a place."

He froze for a second, then nodded. "Right. Sorry." He moved out, shot Jack a look, and went past him to walk behind Teal'c.

When Carter joined Jack again, he gave her a slight nod. "Nice Daniel-wrangling. Of course, you're still new at it. He's being polite. It'll get tougher."

She snorted a laugh and dropped back to follow.

All in all, it seemed like the longest walk of Jack's life, which given his history was saying a lot.

Teal'c led them around a right turn, then a left, then another left. Blank walls, broken by toothless doorways that led into darkness, or into more alleyways. What had Alsiros called this place? *The Great City?* Maybe once, but it had been years since this place had seen anything like civilization.

"Jack!" Daniel's voice, thick and urgent with alarm. Jack paused, turned and looked. The younger man was crouched down on hands and knees beside a pile of fallen bricks.

Jack controlled a flash of pure temper, fueled by pain and exhaustion. "Archaeology later. Shelter now."

Daniel reached behind the rubble and pulled something free. He held it up to catch the last cold blue rays of the sun.

A skull, more yellow than white.

"It's not ancient," Daniel said quietly. "Probably not more than a few months old. The bone's not even bleached yet. There's more back here, but it's all been disarticulated. Torn apart and dumped."

Jack forgot about his ankle. "Animals?"

"I don't see any sign of gnawing. The bones aren't scattered." He sat back, considering. "There's no collar. Some clothing left, but no collar."

Jack looked at Carter. She was frowning, but she lifted one shoulder in helpless commentary. Nothing they could do. They didn't even really know what it meant.

"O'Neill." Teal'c was up ahead, and he stepped back from an open, darkened doorway. "There is more."

The smell warned Jack long before his eyes adjusted to the relative darkness of the room; the roof was missing, but it was still murky.

"What is it?" Daniel asked, coming up behind him.

"More bodies." He counted and came up with twelve. "Fresher ones, smells like." He flicked on his flashlight to take a look, and wished he hadn't. Combat prepared you for a lot of things, but that still didn't make it easy to stomach. Not if you were lucky.

"God," Carter murmured from behind him as he moved to a second corpse. Tough to tell how long they'd been here; decomposition was pretty advanced, to the point that it was difficult to tell the men from the women. "Sir, this one's been hacked to pieces."

"Yeah," he agreed. Behind him, he heard boots scraping, and Daniel bolted outside to heave. Not an unreasonable response; Jack had done it plenty of times. "Whatever happened here, it was violent. Any of these collar things?"

"No sir. None of them have them. The clothes are gone, too. Scavenged, maybe?" She gulped, fighting nausea. He jerked his head toward the exit.

He and Carter stepped out into the relatively cleaner air of the alley – hallway? – and he looked to Teal'c. The Jaffa was silent.

"Goa'uld?" Jack prompted.

"The Jaffa do not kill in such a manner unless no other weapons are available to them," Teal'c replied. "I – have never seen such a thing on any Goa'uld world. Death, yes. But this was not done by Jaffa."

"Somebody's holding the right end of the knives. Swords. Whatever."

"Agreed. We should be alert."

Jack nodded, one sharp jerk of his chin. "You said you found shelter."

"It is defensible, O'Neill."

"Even better."

Teal'c led them around two more corners, a sharp right, over a pile of rubble from another fallen wall that it took Jack two tries to make it over. That raised his pain index another half a point on the scale.

In the shadows, half blocked by another crumbling wall, lay a blind doorway. Darkness inside. Jack held up a closed fist to bring the team to a halt – naturally, Daniel didn't notice at first – and used the penlight to check out the interior. Looked good – one empty room, no windows, no corpses. He limped in and rested his back against one thick wall with a silent sigh of relief. *Damn.*

Teal'c settled at the door, facing out, watching the alley outside. A thin, fading band of sunlight crawled over the outside wall and disappeared, and everything started going dark. Carter, without any prompting, broke out the portable stove for warmth, and began laying out rations. Daniel was drawn over to make some half-hearted jokes about the macaroni and cheese. Jack let his throbbing, protesting body rest up, and nursed a small amount of water like sipping whiskey. The stove radiated a warm orange glow, but didn't do much to heat up the space. Jack finished his water and held up a hand to Carter.

"Yo. Captain. Toss it."

"Anything in particular you're hungry for, sir?"

"Whatever." She tossed one, and he fielded it without effort. He'd long ago formed the opinion that all MREs were the same, it was just psychology to label them differently. But then, as Carter had pointed out back at the SGC, he'd never met military chow he'd actually liked, and he had to admit, the modern MREs were a hell of an improvement over the old crap. "Teal'c? You eating?"

"I am not hungry."

"It's here if you want it."

Teal'c nodded in acknowledgement without taking his eyes off of the empty alley outside. He hadn't forgotten the room back there, the dismembered bodies. Well, Jack hadn't either. He had a hunch he'd be seeing it again when he closed his eyes.

Daniel and Carter were talking in low voices, something about the Stargate and translation again. Jack let the words wash over him without worrying about the meaning, realized he'd forgotten about the MRE in his hands, and opened it up to wolf down the main course – turned out to be tuna with noodles – and the lemon pound cake. Peanut butter and crackers for later, if he got snack-hungry.

Almost before he'd finished swallowing the last sticky bite of cake, he felt his body relaxing.

The wall felt soft as that feather bed he hadn't used, back on Chalcis.

Just before his eyes slid shut, he saw Carter and Daniel, huddled together over the warmth, talking like old friends, and he thought, *if we get out of this alive, we're going to make a damn fine team.*

Then it all slid away, or he did, into darkness.

CHAPTER 5 – SEDUCTION
απoπλάνηση

It was strange, Daniel thought, that he was having the time of his life right now, trapped on an alien planet with the threat of death hanging over him. But for the first time in a long time, he was feeling *useful*. He had puzzles to solve, things to care about, someplace to be and people to belong to. He'd had that on Abydos, for a while. Not so much before. Losing it – and Sha're – had been the hardest things he'd ever endured.

Dan'yel. In unguarded moments, he could still hear her voice, as if she was just behind him, out of sight, and when he slept he woke up believing her warmth was curled next to him. Until reality came into hard, clear, cold focus. Empty bed, empty soul, empty life.

He'd felt useless ever since. This felt... better, being here. Doing this.

Crazy as that was, under the circumstances.

Captain Carter was tugging at her neckband again. He knew how she felt; he kept catching himself pulling on his own, trying to loosen it, trying to find the hidden catch to take it off. When she saw him watching her she gave a guilty little smile. "Itches," she explained. He nodded. "Want something to eat?"

"Sure."

She dug out supplies, and inspected an MRE package with a slight, undeniably cute frown between her eyebrows. "*Country Captain Chicken.* Apart from the obvious jokes, that just doesn't seem very appetizing." She held it out to Daniel, who shook his head. "I'll save it for the Colonel. He'll probably get a kick out of it..."

She made it half a question. Daniel saw her looking toward O'Neill, but Jack's chin was down on his chest, his olive-drab baseball cap pulled down low, his arms folded over his chest, foot elevated to bring down the swelling. Fast asleep. Jack had put on a good front, but it had been pretty obvious to anybody who knew him that his ankle had been bad enough to sideline any of the rest of them.

"Jack? Yeah. Probably."

"I'm just thinking, you know him better than I do."

Daniel paused in the act of reaching for a package labeled JAM-BALAYA. "I do?"

"Sure." Captain Carter's shoulders raised and lowered in a too-careful shrug. "You were on the Abydos mission together. You've logged more time."

"Well... yes. That doesn't mean I *know* him. I mean, I *like* him, and I respect him, but so far as *knowing* him... it's not that easy. Jack's not exactly the type to open up."

"You aren't either," Carter observed.

Daniel felt his eyebrows go up. "And you are?"

"Sure." She ripped open a package – not the Country Captain Chicken, whatever that was – and sorted through the contents. "I grew up a military brat, my father's an Air Force General, I kissed my first boy at 14, and I like fast cars."

"That's it?"

"The highlights." She grinned at him. "I always meant to be an astronaut, until I found out about the Stargate, and then I couldn't think of anything else. End of story. Trust me, I'm not that complicated."

"Captain – Doctor – "

She gave him a sidelong look out of those blue eyes that he couldn't quite think of as military. "Sam. Please."

"Okay. Sam. But only if you quit calling me Dr. Jackson."

"Deal."

"Sam, you obviously think I have some kind of inside track with Jack, but that's just not true. Believe me, the fact that I've known him a little longer doesn't mean he listens to me any more than you... just the opposite. Jack and I, we see things from opposite sides. That helps, sometimes. And sometimes it doesn't." He shrugged and fiddled with the MRE, pulled the heating tab and waited for the entree to cook. "He respects you. He may not seem like it sometimes, but believe me, Jack's good at reading people. If he let you on the team, then he trusts you."

"Nice to know." Her smile was sudden and genuine. "Do you?"

He felt his eyebrows pull higher. "You're kidding, right? I've seen you under fire. The question is, do you trust *me*?"

Her smile switched off, leaving him feeling oddly cold. "I'd trust you better if I didn't understand you so well."

"I'm not sure I – "

"You didn't wait before you bounced out there to talk to a bunch of strangers," she said. "Daniel, if Alsiros had pulled out a knife and stabbed you, we wouldn't have been able to do a damn thing except bury you, and maybe with company. You need to value your life a little higher. I do. So does the colonel."

Daniel had almost forgotten his presence, the Jaffa was sitting so silently, but Teal'c looked over and said, "As do I, Daniel Jackson."

"Hey, wait a minute, guys, I'm not *helpless,* you know…."

"You're a civilian," Carter cut across his protest. "The three of us are trained for situations like this, you're not. From now on, wait until we give you the all-clear, okay? We don't want to lose you."

Teal'c inclined his head a bare degree, then turned his attention back to the outside. Daniel felt his throat close under the grip of something he barely understood – frustration, grief, fierce and aching relief.

We don't want to lose you. All his life, he'd been waiting for someone to say that to him, to give him a sense of belonging. Throwing himself out in front had always been a way of life, not a choice – get noticed, get attention, get people to cooperate. It was going to be tough to undo the habit.

He looked down, stirred his jambalaya, and spooned up a quick mouthful to cover his emotion, then murmured, "I'll work on it. Thanks."

He felt her hand settle on his shoulder briefly, squeeze, and retreat again. She devoted herself to the MRE, and they retreated to the safety of mundane topics, like the merits of Disks, Chocolate, With Crisped Rice, over Disks, Chocolate, With Peanut Butter.

He was dozing before he could think to ask about when he was supposed to wake up to take a turn at watch. Just before he tipped over into true, dark sleep, he felt the remembered tactile sensation of Sha're's soft black hair dragging over his chest, and her warm weight settling in his arms.

In sleep, he could still have her for his dreams. For twilight, waking dreams.

And for nightmares.

"You don't sleep."

Sha're settles on the sand next to him, pulling her robes closer against the night's chill, and draws her knees in close to her chest. He gives her an absent smile and puts his arm around her. Overhead, the moon pours pale light and turns the desert sands to a dry, frozen sparkle.

"You miss it," she says. "Your home. Your people. Your rituals."

"Only some," he replies, and rests his chin on top of her scented dark hair. "Coffee. Showers. Kleenex." Although he hasn't sneezed in weeks now, as his body adjusts to the new climate. "Okay, and toilet paper. I miss toilet paper. I <u>really</u> miss toilet paper."

She laughs. Her English is good, getting better all the time, but some things still strike her as ridiculous. He's had a very hard time explaining toilet paper. Throwing anything away is a foreign concept to the Abydonians.

"I made you <u>chal</u>," she says. "You say it is like coffee."

It's hot, dark, and it keeps him awake. That mostly qualifies. "Yes. Like coffee." He smoothes her hair back and admires the ivory curve of her face in the moonlight. "Sha're?"

"Yes?"

"Why did you..." He can't even put it into words, but she knows, and smiles.

"You were different," she says. "And you were favored of the gods."

"Not sure I like that."

She makes a frustrated gesture. "Not the false gods. The real ones. They mark you."

He isn't sure he likes that either. The ancient gods rarely marked anyone that they didn't plan to play with. Punish. Destroy.

He kisses her hair, her forehead, moves his lips slowly down to touch hers.

"Dan'yel," she whispers in his ear, and puts her arms around his neck.

Close, so close to forgetting...

There is something wrong with him. Something black and thick inside him, like dread, like hunger, and when he pulls away, he sees that there is something wrong with Sha're, too.

Her face is different. The lines are the same, but what lives inside it, what looks out of those eyes, is not his beloved.

Her eyes flash white in the moonlight, brighter than should be possible.

"Worship me," she says, and smiles with Sha're's lips.

He feels oddly remote as he asks, "Who are you?"

"I am moon and fire and the loss of self. I am the death at the end, when the stag can run no more. I am the bursting heart and the flying arrow, the hart and the hare and the spear."

She kisses him fiercely, and they are Sha're's lips, Sha're's hands on him, and he can't resist her.

"Mine," she whispers, and the word breathes warm over his skin. "There is no beauty so complete as in its destruction."

He has a knife in his hand, and he knows what she wants him to do.

"Dan'yel," she says, and her Goa'uld eyes flash again, ordering. "My love."

And he strikes.

Out in the city, someone screamed. It was a long distance off but very clear as it hovered and shivered thinly in the night air. It sent a pure bolt of adrenaline down Samantha Carter's back and catapulted her to a fast, fluid crouch next to Teal'c at the door. He had gone still, listening. When the cry faded into silence, Carter let her breath out slowly and looked over her shoulder at Daniel and the colonel, but they were still sleeping. Good. They were exhausted. Daniel hadn't let on, but that crack on the head hadn't done him any good, and the colonel... damn. She couldn't believe he was walking. She'd have been crawling, if moving at all.

"Captain Carter," Teal'c said. "I will stand watch. You should sleep."

He didn't even look at her as he said it – no flicker of attention off what was going on, or not going on, outside the doorway. She felt amazingly small next to the Jaffa. Colonel O'Neill was a tall, strong man, and he filled a room, no doubt about it, and when she stood next to him she felt included, as if his strength attached itself to hers and multiplied it. Daniel... he was bigger than he looked, and civilian or not, she knew there was a core of endurance to him that would put some gung-ho Marines to shame.

But Teal'c was something else. He was like a mountain, alone and imposing, and when she was next to him there was no sense of being *with* him, only *beside* him, like standing next to the Sphinx in Egypt.

But it felt safe, next to him. Very, very safe.

"I wish we knew what was happening out there," she said. "And I wish we could help them."

"It would be dangerous to leave this shelter," he said. She felt that, too, a strong sense of something out there moving, but just at the corner of their vision. "The scream came from the direction in which Alsiros took his party."

"Damn." Those young kids...

"Do you believe that some enemy hunts this place?"

"All I know is that those people back there didn't decide to commit suicide by dismembering themselves."

Teal'c cast a look at her, fast and unreadable, and she felt that gap again, dark and unbridgeable. She actually understood Daniel a hell of a lot more than she did Teal'c. The colonel had forged an instant bond with the Jaffa, and Daniel seemed to have reached some sense of comfort with him, but she sensed that it might take more time with her. Then again, if she'd been serving Apophis for a hundred years, enduring who-knew-what at the hands of the Goa'uld, she might have been a little careful with her trust, too.

"I will watch through the night," he said.

"No need, Teal'c. I'll take a shift."

"I do not require sleep as humans do. You should rest."

She was thrown. "You don't sleep?" For some reason, that was odder and more off-putting than the idea of the larval Goa'uld stirring in that pouch in his stomach. "You must rest sometime."

He didn't elaborate, his focus entirely on the outside. It was looking a little less murky out there; she risked sticking her head out to see that there was a large white moon rising, larger than Earth's satellite.

Nearly full. It put a silver hush over everything, a silken weight that felt somehow ominous.

"Sleep, Captain Carter," Teal'c said again. "I will wake you at first light."

She wasn't sure she *could* sleep, but now that she thought about it, her muscles were aching and craving oblivion even if her mind wasn't ready. She went back to the stove, turned it to a lower setting, and finally braced herself in a corner of the room, MP5 at the ready, to close her eyes.

I won't be able to relax, she thought, and then exhaustion washed over her in a black tide, carrying her away into moonlit silence.

Running, always running. Feet pounding, back aching, sweat dripping cold down his spine, and the moonlight, silver moonlight freezing everything in cold silence. The city looks like a pillaged corpse, but it is a living thing, hungry and waiting. There are hiding places but they are filled, with others desperate to conceal themselves, and the hunters, behind, are running too, fanning out to flush their prey out of shadows. Some fight when they are caught, but one thing is sure: they all scream.

Before the end, they all scream.

He looks up, gasping, and sees the silver-white gleam of the temple, its flowing columns, its motionless figures standing and watching. So far... too far... he cannot run. Not now.

The hunters are coursing fast behind him. They make no sound, and that is worse, somehow, than if they bayed like hounds for his blood. He risks a glimpse over his shoulder and sees that they are drawing closer, black shadows flickering white as they pass into the open, the moonstones black at their throats like death-clouded eyes. He has retained a weapon, stolen from an old man who was too weak to survive anyway, but he knows that if he turns to face them he will die, and fear drives him on, always on.

He rounds a blind corner, and she is there.

His goddess. Silver white mistress, tall and ethereal, crowned with night and stars. She is majesty and beauty and the stark face of his ending, and he collapses to his knees, staring, spreading his hands in worship. The knife falls free, lost.

Artemis walks toward him, her white clouds of robes drifting in the cold wind, and the alabaster of her skin is like that of the dead, drained of life and blood, but still beautiful, so beautiful.

She puts her cold fingers under his chin and tilts his head up, and he is ashamed to soil her perfection with his sweat, his trembling, his mortality.

She smiles.

"I accept your sacrifice," she says, and there is silver music in her voice, nothing human in it, nothing mortal. "You who once served one dear to me."

Her eyes flash white, pure white with black centers, and then the pack of hunters is on him, and no amount of worship or prayer can save him.

Everyone screams, in the end. His is drawn from him as a blade is driven deep into the vulnerable center of him, and his symbiote is cut and slashed and dismembered. They hold its mutilated, twitching body before him, laughing silently behind their jackal smiles, and their eyes are black and wide and avid.

Then they begin to take him apart, alive.

His last vision is of the goddess of the hunt, smiling, drinking his dying like smooth dark wine.

"Teal'c!"

Jack bolted upright, aware he'd said it out loud but not aware of much else, initially; his heart was thudding as if he'd run a marathon, flat out, and under the thick BDU fabric his whole body was dripping with sweat.

The dream was fading, but the images, the sickening sense of inevitability...

He turned his head and saw Teal'c moving toward him. The big Jaffa crouched next to him, frowning.

"All is well, O'Neill," he said. "There is no cause for alarm." Even so, he looked spooked. Distressed.

"Yeah. Yeah, okay." Jack took off his hat and rubbed his hands over close-cropped hair, then ran his sleeve over his face to wipe off the worst of the sweat. Felt like he was choking, tried to pull at the neck of his shirt and bumped fingers into cold metal.

The collar hadn't been a dream. He tugged at it, but it was as firmly fastened as ever.

Teal'c was still watching him with concern.

"Just a nightmare. Sorry. *Shit.* You didn't dream, did you?"

"Jaffa do not dream."

"Right." Jack looked at him for a second, but Teal'c's eyes were unreadable. "So you didn't see yourself out there, running in the moonlight."

Teal'c changed the subject. "There has been no movement. The dawn is coming soon."

"Good." The word tasted like ashes in his mouth. He tried to remember the dream but it slid away, fish in the night river. He remembered running, and moonlight, and dying. Not much else. *Screw it. Just a dream.* No shock that a place like this would bring up nightmares, considering their nearest neighbors seemed to be dismembered corpses.

Jack tugged his cap back on, seated it carefully with one hand at the back, and gestured for Teal'c to help him up. His ankle had taken the opportunity to swell until his whole foot was numb; that was both a blessing, from a pain point of view, and a curse, from the point of trying not to fall on his ass. He hobbled around experimentally, bracing himself against the wall, until he felt some of the numbness subside and a deep-seated hot ache return.

Ah. Better.

Carter was sacked out in the far corner, huddled up in a small ball but still clutching her MP5. Daniel was on the floor, on his side, facing the wavering glow of the brazier. He hadn't taken off his glasses. They were knocked cockeyed on his face.

"All quiet?" Jack asked Teal'c, who'd gone back to his post by the door. The Jaffa nodded. "You didn't sleep at all?"

"No."

"I'm up now. You take a rest period." When Teal'c didn't move, Jack limped over and nudged him. "Hey. That's an order."

Teal'c nodded, rose from his crouch like some perfectly balanced machine, and moved to the spot Jack had abandoned against the wall. He sat down in a lotus position, put his palms upward on his knees, and closed his eyes.

"I kinda meant sleep," Jack said, but there was no point in pushing the issue. He negotiated his way to a sitting position – too old for crouching, definitely, not to mention the ankle – and laid the weight of his MP5 across his lap. The world outside was dark and quiet. No movement. No moonlight. He was glad of that, even though it would have made things easier to see.

On the other side of the room, Captain Carter made a soft whimpering sound. He glanced over at her, but she shifted position, moving dream-slow, and subsided. A few minutes later, it was Daniel's turn... not so much a whimper as a cry, half-formed. His whole body twitched. Not like Daniel had any shortage of bad dream material to work with, Jack thought. Nowhere near as much as Jack had himself, of course; years of black ops and POW stints were the proverbial winning hand in that area. Well, maybe Teal'c could beat him. No question that Teal'c must have seen and suffered a lot under Apophis; no question that he'd performed atrocities, even if he hadn't been through them himself. Jack wasn't so sure that it was any easier from the side of the aggressor. A lot of his late-night regrets had to do with pulling triggers, rather than getting shot.

He wondered if Teal'c would ever talk about that, and thought he probably wouldn't. The Jaffa didn't seem to be big with the sharing.

Carter whimpered again, then made a louder sound, kind of an eager moan. Jack glanced over at her again and saw that her head was back, light falling over her face, and she was smiling.

At least one of them was having a good dream.

Running. Always running.

She vaults soundlessly over a fallen stone column, lands with perfect balance and continues the chase. She can hear the panicked heartbeat of her prey, loud as thunder in her ears. He is clumsy, and she is elegantly quick. Her skin flashes white in the moonlight as she moves from shadow into the open.

She sees another hunter break cover to run with her, hunting in concert. His grace and strength match her own, and they run, run, pacing and panting, following the prey that clumsily dodges ahead, looking for shelter.

There is no shelter, no mercy, nothing but the inevitability of moonlight. She laughs soundlessly, full of fierce and aching joy, red red joy, and feels the echo of it from the one who runs with her. His hair is lank and sweated to his face in dark points, and he has lost the trappings of who he once was, but she knows him – knew him – as someone else.

His eyes are all black pupil, blown open with fierce desire, and she feels the same rising tide of need and frantic hunger.

They run, chasing the prey.

Just as the prey turns to fight them, just before she tastes blood, she sees that the prey wears Jack O'Neill's face and has a clear moment of sanity that shakes her to the core, and she thinks No this can't be happening no I have to stop now *but then it is gone, and there is only red, and joy, and the screaming.*

Something outside.

Jack came instantly on alert but didn't make an outward move or sound; whatever it was, it was moving slowly, with a faint, rhythmic scrape. It stayed in the deepest shadows, next to the still-intact far wall, and it wasn't until he used his peripheral vision that he spotted what was making the noise.

Human. Crawling.

"Teal'c," Jack said. The Jaffa's eyes snapped open, and he practically levitated up to join Jack at the door. Jack jerked his chin in the direction of the sound. "Cover me."

"You are injured, O'Neill."

Before Jack could tell him to stick it, Teal'c was out the door and moving fluidly across the open ground, staff weapon held ready to fire. Jack got the MP5 to his shoulder and waited tensely, well aware that accurate fire under these conditions was going to be just about impossible, then breathed out a sigh of relief when Teal'c put his staff back to safe position and crouched down in the shadows.

"T?" Jack keyed the radio in his vest and kept his eyes on the Jaffa as he did.

"It is a man," Teal'c said. "I will bring him inside."

"Wait... is he sick?"

"No, O'Neill. He is injured."

"Okay. Go."

Jack shuffled back from the door as Teal'c ducked inside, carrying a limp body as easily as if it was a blanket. Daniel sat up, glasses still askew. Carter went from peaceful sleep to an instantly alert position, fluid and graceful; her MP5 swung into firing position.

"Easy," Jack barked. "Stand down, Captain."

Her eyes cleared, and she let the weapon drop back out of line. "Sorry, sir. What's happening?"

"We're about to find out." Jack flicked on his penlight; the harsh white light made them all wince, first because of the glare, second because of the red glaze of blood that glittered on the body Teal'c laid down next to the camp stove.

The stranger didn't look familiar. Jack looked at Daniel silently, but the other man shook his head; not one of Alsiros's party, then. If the numbers held true from one tribute party to the next, there would be at least thirty running around they hadn't yet met.

Carter moved forward, MP5 slung over her shoulder, and folded back the black draperies of the man's outer robe. Under it, he was wearing a pale yellow tunic, ripped and soaked with blood. Jack felt his face tighten, and some fragment of a nightmare came back to him.

Running, always running. He looked suddenly at the man's feet. His sandals were gone, and his feet were battered and bloody, scraped raw.

"Carter?" he asked. She shook her blonde head silently and used her knife to slice open the tunic to the man's waist, folded it back to reveal a bloody mess. She pushed on his shoulder to roll him up on his side and then eased him back down.

"He's going, sir. There are stab wounds all over him, including his back. He's just about bled out."

The victim opened his eyes at the sound of her voice, saw the knife in her hand, and panicked. He reached out and grabbed Carter's wrist in both hands, trying to hold the knife away from him. She tried to jerk back, but he had the strength of terror. Blood oozed from the corner of his milk-pale mouth, and panic shone silver in his eyes.

"Carter!" Jack said sharply. "Drop it."

She looked up at him, and for a bare instant he thought he saw a flash of something strange in her eyes, but then she let go, and the knife bounced away on the stone floor. Daniel wrangled it, holding it at his side, watching.

The victim didn't relax. He was a middle-aged man, gray in his curling hair; in normal life he might have looked plump and happy, but this wasn't anything like normal life. Or a normal death.

"Who did this to you?" Jack asked him, and reached down to raise his head and shoulders. The man was drowning in his own blood. "Can you hear me? Who did this?"

The lips moved, and he whispered, "Wolves... Dark... Company..." He choked on another arterial-bright gush of blood. Carter was right, the man was done for. Jack held him up anyway, took his hand and held tight as the man gripped hard, searching Jack's face frantically for something. Rescue, probably. Safety.

Those eyes focused somewhere below Jack's chin, on the cold weight of metal around his neck. The man let go of Jack's hand to reach up and brush fingertips across the stone on the collar, then looked over at Carter, crouched across on the other side. He pointed at her collar with trembling insistence.

For a second, Jack couldn't see why, and then it clicked.

The dying man's collar stone was pure milky-white, like the moon. Carter's had a flaw in it of some kind, a streak of black on the right side occluding part of the disc.

The man lying between them rattled in one last breath, or tried to, and his body went into death spasms. Jack held his hand tightly until it went limp, then folded it carefully over the bloody chest. On the other side, Carter did the same.

"Jack?" Daniel cleared his throat. "What should we do... "

"Best we can do is leave him here and move out," Jack said. "Carter? Use an extra blanket, wrap him up and tie it off. Everybody, watch your backs."

She nodded and turned away to pull one of their thin thermal insulation blankets out of the field pack. Daniel, without being asked, helped her spread it out on the floor and rolled the body onto it, then took over the task of tying it into a makeshift mummy wrapping. He'd probably had practice, back on Abydos, Jack thought. He seemed to take it as a solemn duty, fastening the knots carefully and smoothing them in place.

"O'Neill," Teal'c said quietly. He was standing in the doorway; Jack hadn't even seen him leave, but here he was, back again. "I have followed the trail of his blood. He crawled for several streets. I believe he was attacked earlier in the night. Captain Carter and I heard a scream."

"Any sign who attacked him?"

Teal'c held out a bronze dagger, triangular in shape, with a ram's head handle. It was smeared with blood. "One of the other tribute sacrifices," he said. "Perhaps some of them have formed hunting parties."

Jack felt dizzy for a second, because he recognized that knife. *Deja vu.* He'd seen it in his dreams, only… only it had been killing Teal'c.

"Jack!" Daniel's sharp, urgent call. They all turned to look.

He held up a silvery mesh collar, loose and unfastened, with a white moonstone. Not his own; his was still around his neck. "It came off," he said, and indicated the dead man. "I heard a click, and it just slid apart."

"What did you do?"

"Nothing."

"Okay, what did you *touch*?"

"*Nothing,* Jack. I'd tell you if I had." Daniel sounded as frustrated and irritable as Jack felt. "I was tying off the blanket at his feet. I looked up when I heard the sound. Nobody touched the collar."

"Let me have it," Carter said, and reached out. Daniel dropped the heavy weight of it into her open hand. "Maybe I can open it up, see how it works."

Nobody had any better ideas. She set to work with tools.

Dawn came, bringing a pale blue wash of light but leaving a significant chill in the air. Jack thought longingly about the brand-new standard-issue jackets he'd refused in the Quartermaster's office back at the SGC. Hypothermia was a concern; best to keep everybody moving until the weak sunlight warmed up enough to be useful.

Carter, despite using every trick she had in the bags, including Teal'c's brute strength, hadn't been able to make a dent in the unlocked collar. Jack could tell it was driving her crazy. Carter didn't like to be thwarted, especially by something mechanical. "I *should* be able to open this," she said finally, and tossed her toolkit off to the side to rub her forehead. "Dammit. I don't know this metal, but it's as tough as the stuff the Stargate's made of."

"Maybe the same stuff?" Daniel asked.

"Without a full lab, I can't determine that. Nothing I have here will scratch it, and I haven't found any kind of pressure point or catch or fastening. However these things work, I'm not going to figure it out any time soon."

"Bag it," Jack said. "Let's move. I don't feel too comfortable staying over. Let's get moving."

"Are we still making for the temple as Alsiros suggested, O'Neill?" Teal'c asked.

"Unless you've got a better plan, in which case, hey, toss it out." Teal'c shook his head. "Then we keep moving until we spot something we can use."

"Shouldn't we… I don't know, say something?" Daniel asked, as Carter shouldered her field pack and prepared to move out. He was looking down at the body left behind, wrapped for the afterworld. Jack and Teal'c paused in the doorway to watch.

"Sure," Carter said, and let the pack slide off. "What do you want to say?"

"I don't know." Daniel was frowning in concentration, staring down. After a short pause, he said, "I'm sorry you came such a long way to die, and I'm sorry we couldn't help you. I hope you left someone behind who remembers you."

It had something personal in it, Jack thought, and remembered Daniel leaving on that first mission to Abydos – homeless, friendless, joining up with a bunch of hard-assed military guys who didn't have much respect for a trunk full of books.

I hope you left someone behind who remembers you.

"Amen," he said quietly, and limped away before Daniel could look at him. Outside, he slid on his sunglasses, checked his compass, and left a black-ops style mark on the wall, right around knee level. At least he'd be able to tell if they went in a circle. Not that the dead guy inside wouldn't give it away.

"O'Neill," Teal'c said, and caught up to him in two strides. "I have taken a sighting from the top of that wall." He pointed to one that looked really, really high. "There is an Acropolis in the center of the city, as Alsiros said. It is many miles to get there, and there appear to be no streets that travel in a straight line."

"Who builds a street that doesn't… never mind. What you're saying is that this place is a maze, right?"

"Almost certainly, it was built with that intention," Teal'c agreed. "Perhaps it was meant to foil invasion."

"Whatever it is, it's a total pain in the ankle." Jack grimaced, to let Teal'c know it was a joke, only not really. "Take point, and keep your eyes open. If somebody's running around dispatching new arrivals, let's stay off their dance card."

Teal'c's eyes were wide, suddenly. "Is there a possibility of dancing, O'Neill?"

"Figure of speech. It means, let's don't get killed."

"Indeed."

Daniel came out of the night shelter, and stopped, blinking in the bright sun; Carter's hand closed over his shoulder and more or less gently steered him out of the way. "Colonel?" she asked, in that way that reminded him it was time to get moving.

"Waiting on you slackers," he shot back. Carter looked up, a flash of bright blue eyes that were surprisingly cold. She'd taken it personally. Odd, he usually had pretty good radar for who he could needle, but hey, bad night, dead guy, he could see how it might screw up a generally good attitude. Daniel, on the other hand, shrugged it off, as Daniel typically would.

Time to mend fences. Jack quirked his eyebrows at Carter and said, "I'll take rear today. Keep Teal'c company."

She nodded, a bare quick movement, and moved around him to fall in behind the big Jaffa. Jack made an *after-you* to Daniel, who gave him a doubtful look but set off after Carter. The ankle wasn't so bad today – rest and anti-inflammatories had cut the pain by about fifty percent. He wasn't up to sprinting, but he could hobble along at a brisk clip. Jack kept his MP5 in a comfortable two-handed position, ready to bring it up with a snap if a situation presented, but the morning seemed quiet. Even the wind had let up, and the place smelled of nothing but dust and a faint, universal aroma of decay.

He caught a flash of something, just a dark shadow, moving fast, and turned to bring his weapon to bear. Nothing – no. There'd been something. Maybe human.

We're being tracked.

Jack checked their six at regular intervals, but there were no shadows behind them that he caught sight of. Night seemed a long way off, left behind, and as the sun warmed the air the place seemed a little more inviting.

Particularly, of course, to Daniel, who slowed down at every new corner, in front of every piece of rubble or carved stone. He got into the habit of darting up even with Carter, detouring into a likely pile of rubble and doing what Jack could only think of as hit-and-run archaeology – shoving aside piles of stone and rubble, looking for artifacts. The third time, he came up with something that looked like pieces of broken pottery; he jotted down notes and sketches on the move, dropped the pieces into a padded bag and stowed it in his pack. There were lines of stress around his eyes and mouth, a kind of wildness in him Jack didn't understand, until he looked at it from Daniel's perspective. After all, not only were they in a ruin – which was enough to make the man salivate like Pavlov's dog – but a ruin with a *mystery*.

Jack hobbled up next to him, sometime about an hour in, and peered over the man's shoulder at a scribbled notebook covered with stuff that might as well have been hieroglyphics, so far as Jack was concerned. Okay, it probably *was* hieroglyphics. "How's it going?" he asked. It was an innocent enough question.

It opened the floodgates. "This is so *frustrating!*" It burst out of Daniel, steam under pressure. "Jack, this place is a treasure trove, who *knows* what's in here, my God, it stretches for miles and there are probably artifacts in every one of these rooms – all these carvings, all these statues – " He gestured helplessly at it all. "I'll never get it all. I couldn't get it all if we spent a year here. This needs a team, a full-scale archaeological – "

"Probably a good time to mention that if we die, you don't get *any* of it."

"I know." Daniel frowned ferociously at his notebook, sighed, and flipped it closed. "It's just – I never expected to see anything like this. It's beyond my experience. Like Abydos and Chulak, only times ten.

Times a hundred. All these *rooms*… "

Jack put a hand on his shoulder, aware of the flinch that ran through Daniel's body; not antipathy, just gut-deep reaction. It probably said a lot about Daniel's childhood, now that he thought about it. Sha're was the only person Jack had ever seen touch him without causing that defensive reaction. "Daniel," he said. "We could be walking into anything. You know that, right?"

"I know. I'm trying not to slow you down, and I'm watching out, really. I am." Daniel looked up ahead, to where Carter was standing at the next corner, watching them with a tilted head. She beckoned for them to get a move on, then stepped out of sight. "She seems… different today."

"Bad night," Jack said. Daniel started walking, without any protest; Jack fell into stride next to him, with frequent glances back over his shoulder.

"Jack, did you dream?" Daniel asked.

Jack nearly missed a step, covered, and was grateful for his sunglasses and hat to hide most of his expression. "Nope."

"I did," Daniel said.

Jack waited for more, but that was it. Daniel lengthened his stride, sprinted on up ahead to grab hold of a broken hand-sized statue and examine it avidly, stroking his hands over it like a lover's body.

Jack shook his head, checked their six, and wished alternately that the place wasn't so damn deserted, and that it would stay that way.

Something weird happened, when Jack called a rest period. Well, not *weird* weird, but definitely out of the ordinary.

He had just eased himself to a half-reclining position against a handy fallen piece of masonry when he saw Daniel take his M9 out of its holster. If it had been Carter, Teal'c – hell, anybody else related to the SGC, up to and including the dour Airman Collins on the chow line – he wouldn't have taken much notice, but Daniel didn't *handle* guns. He wore one, reluctantly, but it was a necessary evil; he didn't exactly bond with them.

Have to work on that.

He watched as Daniel looked at the weapon, tilted it curiously this way and that in the sun, and smoothly slid the magazine out and then back in. Fast, fluid motions worthy of a trained military man.

Which Daniel wasn't.

And Daniel didn't holster his sidearm; he held it at his side, close to his trouser seam, and walked over to Carter. She was sipping water; he bent over and asked her something, and she smiled and nodded.

"What's that about?" Jack asked. Teal'c, sitting next to him, looked in the direction Jack pointed.

"I do not know."

Daniel cleared the M9 clip, pocketed it, and ejected the shell from the port to make it safe. He showed it to Carter, who nodded, and then he slapped it all back together again. She watched critically, made a couple of corrections, and had him do it again.

"Huh," Jack said. "Okay, now, I *really* think we're not in Kansas anymore. Since when does Daniel actually train? Without anybody making him?"

"He has had little instruction from your warrior-teachers," Teal'c said. "Is it not natural that he wish to continue to expand his knowledge of the weapon?"

No. Not Daniel.

Carter came over to squat next to him. "Colonel, Daniel wants to do some target practice. What do you think?"

"I think that stealth and gunfire are mutually exclusive." Jack watched Daniel sight down the pistol and dry fire it. "Why?"

"Sir?"

"Why does our peacenik archaeologist suddenly want to shoot bottles off of rocks?"

"Might have something to do with the dead bodies back there." She shrugged fluidly. "Not to mention the man who died this morning... Sir, I just think it's better if he gets some practice in. He might need it before too long. You never know – "

She wasn't wrong, although it still gave Jack an itch between the shoulder blades. "One clip."

She flashed him one of those luminous grins and went back to Daniel. Jack leaned his head back against the wall and watched through slitted eyes as she put Daniel into firing stance and walked a full circle around him, correcting him with touches and small shoves.

Then she moved in behind him and gave him the signal to fire.

Crack. She ordered a halt and checked the target.

"O'Neill," Teal'c said. "This morning, you asked if I dreamed of running in the night."

"Yeah. You said Jaffa don't dream."

"We do not. What I experienced was not a dream."

Teal'c's face was closed and still as he studied Carter, who moved to Daniel to give him some correction in his stance. She stepped up behind him, front to his back, and reached under his arms to lift them up and lean him into the stance. Very intimate. *Well, that's probably against regs,* Jack thought, *not to mention going to make him flinch like a mother...*

Only it didn't. Daniel didn't pull away. Well, look at that.

Crack. Two shots down. *Crack, crack, crack.* Five.

Teal'c had said something important, Jack realized, and he scrambled to catch up. "What exactly did you experience?"

"I had a vivid hallucination in which I felt I was being chased through this city, and was killed," Teal'c replied. "By Daniel Jackson and Captain Carter. It was..." He seemed to think about the word for a long time before choosing, "... disturbing."

Jack's dream washed over him again, thick and slow, heavy with dread. *Disturbing.* Kind of like watching those two so close together, dusty brown head bent close to dusty blonde one, examining the results of Daniel's target practice. Unconsciously in each other's personal space. *Well, you wanted to see them bond.* Yeah, just not in a predatory wolf-pack kind of way.

If that was what it was.

"I hate this place," Jack said, and shoved himself back to his feet. "Yo. Carter. Let me do that."

He hobbled toward them, cursing the drag in his foot, and they both looked up to stare at his approach.

Identical blue-eyed stares, and for a second, the dream – hallucination? – he'd apparently shared with Teal'c in the night took on weight and texture and certainty.

Daniel stepped back to let Jack see the tight grouping of shots on the wall. "I never thought I'd hit the broad side of a barn. She's a good teacher."

"Yeah," Jack agreed, staring at that tiny, expert impact zone, and imagining it in somebody's bleeding chest. "Enjoying yourself?"

"Not really." Daniel was frowning now, and there was genuine wariness in his blue eyes. "Jack... I thought you'd be pleased. If I get better, I won't slow you down, I won't be a liability in a fight..."

"Yay?" Jack loaded it with sarcasm, and jerked his head at Carter. "Playtime's over. Let's get moving."

She didn't. "Sir, you said one clip..."

"And now I'm saying I'd rather be six streets away before anybody comes to investigate what that racket was, Captain. Any questions?"

For a genuinely cold second, he saw resistance in her eyes, and then she smiled and it was gone. "No sir. Good work, Daniel. Maybe later."

He nodded, cleared his weapon and holstered it.

Wasn't I saying he needed more practice? Yeah, I did. Which bothered Jack at least as much as the fact that he couldn't make himself be happy with either outcome.

CHAPTER 6 – MOONLIGHT
φεγγαρόφωτο

They ran into Alsiros again just after the sun touched the center of the hollow sky.

Or rather, what was left of him.

"Colonel!" Carter's sharp yell jolted him into a lopsided jog, pain or no pain; he slowed down to scale a waist-high rubble pile made by a couple of collapsing walls, and slid down the other side to find Carter and Teal'c standing together in what looked like another big courtyard. Agora. Whatever. Like the one in Chalcis, this one was tiled, and it had a big fountain in the center. The water still trickled from broken, mutilated statues, but the stuff in the square pool looked brackish and foul.

It looked like a war zone, post-occupation; destroyed buildings, burned fragments of timbers, jagged broken foundations and fallen columns. A giant statue that must have once been some god or other lay on its side, shattered into four pieces. One massive hand held a golden globe with intricate symbols all over it.

The place was a treasure trove. There were pieces of gold glittering everywhere. Over by the fountain, coins and jewelry spilled out of a rotting, beautifully painted wooden chest. Tattered silk flapped like sun-faded ghosts with the wind.

Human beings collected shiny things. The fact that they'd left it here, abandoned, told Jack about as much as he wanted to know about how desperate things had gotten here, before the end.

And whatever came afterward.

Grandpa Preacher – Alsiros – was kneeling with arms spread out to each side, on the cracked steps of what had once been a massive marble-faced temple. It was shattered now, nothing but jagged walls and broken columns. Whatever holiness had once been inside was long destroyed.

"Alsiros?" Jack took a couple of steps closer, saw the man's graying hair blow in a sudden gust of wind. The black robe he was wearing flapped restlessly. "Hey. You okay…?"

"Careful, sir," Carter murmured, her MP5 still locked in firing position. Teal'c stood with her, tense and ready to jump forward, but the old man just turned his head toward Jack without making a sound.

He was splashed with blood. Dried blood, turning rust-brown, spidering over his face and neck, coating his hands as if he'd washed in it.

"Hey," Jack said again, more slowly. "So… you okay, there?"

"Dead." Grandpa wasn't preaching anymore. His voice was hollow, broken. Haunted. "So many dead."

Jack slowly sank into a crouch next to him. "Alsiros. Who's dead?"

A blood-smeared hand rose, gestured vaguely toward the far end of the courtyard. Jack looked over his shoulder at his team, fixed on Teal'c, and nodded. Teal'c nodded back and took off at a run across the courtyard.

Carter's frown deepened. She still had her finger on the MP5's trigger, and was watching Alsiros with way too much focus. Jack caught her eye and sent her a silent *stand down*.

She didn't.

"Captain Carter," he said, quiet but firm. "We're okay here."

She blinked and let the weapon slide down to a resting position.

Daniel, oblivious, had moved forward next to Jack. "Alsiros? Remember me? Daniel Jackson? What… what happened to you?"

The old man looked blank. Unoccupied. But as the eyes focused on Daniel's compassionate face, something snapped back in place, with a vengeance.

He grabbed Daniel's shoulder, hard enough to make the younger man wince. Jack didn't move, but his finger stayed close to the trigger.

"*She*," Alsiros said fiercely. His eyes were wide and full of horror, fury, something too big for a human body to hold. "I gave her worship, but *she… she* craves only blood. Only death."

"Who? She, who?" Daniel said, holding Alsiros's hand on his shoulder as if he wanted to reach out to him but didn't dare. "Alsiros, *who*?"

"The goddess," the old man whispered. "She chooses... she knows... I saw her face last night, cold and beautiful, her eyes as bright as suns..."

Jack met Daniel's wide eyes. No question, that was the description of a Goa'uld... Daniel fumbled in his pockets and came out with the single photograph he had of his wife. He offered it to Alsiros. "Is this – is this the goddess?"

The old man barely glanced at it. "No."

Jack sighed under his breath, and heard Daniel echo it; the last thing they needed right now was the prospect of fighting Skaara and Sha're. Bad enough there was some other snake out here running around, probably with a small army of Jaffa at her command....

Teal'c had reached the far side of the courtyard. Whatever he found, he found it quickly, and came loping back fast.

"Two are dead," he reported. "I believe the others in this party have fled separately, farther into the city. They no longer appear to be traveling together."

"Faithless," Alsiros murmured. "They were faithless and the goddess punished us. She came in my dreams... in my dreams... laughing..."

He let go of Daniel's shoulder and began to wring his hands, over and over, dried blood flaking from his skin.

Teal'c said, over Jack's shoulder, "I do not believe a Goa'uld killed them." Jack turned to look at him, and Teal'c sent Alsiros's stained hands a significant look. "They died as did the one we found before."

"Stabbed?" That was from Carter, who'd moved up behind Daniel. Teal'c nodded.

"Hey. Alsiros." Jack got the full-on crazy stare in response. "Don't take this the wrong way, but... let me have the knife."

Alsiros looked briefly confused. He had nothing with him, nothing but the black robes, and some other kind of robes underneath... and then he slowly reached inside the black and came out with red-streaked metal in his hand. Same style of dagger as before. Triangular blade, ram's head at the top. Probably from an armory of some kind. Maybe each of the tribute offerings had been issued one along with the black robes, the better to kill you with, my dear.

"Okay, just hand it to me now," Jack said in his best, kindest voice. Alsiros started to, then hesitated, staring down at the bloodstained bronze. "Don't think about it. Just hand it over."

But he didn't. When the old man looked up, his eyes were bright and sharp again, glittering with tears. He stared at each of them in turn, as if he'd never seen them before, finally focusing his gaze on Sam Carter.

He handed *her* the knife. She frowned, her hand closing around it, staring down at it for a few seconds before shoving it into her pack.

"Alsiros," Daniel was asking urgently, "did you do this? Did you kill them?"

"Not I."

Jack bent his head toward Daniel and said in an undertone, "I'm no detective, but I'd say bloody knife plus bloody hands plus dead guys equals guilty."

"Not necessarily," Daniel muttered back. "Maybe he was trying to, I don't know, save them. And picked up the knife for self-defense."

"Thank you, Perry Mason. No unprotected backs and sharp objects for him. You can appeal later."

Alsiros wasn't watching them; he was focused on Carter, his hand touching his moonstone collar. Like Carter's, it was flawed. Alsiros's was more than half dark, occluded like there was some invisible eclipse going on inside of him.

"Okay," Jack said with false heartiness. "Daniel, you're in charge of Alsiros, here. We need to get moving; if we're making for the Acropolis, we've got a long way to go."

"I will stay," Alsiros said. He turned his crazy gaze back toward the destroyed temple, with its broken-teeth columns and shattered gods. "If the goddess wills it, I will come to you."

Which had more than a little aroma of genuine psychosis to it, and when Daniel raised his eyebrows at Jack, Jack shrugged and took a step back. Daniel moved closer to him to whisper, "Ah, we're not just going to *leave* him here, are we?"

"Let me put it this way: Yes. Yes, we are."

"But Jack – "

"Daniel, I am *not* dragging along a possibly homicidal crazy guy against his will. He doesn't want to come, fine. We're moving on."

"Jack!"

"Leave him food and water." Jack let the command seep into his voice and level stare. "You heard him. Maybe he'll come to us." *With a nice, shiny knife in his hand.*

Daniel had more argument left, but he was wise enough to store it up for later. He left a short supply of MREs for Alsiros, painstakingly explaining how to open and prepare them, and then they were on their way, heading farther into the guts of the destroyed, dead city.

"O'Neill," Teal'c said, and gestured with a jerk of his head off to the right-hand side.

Someone was standing on top of a pile of rubble. Dark tunic, a fluttering tattered cloak. Holding something that glittered metallic in the light.

And then, like a ghost, he was gone.

"Tell me you saw that," Jack said. Teal'c nodded. "What do you think?"

"I think that they move very swiftly," the Jaffa answered. "And they have been following us for some time now."

"The Dark Company?"

"Those I have seen wear dark clothing."

"Well, that's just never good. Keep your eyes open." Jack looked toward Daniel and Carter, standing out of earshot. "And Teal'c. Watch them, too."

Jack set a faster pace, as fast as he could possibly hobble. *We've got to get the hell out of here.* He felt the pressure more with every passing hour.

For the rest of the day, they hiked arduously over shattered rubble and around blocked streets, trying to keep more or less on the compass heading Teal'c had given for the Acropolis. Teal'c, Carter and Daniel took turns with sightings, scaling walls and, on one memorable occasion, a broken marble plinth that still had the dismembered marble legs of some statue attached to it. Daniel had looked particularly weird, standing up there gazing at the horizon, hugging those giant marble ankles. When he'd shimmied down again, he'd reported that they'd only covered a half a mile or so toward the goal.

Which put it still at least two days away, assuming they kept to the same pace. Great. Jack *really* didn't want to do any more camping in Crazy Killer Theme Park, but he didn't see any way out of it.

Of course, some traitorous part of his brain whispered, *maybe you get there and all you find is some nice roomy marble tomb of a place, and nothing to help you fix the DHD. Maybe it's a one-way trip, after all.*

That wasn't strategically useful, even if it might be true. He rejected it and focused on the matter at hand.

"Getting dark," Carter noted. She'd been very quiet today, talking in monosyllables when spoken to. He couldn't gauge her – was it just that the little voice in her head was louder, and she was convinced this was a waste of time? Or when it came down to brass tacks, did Captain Carter not have what it took to carry on in the face of over-whelming odds? No, he had better instincts than that. Carter was okay. She'd hold together. If he'd ever misjudged anybody on that score, it had been a geeky, sneezy scientist on a mission to Abydos... who'd ended up saving his ass.

"Find us some shelter," Jack said, and took the opportunity to sit down on a handy stone block that had once been part of somebody's home, somebody's business. Daniel was, as usual, grubbing around in the rubble. This time he came up with something that slithered through his fingers almost like a living thing, and Jack felt that instinctive tightening along his spine. Nope. Not a snake. This was gold, where it caught the light.

"Necklace," Daniel said, and carried it over to sit next to Jack. He bent his dusty head to examine it more closely. "God, it's beauti-ful. The artistry – these links are so small, they're almost invisible." Jack's first impression had been right after all, it was in the shape of a snake, with a thick triangular head and ruby eyes. Daniel's voice was hushed and almost worshipful. "Here. Hold it."

Jack waved him off. "No offense, Daniel, but you've found about a hundred trinkets so far. Doesn't the new ever wear off for you?"

Daniel, who'd taken off his glasses to examine the piece more closely, looked up at Jack and gave him that little strange smile. "No," he said. "Jack, somebody *made* this. Not a factory, not a machine, a human being. He had to smelt each of these tiny links and fit them together, it must have taken months of backbreaking work. Then he sold it to someone else, who put it around her neck and wore it… it may have been the only nice thing she ever owned. It may have been a gift from a lover, or a husband, or a father… Jack, this is the history of *people*. Each of these things, they mean something. Touching them… it's like touching all of human history."

Jack stared back at him for a second or two, then reached over and took the necklace. He held it, feeling the weight of it, the cool and almost living movement of the tiny links. The ruby eyes winked at him. He wanted to see what Daniel saw, the magic that Daniel felt holding these things. All he could think of was a Goa'uld, ready to sink its evil little self into the back of his neck.

He managed a smile and handed it back. "Yeah," he said. "Pretty fabulous."

Daniel beamed, and wandered over to show Teal'c his find.

That was when Jack felt they were being watched. Again.

He sat for a few seconds, then levered himself back to his feet and made his way over to where Teal'c and Daniel were talking.

"Teal'c," he said, interrupting Daniel's monologue. "Take the side street over on the right, circle back. We've got visitors. Daniel, don't look. Just keep talking."

"About, ah, anything in particular?" Daniel asked.

"Don't suppose you know anything about hockey?" Dumb question. "Watch *The Simpsons*?"

"Um…"

"Okay, talk about the snake."

Daniel launched into another voluble explanation, this time about mining and cutting rubies, and Jack nodded wherever there was a pause that looked like it might need a response. As he listened, he casually turned them around so that he was facing back the way they'd come. Daniel didn't even notice… or if he did, he played along well. No sign of Teal'c. No sign of anything moving out in the rubble.

Could have imagined it. No, probably not, that sensation had saved his life too many times to be just nerves.

He caught a flicker of movement off to the right. Daniel was saying, " – hand-polished the gems using sand cloths – " and then, blindingly fast, Teal'c was in the open and moving to attack. Jack grabbed Daniel and threw him behind cover, brought up his MP5, and Teal'c

dived behind a thick nest of boulders and came out holding two struggling figures.

After a couple of seconds, the faces clicked in. Teal'c had hold of
the brother and sister from Alsiros's party. The boy was fighting, but
that wasn't having much of an effect on Teal'c, who had hold of both
of them by the backs of their tunics like a couple of stray puppies. The
girl looked doe-eyed and scared to death.

Jack saw the intention in the boy's set face a second before he saw
the knife, and yelled, "Teal'c! Watch yourself!" just before the boy
slashed with a familiar-looking bronze knife. He scored a shallow
scratch on Teal'c's tac vest.

With no memory of having moved, Jack was suddenly over the
pile of rubble between them and grabbing the kid, wrestling the knife
away with a quick, efficient turn of his wrist. The boy – Pylades? –
yelled out his rage and hatred, and struck blindly with fists; Jack got
him in a sleeper hold and took him down to his knees. The girl, by
contrast, was almost catatonic, tears streaming down her face.

"Teal'c? You okay?"

"I am uninjured, O'Neill," he said, and drew a finger across the
slice in his vest. "However, I am grateful for the warning."

Daniel joined them, sliding down the mound of rubble – damn,
that thing was tall, Jack hadn't realized it until then – and came to a
stumbling halt, looking from Jack and the boy to Teal'c and the girl.
"Pylades? Iphigenia?"

"Let her go!" Pylades yelled at Teal'c. Teal'c, after a raised eyebrow at Jack, released her. The girl dropped to her knees next to her
brother and put her arms around his neck. Jack let the boy loose, too,
and he wrapped Iphigenia in a protective hug. "I swear, I will kill any
who try to hurt her – "

"Easy," Jack said, and stowed the knife in his tac vest pocket to
show empty hands. "Nobody's hurting anybody. You okay? Both of
you?"

Pylades slowly, unwillingly nodded. "We ran," he said. "I hid her
here, when she couldn't run any farther. I was coming back for her
when I saw you."

"Don't leave me," Iphigenia whispered to him, and buried her face
in his chest. "Please don't leave me again!"

"I won't," he soothed her, and stroked her tangled brown hair. "It was the only way. You couldn't outrun them. But you're safe now."

"Safe from...?" Daniel asked. "Pylades, it's okay. You can trust us. We're not going to hurt you, either of you. You'll be safe with us."

From the narrow set of the kid's brown eyes, he wasn't buying it. Iphigenia, though, was; Jack could see it in the way she sneaked glances at Daniel, color rising in her cheeks. *Oh, great.* Daniel seemed to have that effect on the young, innocent ones. And just as clearly, Daniel had absolutely no clue.

"Who was chasing you?" Jack asked. "Jaffa?" He gestured at Teal'c, with an apologetic shrug in the man's direction. Teal'c accepted it stoically.

"They were from Mycenae," Pylades said. "I did not know them."

"How do you know they were from Mycenae?" Daniel asked.

Pylades frowned at the question. "It was obvious."

"From...?"

"They wore the colors."

Well, at least the bad guys were color-coded. That helped. "What colors would those be?"

For answer, Pylades produced a scrap of fabric, bloodstained – pale yellow. Jack rubbed his fingers on it, thinking, then handed it to Daniel. "Look familiar?"

"It's like what the man this morning was wearing."

"So he was from Mycenae." And maybe Pylades had been the killer. Damn. Nothing confusing about this, was there?

Daniel must have seen the thought passing over Jack's expression, because he shook his head and gestured toward Pylades' tunic, which was torn and grubby, but not bloody. "He'd be soaked, Jack. Like Alsiros."

"Alsiros!" Iphigenia suddenly grabbed at Daniel's hands and held them tight. "Is he alive?"

"He's fine," Daniel assured her, and gently extricated himself. "He's, ah, praying. We left him food and water. He'll be all right."

Pylades and Iphigenia exchanged a look, and Jack saw the grim light come back into Pylades' eyes.

"What?" he asked them.

Pylades focused on him, and said, "Alsiros killed two of us. He went mad. You should have slain him where you found him. I would have, only…" He glanced at Iphigenia, who had tears in those big brown eyes. "… Only my sister was so frightened. We ran, like the rest. Then the men of Mycenae came after us."

So, bad guys *not* color coded. Not a help. "Daniel? What the *hell* is going on?"

"I don't know. Pylades – before Alsiros went mad, did he say anything, do anything…?"

"He slept," Pylades said. "I kept watch. I saw him wake and stand, looking at the moon, and then he took his knife and went to Kalman, who was asleep. Before I could raise the alarm, he had stabbed him. Not – not killed him. Kalman ran, and Alsiros – he ran after. We all saw him – " He stopped, unable to go on. Jack realized suddenly just how young the kid was. Strong, yeah, but nowhere near old enough to handle something like this. "When Kalman was dead, Alsiros came back. We ran, we all ran, but he caught Siria…"

"But he didn't say anything?" Daniel asked gently. "You're sure?"

"He said… something about the moon. About running in the moonlight. It didn't make any sense."

Jack had a sudden hot, vivid flash of the dream, of running in the cold silver moonlight, hunters swift and fatal on his trail. He thought he saw something in Daniel's eyes, too, but then the younger man looked away.

"It's getting dark," his sister said. She was sitting, with Pylades, in a deep shadow thrown by the walls; her disordered long hair glowed orange in the setting sun. "We should – we should hide."

Pylades nodded. "We're safe now," he said. "Look at their weapons. They're fierce warriors. They will protect us now, and no one can harm you."

Jack looked up just an instant before the rubble shifted; Carter appeared at the top, face stained with sunset. Her eyes were unreadable as she looked down at them. "Found something, sir," she said. "It's not great, but it's pretty defensible."

"Big enough for a couple of houseguests?"

"Don't see why not."

"Lead on, Captain," he said, and hoisted Pylades up by an elbow. Pylades kept hold of Iphigenia's hand, drawing her with him. "Kid. Stay with us, right? Safety in numbers."

Pylades nodded.

Dinner was another round of MREs, washed down with tepid water and – in Daniel's case – instant coffee. Pylades and Iphigenia gamely tried everything. The Chili Mac went over gangbusters, along with the fruit; Iphigenia nibbled on her oatmeal cookie and abandoned it, and Pylades ended up scarfing them both. Jack, drawing the short straw, ended up with the Escalloped Potatoes and Ham, which he'd always pretty much loathed. He tried to talk Teal'c into swapping, with no luck. Invoking command privilege over entrees seemed a little petty.

Daniel, who didn't seem to notice or care what the hell it was he was eating, was busily grilling Iphigenia about life on Sikyon. She was shy, but eager to give him details about everything from hair styles to shopping in the market; Daniel made copious notes. Pylades, after watching with a brother's jealous care for a while, must have decided that Daniel posed no threat to his baby sister's virtue; he came to sit next to Carter instead.

"You are a woman," he said.

Carter's quick, vivid smile flashed for the first time in hours. "Yeah, thanks for noticing."

"On Sikyon – women do not carry arms. Or fight. Men do that for them." He sounded defensive about it, Jack thought. "It is not seemly. Do not your men defend you?"

Jack choked down a grin. "Wanna field that one, Captain?"

"It's not quite that simple, Pylades. My people believe that anyone should be free to choose their own path – men or women alike. If I'm suited to be a fighter, then I can be a fighter. Although personally, I admit I like flying." Pylades gave her an uncomprehending stare, as if the word didn't translate. "Flying. In the air. In machines."

"Your words are foolish," Pylades said. "Men cannot fly. – Women," he added belatedly.

"Well, they can with a little help."

"No one should wish to *fly*." Pylades shook his head, and pointedly looked away to end the conversation.

"Who in their right mind doesn't like flying?" Jack asked, with a quirk of his eyebrows.

"Army, Navy, and Marines, sir."

"And there's a reason they're not on my team, Captain. I believe I did qualify it with *right mind*."

She gave *him* the smile, then. The uncomplicated approval of it eased some of the tension that had accumulated in his guts. Maybe she hadn't been acting odd, after all. Maybe that black spot on the necklace had nothing to do with it – Daniel's was still pure white, after all, and he'd been the one popping off shots and channeling Wild Bill Hickok. "Any thoughts about tomorrow?" he asked her.

"I guess we have no choice but to keep heading for the Acropolis," she said. "Every other building we've seen has been gutted or destroyed. The place is a complete ruin. The chances of finding anything to help us get home in any of these wrecks is, well, pretty small."

They were camped in one of those wrecks; this one, according to Daniel's enthusiastic flood of explanation, had probably been a private home, and they were bedding down in what would have been a front receiving room. It still had a roof and four walls. Jack wasn't entirely happy with the open back door, which looked out on a dead, dry garden and a broken fountain, not to mention a warren of other partially destroyed rooms, but it was the best they'd found. Teal'c was keeping watch at the back, Jack at the front, and they'd be taking shifts through the night.

They'd found bodies here too, long-dead skeletons that probably dated from when this city had died. Daniel couldn't tell much about them, except that at least three had been children, one just a baby. They'd left them huddled together in the back room where they'd found them. Jack, seeing a glint of gold around the baby's bony arm, had gestured to Daniel; Daniel had just shaken his head and walked away.

Jack already liked him, but he liked him a hell of a lot more for that.

"Let's get some sleep," Jack said, loud enough to cut through the still-enthusiastic dialogue going on between Iphigenia and Daniel. "Carter, Daniel, we'll wake you at 0300."

Nobody protested; truthfully, Jack thought, every one of them with the possible exception of Teal'c was pretty much wrung out. Daniel and Carter stretched out on the thin bedrolls, pulled blankets over their heads, and within minutes Jack heard the light sound of Daniel's snores. Carter slept silently – military training – and Iphigenia and Pylades curled up in the corner together, back to back. No self-consciousness about sleeping so close together, Jack noticed, but then, different planet, different customs. Daniel and Carter had unconsciously left a good amount of space between them, even though the chill was settling in deeply.

Jack blew out a breath, saw it spread out silver on the air, and hugged his hands under his armpits.

It was going to be another damn long night.

Hours passed in silence. Jack watched the night go from ink-black to silver, washed in the thick moonlight; nothing moved out there, but there was a feeling to it. Sinister. Maybe it was imagination, but he didn't think so. He remembered the mosaic back on Chalcis, the ruined city, the moonlight, the sense of danger lurking in shadow. It occurred to him, kind of cheerfully, that somebody had been here to see that scene, so maybe there really was a way off this rock.

Although it was way too easy to believe, here in the darkness down the throat of night, that there wasn't any hope – that all that was left was a futile, desperate struggle and an ugly death. But he'd faced that before, many times, and it didn't drag on him the way he knew it would the others. Daniel might be resistant to it, too. For all his imagination and quick intelligence, Daniel could be amazingly dense when it came to recognizing danger. Carter, on the other hand... all the sensitivity, none of Jack's hardening. He knew she was tough, or he wouldn't have picked her for the team, but she hadn't been tested the way Daniel had, or Teal'c. It took special hardness to make it through something like this without breaking.

And now she was whimpering in her sleep again, making sounds of real distress.

Jack left his post and shuffled over to her, wincing at the strain in his still-sore ankle, and put a hand on her shoulder and shook gently. "Captain," he whispered. "Captain Carter."

She came awake with a galvanic shudder, straight up, and he saw the shine of sweat on her flushed face.

She also came up with her combat knife in her hand. Jack threw himself back instinctively, before his brain even reported the flash of movement, and felt the tip of the knife dig into his tac vest a second before ripping free in a diagonal line.

"Captain!" he barked, and grabbed her arm. He twisted, *hard*, felt her fighting him but adrenaline and training, not to mention superior upper body strength, won out. She dropped the knife with a metallic *klang* and spun up to a fighting crouch. "*Captain Carter!*"

Everybody woke up. Teal'c came to his feet, but didn't abandon his post.

It took long sweaty, skin-crawling seconds before the sanity crept back into those wide eyes, and finally Carter swallowed hard and whispered, "Colonel?"

"What's left of him," he said in disgust, and looked down at his vest. Another inch, and he'd be picking up his guts with both hands. "Any particular *reason* you want to field-dress me, Carter?"

She sucked in a deep, shaking breath. "Sorry, sir. I was – "

"Dreaming, yeah, got that." He engaged her eyes and held them. "You okay?"

"Yes sir."

"I'm not asking for the P.C. answer, Captain."

"And I'm not giving it." A deep, convulsive breath. "I'm good, sir."

Daniel, up on one elbow watching the drama, had frozen in place, as had Teal'c; when she followed up the declaration with a murmured, "Sorry, bad dream," Daniel rolled back flat and closed his eyes in relief.

Teal'c kept watching, expressionless and tense.

Jack wasn't buying her apology; she had a pale, shaky look he didn't like. And it might have been his imagination, but she looked fevered – flushed, eyes glittering. Reaction time a little too fast. In the pale reflected moonlight and the half-light of the camp stove that kept the room moderately warm, he caught sight of her collar, and the moonstone in the center.

The dark mark on it was larger, nearly a full quarter. Like Alsiros's.

"Turn around, Captain," he said, and made a twirling motion when she didn't respond. She did, unwillingly, and turned her head to try to catch sight of what he was doing. "Nothing personal, Carter." He moved her hair off her neck and looked first at the unbroken skin – no stealth invasion by Goa'uld, at least – and then at the silvery mesh of the collar. It was seamless. He probed at it with his fingers, looking for some kind of catch, then had her turn to face him again. This close, it was impossible not to feel some discomfort. He compensated by focusing hard on the objective – the damn collar. She was breathing shallowly and fast.

When he reached out, she blocked him with a fast upraised arm. "Don't, sir," she said hoarsely. "Don't touch it."

"Why not?"

"Because – " Her eyes were a little wild. "Just don't."

He felt his frown groove deeper. "Carter – "

She put a hand up over the collar, not as if she was trying to rip it away – which was what he wanted to do – but as if trying to keep it *on*.

Okay, something was deeply wrong here.

"Why me, sir?" It burst out of her in a shaking rush. "Why is this happening to *me*? Why nobody else?"

"I don't know, Captain."

"Is it just that I'm the only woman, or – "

"Alsiros went faster than you did," he reminded her. "One or two nights, he was over the edge. Maybe it's body chemistry. Maybe it's magnetic waves. Hell, Carter, for all I know, we're right behind you. Stay focused. You're not crazy."

"Maybe not yet," she said, and forced a shaky smile.

"Maybe not ever."

They both flinched at the high, thin, panicked sound of a scream. It ripped the fabric of the night, echoed, multiplied. Echoes? More than one voice? Jack took a step back, saw Teal'c turning to face him too, face wiped blank in concentration. Daniel rolled groggily up for the second time.

The screaming was *close*. Very close.

Carter darted around him, grabbed her MP5, and hit the door at a run.

"Captain!" he yelled, but she was already gone at a dead run. "Captain, *halt!* That's an order!"

No way he could keep up with her, not with his ankle; he tried anyway, running until the fiery ache crippled him and he had to sag against a crumbling wall, hissing in pain. Somebody ran past him, flat out – he thought it was Teal'c, at first, until he felt a ham-sized hand closing on his shoulder to support him from behind.

Daniel. *Daniel* had been chasing after Carter. Going like a god-damn track star.

"I'm fine!" Jack lied. "Go go go!"

Teal'c abandoned him and loped on, running after Daniel, and *damn*, where had Daniel learned to run like that? Well, Abydos, prob-ably. He'd had plenty of time toning up, chasing after the Abydonian kids up and down sand dunes. He would have been training them, same as he'd trained them to use the ordnance that the first Stargate mission had abandoned there.

Bad time for Daniel to decide to be a hero, and *dammit*, there was no way Jack was going to keep up, his ankle was folding up like wet cardboard the harder he pushed it. It was pulsing now, sickening red/ purple pulses that thudded in time with his heartbeat.

He rounded the next corner in time to see Carter climbing a moun-tain of rubble, cresting it, and disappearing on the other side. Teal'c and Daniel were kneeling next to a crumpled dark shape in the moon-light – another black-robed tribute victim, this one a woman, her throat slashed. Blood slid in dark sheets over the stone, and Daniel's hands were covered with it as he tried to stop the bleeding.

No good. Daniel sat back and looked up at the moon. Blood-flecks on his glasses, splashes on his face. He looked exhausted and ill.

Jack remembered the flash of the knife in Carter's hand, and felt a sickening drop at the pit of his stomach. *God, no.*

Daniel must have read the thought in his face. "She didn't do this," he said. "She – she went after the one who did."

Jack keyed the radio. "Carter! Captain Carter, break off pursuit and get your ass back here, *now*!"

"She can't," Daniel said, and scrambled to his feet. "She can't stop now."

"Daniel!" Jack barked, and hobbled toward them as fast as possible. "Stay, dammit – "

But it was like Daniel couldn't hear him, or didn't care; he hit the pile of rubble at a run, scrambled up with hands and feet, and slid over the top out of sight.

Jack felt a sudden strength-sapping wave of weariness, outright *fear*, and looked at Teal'c. Was it just his imagination, or was there something there, too? Some sense of futility, of uselessness, of inevitability?

"Teal'c," he said hoarsely. "Go after them."

The Jaffa nodded and took off after Daniel and Carter. Jack sucked in heavy, blood-tasting breaths and looked at the scene again. Bloody corpse, bloody footprints leading up to the mountain of rubble.

This is going so far south it's meeting north.

And he didn't understand why. Daniel was headstrong, but he wasn't stupid; he wouldn't go after Carter against orders, he *knew* he'd be lousy as backup. And Teal'c should have been way ahead of him. It was as if...

As if they'd all changed, in small but telling ways.

Yeah? Is that why you weren't faster on the uptake? Why you didn't grab Carter and slam her down before she could make it out of the shelter? Why you couldn't stop Daniel just now?

Jack turned, a slow, limping circle, looking around. There was a dark doorway to his left. He took it, found a half-fallen wall that he managed to roll himself over, then a shortcut past the massive pile of fallen wall that blocked the street.

He limped grimly on, knowing that whatever was happening, he was going to be too late to stop it.

We left those kids alone back there. In the fast press of events, he'd forgotten Pylades and Iphigenia, and that wasn't like him, he should have snapped out orders to protect the camp, should have kept command...

Worse, he left them with the supplies. *Dammit.* If those were gone, they were deeply screwed.

He took another shortcut, then another, listening for the sound of pounding footsteps, and came out less than a hundred feet away from Captain Carter.

She was standing very still, her MP5 trained on a man lying on his back, hands flung wide. There was a bronze ram's head dagger in his right fist, but he wasn't making any threatening moves. He was staring up at the moon like a blind man, face open and weirdly ecstatic, and as Jack watched, his back bowed and he had some kind of seizure, foaming from the mouth.

He saw the fury twist on Carter's face just an instant before her trigger finger tightened.

Daniel exploded around the corner, reached Carter and knocked the muzzle of her rifle up into the air just as she let loose a full auto burst that would have shredded the man lying on the ground into hamburger.

It would have been stone cold murder. Jack felt that settle over him like frost, even as Carter rounded on Daniel with a snarl like nothing he'd ever heard in his life, animal and furious, and swung her MP5 straight at his head like a club.

Daniel ducked fluidly and decked her with a backhanded blow to the face. Flat out on the stone next to the man with the knife. He went down with her, knee in her chest, holding her flat as she struggled, and wrenched the MP5 away from her with one hand.

He lifted it with a snarl, ready to slam it down into her face.

"Daniel!" Jack roared, and saw the man hesitate, every muscle in his body trembling, and then Daniel dropped the gun, hit Carter hard on the chin again with his fist and rolled away.

Carter went limp.

Daniel fell over and curled up on his side, shaking, as Jack limped forward and grabbed the MP5, slung it over his shoulder, and kicked the knife out of the reach of, well, everyone.

He stood there in the moonlight looking down at Daniel, at Carter, not knowing what exactly he should be feeling but knowing what he *did* feel, inappropriate as it was.

He was scared shitless for them. *Of* them.

Teal'c rounded the corner and advanced slowly, staff weapon held at cautious half-staff, and some of Jack's irrational fear eased a little.

"Teal'c, nice of you to join us. Zip-cuff that guy," Jack said, and jerked his chin at the foaming, spasming figure of the killer still lying on the ground in some kind of ecstatic frenzy. As Teal'c moved to comply, Jack carefully eased himself down on one knee next to Daniel and put his hand on a shaking shoulder. "Daniel. Hey. Easy…"

Daniel flinched. More than ever. Then he rolled painfully over on his back, and stared up at the moon; there was some of the same blindness in him, as if he'd been drugged. His pupils were hugely dilated.

"Oh, God, Jack," he whispered, and shut his eyes. "Help me. *Help me.*"

"*How?*"

"I – " Daniel threw his arm up, blocking out the light. "Get us inside."

Carter was out, but starting to stir. Jack stared at her for a second, remembering the bright silver shine of her eyes, the fluid ferocity of the way she'd run, the coldly calculating way she'd sighted down the MP5 at a helpless captive.

"Teal'c," he said, feeling exhausted to the bone. "Do Carter, too."

Teal'c pulled the zip-cuffs tight around the black-robed murderer's wrists and looked up, plainly doubtful. "O'Neill?"

"That's an order."

Teal'c pulled another set from his vest, flipped Carter over on her face, and fastened her hands behind her back. She woke up halfway through the procedure and started fighting him, fierce and focused; Teal'c added ankle cuffs, stood and dumped Carter unceremoniously over one broad shoulder.

Daniel was up on his own, pale but still in control. He even managed a faint, scared smile, and said, "She's not going to forget that."

"Hope not," Jack said somberly. "Let's all live to regret it."

Some of the tension in Jack's guts eased when they found Pylades and Iphigenia still in the shelter, safe and sound, along with the supplies. Pylades had a sharp-edged stone scavenged from a pile in the corner, and looked determined to beat the fool out of anybody who came in without authorization. Jack talked him down and got Daniel settled in one corner as Teal'c gently deposited the still-struggling Carter in another. She was eerily quiet, breathing fast, eyes shining, but saying nothing at all. She devoted all her strength to the zip-ties.

"She will injure herself," Teal'c said, frowning. It looked likely; she was already rubbing her wrists raw on the plastic. "Do you not have some medicine that will calm her?"

Jack nodded and dug in Carter's pack for the first aid kit. There were self-contained shots of painkillers and sedatives; he went for the sedatives, promising himself a celebratory morphine shot later, in the safety of the SGC. He sliced open her BDU sleeve to reach bare skin on her arm. She hissed when the shot went in, thrashed even harder, then began to weaken and go still.

When her eyes closed, Jack patted her on the shoulder and nodded Teal'c back to door sentry duty. Then he went over to Daniel.

"Hey," he said. Daniel was sitting with his head in his hands, elbows propped on his knees; he didn't look up. "Okay, you're the scientist. Enlighten me. What the hell is going on?"

"She's – " Daniel dry-washed his face with his hands, then looked surprised and sickened at the blood still smeared on his fingers. Jack tossed him a wet-nap; Daniel wiped his face and hands and went for a second towelette, then a third. When he reached for a fourth, Jack cut him off, knowing post-traumatic obsession when he saw it. Daniel settled back, newly clean hands limp in his lap.

Daniel drew in a deep breath and finished, "I think she's infected."

"Infected?"

"Yeah… if I think of a better term, I'll let you know." Daniel's hand covered his own collar. "Dark spot, getting bigger. I think it's some kind of indicator. It shows who's been compromised."

"So… black marks show the hunters," Jack said. "As opposed to the hunted."

"Yeah." A dry laugh, without much humor in it. "Artemis is the goddess of the hunt. One of the most famous Greek myths was about a hunter, Actaeon, who saw her bathing. She turned him into a stag and had his own hunting hounds tear him to pieces."

"So she's a charmer."

"Apparently." Daniel rested his head back against the wall; he was still sweating, hair clinging to his face in dark jagged points. Without his glasses, he looked incredibly young and way too vulnerable. "I think the collars are receivers. We're all being broadcast a message; some of us receive it, some don't. Those who do become the hunters. Otherwise…"

"Otherwise, we run."

Daniel's eyes flashed open. His pupils were still unnaturally dilated. "Yes. The dream. You remember?"

"I remember running." He remembered more than that, but there was no point in dwelling on it.

"Running." Daniel's voice was dry, devoid of emotion. "Yes."

He dreaded asking. "You?"

That strange, defeated smile. Daniel let his hand fall away from the moonstone, and in the glow of the camp stove, Jack saw the slender crescent of black cutting into the white. "Oh, I'm running, too," Daniel said. "With Sam."

Daniel was becoming a hunter.

CHAPTER 7 – MAENAD
βακχίδα

There was no question of Daniel taking a watch, obviously. Teal'c stayed vigilant at the door, facing out. Carter slept the sleep of the wickedly stoned, over in the corner, and so far as Jack could tell Iphigenia and her brother followed suit after about an hour or so.

And Jack was getting tired. He'd been running on the ragged edge before the dust-up; the fading adrenaline was taking the rest of his energy with it. Sleeping wasn't an option. After a silent debate, he checked the medical kit for stimulants, palmed a couple and downed them with instant coffee.

"Sure you want to do that?" Daniel asked quietly. He wasn't sleeping, either. And, from what Jack could tell, wasn't likely to.

"No offense, Daniel, but I don't think either of us wants you awake with access to a sidearm, and by the way – " Jack held out his hand and snapped his fingers. Daniel sighed and pulled his weapon, offered it butt first. "Thanks."

Daniel silently followed with the k-bar knife as well. No reluctance. The momentary burst of violence Jack had seen outside in the moonlight seemed to be totally gone.

"Thanks," he said after a few moments, very quietly. "I don't know – I don't think I can fight this thing."

"Yes you can."

"Jack…"

"*Yes you can,* Daniel. I know you."

"No, you don't. You used to know me, a couple of days worth, about a year ago. But you don't know me now."

"Bullshit. You're the most stubborn man I ever met, including me."

"*No.*" Daniel banged his head against the wall behind him, eyes closed again. "Look, I admit, I don't know Sam very well, but I know that if character meant anything, well, she wouldn't be drugged and cuffed in the corner."

"I didn't say you had character. I said you were stubborn."

"Ah." Daniel raised one finger. "Point taken."

"Just rest, okay?"

"No."

"Daniel – "

"I don't want to dream."

No arguing with that. Jack settled back against the wall, faced the exit, watching the silent moonlit night. People were probably dying out there, somewhere in the ruins. Hunters hunting, victims running.

Hunters like Daniel. Hunters like Carter.

Victims like him. Teal'c. The kids in the corner.

Jack waited for the stimulants to kick in, staring out at the unchanging scenery, and heard the light, fast rhythm of Daniel's breathing start to slow. *Should have given him some drugs, too.* Except there weren't all that many, and Jack knew he might need them later, if things got worse.

"O'Neill," said Teal'c softly from across the room. "I will keep watch. You should rest."

"Can't watch two doors at once," Jack pointed out. "I'm good. Better living through chemistry."

"I did not enjoy harming Captain Carter."

"Good. But if it makes you feel any better, Daniel's the one who clocked her."

"Clocked…?"

"Knocked her out, Teal'c."

"Daniel Jackson is a formidable warrior," Teal'c conceded. "I did not know he had such strength and speed."

"He usually doesn't," Jack said. "Just part of the fun on Adventure Planet." He leaned at a better angle against the wall, the better to prop his head up and give his neck muscles a much-needed rest. "Look. If he's right, this thing may have delayed onset, so we need to watch each other just as much as we watch them, right? Stay alert for any signs of… weird behavior."

"Such as a tendency to violence." Teal'c was quiet for a minute or so, then asked, "How will we then recognize a difference?"

"Teal'c! Was that a joke?"

"I do not believe it was, O'Neill."

Jack snorted and cut his eyes toward Daniel. Yep, the man was napping, head down. Too bad. He'd have liked to have had a witness to that; it had to be a landmark occasion.

"Do you believe we will survive this?" Teal'c asked.

"Hell yes. This is just another Goa'uld. We've kicked their bony butts before. There wasn't enough of Ra left to fill one of those canopic jars Daniel likes so much. By the time we finish here, Teal'c, this *goddess* is going to wish she'd never heard of Earth."

"I do not believe she *has* heard of Earth."

"Figure of speech."

Teal'c turned back to motionless vigilance. Jack shuffled around, sighed, and finally stood to stretch. "Change places," he said. Teal'c rose and settled in by the front. "Back in five."

"I do not think it is wise to explore at this time."

"Not exploring, Teal'c. Finding the facilities." No comprehension on Teal'c's face, until Jack took the explanation out of euphemisms and into gestures; at that point, the Jaffa simply nodded and resumed his watch.

Jack stepped out into the moonlight.

Instant chill. There was a surge of adrenaline – maybe from the stimulants, but he didn't think so – that left him with a slight unsteadiness. He limped around the shattered wooden corpse of what looked like some kind of couch. The fountain in the center had a recessed cracked pool with a thin scum of water left in the bottom; Jack unbuttoned his fly and watered the concrete, feeling a hell of a lot more exposed than usual, and finished with a mental promise to cut down on the coffee. As he was fastening up his trousers again, he heard – *felt* – something shift behind him.

Air.

He turned fast, bringing up the MP5 with a rattle of metal, and found himself facing...

... a goddess.

He wasn't prepared for her to be pretty, although he'd known all along the Goa'uld liked pretty hosts – witness Ra, and Apophis, and Sha're. But she was... beautiful. A heart-shaped face, wide brown eyes, curling brown hair piled in a complicated arrangement on top of her head and fastened with a silver crescent moon diadem. Tall as

Captain Carter, long strong legs exposed by the short white tunic she wore.

The only thing that didn't fit the Greek image was the metal brace on her left arm. He'd seen that before, on Apophis. Definitely Goa'uld manufacture.

"Kneel," she said, and her eyes did the white flash thing.

Kiss my ass, he was about to snap back, but then his knees went out from under him and he went down hard, and no matter how much he wanted to give her the benefit of his acid disbelief, he couldn't get the words to come out of his mouth. He raised one hand and fumbled with the collar, tugging at it.

"You waste your time," she murmured, and reached out to trail cool white fingers over his, over the collar, over his sweating skin. "You are not of my worlds, stranger. How do you come here? Who offers you as tribute to Artemis?"

He was free to answer that one; he could feel his tongue and throat unfreezing. It took a huge effort to keep the words back. *Not doing what you want, bitch.*

"Speak." Her fingers lifted his chin and forced him to meet her eyes. "You are a warrior, I see it in your eyes. I like warriors. They make good sport."

"Bite me," he managed to whisper. She smiled – cold silver lips, a sweet schoolgirl smile. He didn't let it defuse his rage. She'd stolen that body, murdered the person it had housed. A snake with a nice face was still a snake. "I won't run for you."

"You will." Her fingernails bit into the tender skin under his chin, drawing blood, and then she let go and walked a few steps away. "I smell the fear in you, warrior. It rises up like the smoke of sacrifice. Your comrades already understand their place. You will hunt and be hunted soon, all of you. And that will please me."

Move the gun. Bring it in line and fire. She can only kill you once. He tried to force his muscles to obey, but they were locked, held tight in her control. The collar. The damn collar. Had to get it *off*…

"Your world," Artemis said, and seated herself on a nearby cracked marble block, with one crisscrossed sandaled foot dangling and swinging. "Which god rules you?"

"You aren't a god."

"Indeed not. I am a goddess." She gave him another rich smile and a charming little giggle. "This world was ruled by my brother, Apollo. He gave it to me as a toy. For a thousand years I have played here, but I grow bored with the hunting. The prey is too simple. Is your world better?"

Teal'c had to have heard the voices. It was just a matter of time before the Jaffa charged out and gave this Goa'uld a smoking hole where it would do her the most good... "Oh, yeah. Cable TV. Air conditioning. Flush toilets. You'd love it."

"You mock me." The smile disappeared. "*You mock me.*"

"Damn straight," he croaked, and swallowed a mouthful of bile; fighting his own fear, the fear this damn collar was pumping into him like poison, was making him sick. "You Goa'uld. No sense of humor."

Her eyes widened, and she came off the block in a fluid move that sent the tunic swirling like white smoke. "*What did you call me?*"

"Goa'uld. Want me to spell it? Wait... don't know how." He was shaking now, but her control didn't seem quite as complete. His throat wasn't seizing up, anyway.

"You know of the Goa'uld?"

"Sure. Ra, Apophis... been there, kicked that ass."

"You lie!"

"Call Ra. You'll get his answering machine, because he's a little dead." He forced himself to meet and hold her eyes. "You're next."

Her eyes flashed white, and she held out her left arm, and he just *knew* that he was going to have his brain pureed into cream cheese, but then he heard something from inside the room where SG-1 was taking shelter.

Yelling. *Screaming.*

Artemis smiled, lowered her arm, and said, "I have no need to punish you. You will be punished enough, before I am done with you."

She pressed a button on that silver arm-guard, and a pile of rings fell out of the sky and stacked around her; she vanished in a blue flash. Jack craned his neck up at the night sky and saw something black slide soundlessly across the moon.

Great. The bitch had a ship.

"O'Neill!" Teal'c was yelling.

Jack clawed his way to his feet and went to help.

It was Carter. The sedatives had worn off, and she was screaming and thrashing like a wild thing. Daniel and Pylades were trying to hold her down. As Jack limped back inside, Teal'c returned to his post by the door, ready for an ambush. "Dr. Carter! Sam!" Daniel was yelling her name, over and over, kneeling over her and pressing her shoulders flat while she bucked and tried to throw him off. Pylades was gamely holding down her legs and looking like he was having second thoughts about this whole *you're safe with us* theory. "Sam, *stop!*"

"She can't hear you," Jack said tersely, and rifled through the medkit for another sedative. Not a huge supply of those, either. He pressed the pod against her bare skin and activated it, full dosage. "Hold her down." The way she was thrashing around, she was in danger of ripping muscles.

Once the worst was over, Jack rolled her on her side to look at her wrists, and winced at the state they were in. "She needs bandages," he said. "Is she out?"

Daniel lifted her eyelids. "Looks that way."

"Okay, both of you, get back. Teal'c – "

"I am ready, O'Neill," Teal'c assured him. Pylades backed away, to where his sister was cowering wide-eyed in the corner; Daniel withdrew to just a couple of feet away, hovering anxiously. Jack cut the zip-ties, got the bandages from the kit and started wrapping her bloody wrists. She hadn't cut anything vital, at least. When he'd finished binding up the wounds, and adding an extra layer for padding, he pulled another set of restraints from his vest and tied her up again. Daniel winced but didn't protest; he knew as well as Jack did just how dangerous Carter was in this state.

"She'll sleep a while," Jack said, and looked across at Daniel. "How you doing?"

"I'm not going to go for your throat, if that's what you're asking. Not yet, anyway."

Jack checked his watch. "Still got hours to go until sunrise. Get whatever rest you can. I'll watch you."

"Jack. You won't hesitate – "

"If it comes to it, I'll hog tie you next to Carter."

"Thanks." Daniel gave him that faint, rare smile. "I think."

He went back to his corner, wrapped himself up in blankets and, to all appearances, went back to sleep. Jack let a decent amount of time pass, until he was sure everybody was out of it, then met Teal'c's gaze across the room.

"Next time you hear me having a nice chat with a Goa'uld outside in the back, feel free to step in," he said.

Teal'c's eyes widened. "You spoke to no one, O'Neill."

"Trust me, I did. Nice girl, name's Artemis, glowing eyes. Crazy as a bedbug, even by Goa'uld standards." Jack frowned when Teal'c's expression didn't change. "You didn't hear us?"

"I heard nothing."

Jack ran it over in his head, but he *knew* it had happened. Hadn't it? He could still feel the sharp dig of her fingernails in his throat, and when he touched the sore spot his fingers came away with a light smear of red.

"Never mind," he said. No point in beating Teal'c up about it. If Artemis could alter behavior with these damn collars, could make Carter a killer and drive Daniel to violence, it was a piece of cake to blot herself out of Teal'c's awareness while she had a private chat. "Nobody moves alone from now on, not even to piss. We go on the buddy system."

Teal'c inclined his head, acknowledging both the order and the wisdom of it, and then settled in for the long, hopefully quiet night.

Running. Always running.

Sam running next to him, dressed not in heavy BDUs but in a short white tunic, her long legs flashing pale in the moonlight. She grinned at him, the grin of a wolf, a predator, and he felt himself grinning back. He'd never felt this free. There was nothing in him but the wild red beauty of letting himself loose. Doubts, regrets... those were old things, human things, left behind in the dark.

Knife in his hand, warm as the blood in his veins. The prey, running, panting and scrabbling ahead. He laughed at its clumsy progress and separated from Sam, darting around the shadows to close on it from the side.

They pounced together, took it down and tore at it with nails and teeth and knives, bathing in the blood and moonlight and choked, desperate screams, and it was sweet, so sweet...

Daniel looked at Sam across the limp, trembling body of the prey, and she was the most beautiful thing he'd ever seen in his life. Flushed, fevered, blood-spattered and vividly, violently erotic. She lifted a hand brimming with blood to his lips, and he drank the thick salty copper from her fingers, and he had never felt so much a part of anyone, anything...

"Dan'yel," a voice whispered. It wasn't Sam, who was voiceless now, except for the sounds of the hunt. He looked around in the still moonlight, then down.

Down at the bloody, dying prey.

Down at Sha're, whose wide dark eyes were full of despair and fear and love. Reaching out to him in helpless entreaty.

Oh God no no no no...

Daniel jerked awake and let out a shaking moan as he curled in on himself in a protective ball. His hair was matted with sweat, his clothes soaked with it; his breath was coming fast and thick in his chest, and he wanted to tear it all off and run, *run...*

That's what she wants. She wants you to run.

He swallowed, tasted blood and froze. *Just a dream, it was just a dream.* Sam was still lying on the other side of the room, tied up. Her eyes were open, and her breath coming in short gasps, but she hadn't been outside in the moonlight. They hadn't...

... hadn't killed together.

Yet.

The sun was a pale blue mist on the horizon, just rising.

Jack had fallen asleep, sometime during the night; he was leaning against the door, eyes shut. Daniel rolled up his blankets and stowed his gear, then crawled over to Teal'c. The Jaffa hadn't slept at all, that he could tell.

"Daniel Jackson," he greeted him. "O'Neill should rest another hour to maintain his strength."

"Yes. Sure....Teal'c, did I – "

Teal'c knew what he was asking. "You slept."

Daniel nodded, and couldn't meet the Jaffa's knowing dark eyes. He moved over to Carter, who had wriggled herself into a sitting position against the wall. Her eyes were clearer now, and touched with the same appalled expression he still felt himself.

"Oh God," she said in a whisper when Daniel came close. "What did I do?"

"Nothing. Well… you tried. We got to you in time."

Her eyes welled up with tears, and she blinked them furiously away. "I dreamed – God, Daniel, I dreamed about killing people. About… *eating* them. And –"

"And it felt good," he finished softly. "I know. I dreamed it too." He settled in next to her. "How are the wrists?"

"Painful," she said with a fragile smile. "What did I do? Try to gnaw them off?"

He touched her shoulder gently. "Captain – Doctor – "

"After all this, I'd think you could call me Sam."

"Sam," he repeated. "Sorry. How are you feeling?"

"Like I spent the night in cuffs." Her eyes stayed on his face. "Ah. You mean, do I feel like ripping any throats."

"Something like that."

"No." She let her breath out in an unsteady rush. "At least, I don't think so. I didn't know – I just thought that yesterday I was – I *hate* this. Why is it me? Why is this happening to *me*?"

He'd had the same chorus running through his head since waking up, and he didn't know the answer. He touched her shoulder instead and indicated the cuffs. "Look, I'd take these off, but – "

"It's the Colonel's decision," she finished for him decisively. "I understand. I'm okay, Daniel. Thanks for – thanks for not making this worse."

He met her eyes squarely, this time. "It'll probably will get worse, you know. For both of us."

"Then I guess we'll just have to rely on each other."

"Not so sure we should," he said somberly. "I'm not sure either of us are any too reliable right now."

Her blue eyes were very clear, very direct. "Do you think the Colonel is thinking any more clearly than we are?"

Another unanswerable question; Daniel remembered the flash of – *something* – in Jack's eyes, his inability to react when Carter stood over a helpless victim with MP5 ready to fire. The old Jack O'Neill would have stopped her, with force if words wouldn't suffice.

He'd been assuming that the influence of the collars had been making him and Carter stronger, faster, more violent; maybe that was true, but maybe the *opposite* was true for Jack and Teal'c. Weaker, slower, more passive.

Victims.

Victims and predators. Dividing them.

"Teal'c," he said; the Jaffa turned his attention toward him and came at his gesture. "Let me borrow your knife."

"I do not think this is a wise course of action, Daniel Jackson."

"She's all right. We're all right, as long as the – " He gestured vaguely up at the ceiling. " – sun's up. It only takes hold in moonlight."

"So you believe."

"Yes," he nodded. "So I believe. Now that we know, we can resist it during the day. Teal'c, we can't leave her tied up. You know that."

He held out his hand, watching Teal'c's face; the Jaffa thought it over, then silently drew the blade from its sheath and handed it over, hilt first. Daniel bent and slit the ties holding Carter's wrists; she sat up, rubbing the bandages, and stood up with a fast, fluid motion.

The moonstone on her collar was straight up and down, a clear half-moon.

If this is what she's like when she's only half under the influence...

He couldn't finish the thought. He became aware of the knife still in his hand, warm and oddly familiar, and handed it back to Teal'c with a nod.

"You're going to have to restrain us at night," he said. "And no matter what happens, don't let us loose."

From the far corner, the boy Pylades said, "If you had any courage, you would use that on yourself. Her, then you." His voice was soft but clear. They all turned to look at him, and Daniel caught the cool shine of Carter's eyes a second before they softened into something more rational, more normal, more *Sam*. "I will not let you kill my sister. I'll cut your throats as you sleep, first."

"We're not going to hurt you," Carter promised. "We're going to find a way out of this. You have to trust us."

He gave her a scornful look – Daniel couldn't imagine having that much self-possession at that age, especially under circumstances like these – and pulled a bronze knife from under his robes. Triangular, with a ram's head. "I wouldn't let you hurt us," he said. "Touch my sister and I'll give you back to the gods."

"Fair enough."

They settled down next to the camp stove, and sorted out breakfast as Jack slept on.

Damn.

Jack woke slowly, feeling exhaustion drag at every cell of his body, and blinked at the bright light facing him. Morning. *Crap.* He'd fallen asleep on watch. He groaned as he pulled himself out of the awkward sitting position, and his ankle set up its trademark throb to remind him that all was not well with the world.

So, nothing new.

Except that Carter was up, unrestrained, calmly drinking coffee and talking in undertones with Daniel across the room. For a second Jack couldn't remember why that was wrong, and then it flooded back with a vengeance. Moonlight. Running. Carter's finger on the trigger.

"Teal'c." He made the name a snap, and saw the Jaffa draw himself up to a more formal angle and put down his breakfast. "Restrain her."

Carter slowly put her coffee down and raised both hands. "Sir? I'm okay. Really. Daniel thinks it only happens at night."

Jack levered himself up to a standing position and had to grab wall to keep upright. He didn't let his stare waver. "Did I *ask* for Daniel's opinion, Captain Carter?"

"Jack, she's unarmed…" Daniel indicated the MP5, sitting in Teal'c's possession, and the Beretta and knife bundled together by the Jaffa's pack. "You can't keep her tied up all the time."

"Watch me. Carter? Nothing personal. I just don't want to have to shoot you. Looks bad on my record." He yanked another set of zip ties loose from his vest and tossed them at Daniel.

Who just let them lay there at his feet.

"Daniel…"

"No, Jack." A muscle flickered in his tensed jaw. "She's not insane. *I'm* not insane. As long as the sun's up, we can cope with this. You have to let us try."

Two against two. Even though he and Teal'c had the superiority in strength, training, and – admit it – longevity, Jack's tactical spider sense was warning him that the fight would get brutal. Daniel would go down, but not easily; Carter would do damage, and they'd have to do unto her in return. Add in his bum leg…

Jack kept his face blank, the calculations secret. "One hour before sunset, we find a defensible camp, and you and Carter get tied up. No arguments. And if I see *anything* before then that makes me itchy – "

Daniel nodded. After a few seconds' lag, Carter followed suit.

"And you," Jack said, pointing at Teal'c. "Next time, wake me up."

Teal'c inclined his head, more in acknowledgment of the words than a promise to obey. Jack gave up, hobbled to the group, and fished a breakfast packet out of the pile. Daniel wordlessly handed over a cup of instant coffee that went down hot and bracing.

Across the camp stove, Iphigenia leaned over to whisper something in her brother's ear, blushing furiously; the boy took on a rose-colored hue, too, then looked helplessly around the room, fastening on Captain Carter. He cleared his throat and said, with stiff formality, "My sister asks that you accompany her."

"Where?" Carter asked, nibbling on a strip of reconstituted bacon, and then glanced at the girl's blush and averted eyes. "Ah. Bathroom. Could use one myself, actually."

She grabbed a pack of tissues from her pack and stood up, offered a hand to Iphigenia, and the two walked out the back entrance. Jack exchanged a look with Teal'c and nodded once; the Jaffa moved to the door. Privacy was a risk they couldn't afford just now. With his experience at Apophis's right hand, Teal'c had probably perfected the art of watching without looking…

The women were back in five minutes, about the time it took Jack

to swig down another cup of coffee and wolf down a fast, cold breakfast, and then they broke camp and took bearings again – Carter this
time, using her enhanced athletic abilities to scale a nearly sheer wall
and take a view of the maze. Wind stirred her blonde hair as she
shaded her eyes; and she pointed decisively in the same direction
Jack's compass heading confirmed. Good enough. At least the place
wasn't reorganizing itself during the night.

Carter thumped down flat-footed in front of him, cheeks flushed,
eyes sparkling. The picture of health. He felt old, looking at her, not
to mention cranky and damaged.

"There's another open area up ahead," she reported. "Looks like
some kind of camp there."

"People?"

"Five or six that I could see."

Could be good news, could be bad… he was leaning toward bad,
this morning. "Move out," he said, poker-faced. "Daniel. Take point,
and *don't* pick up any souvenirs today. Hang back when you approach
this camp. Kid – Pylades – you and your sister, stay with Teal'c."

Daniel hitched his pack into a more comfortable position and put
on his boonie hat, which looked oddly at home on his head, then set
off down the narrow, rubble-strewn path. The wall next to them had
intricate carvings; Jack watched the man's eyes slide longingly over
them, but he didn't slow down. *Might make a soldier of you yet.* The
thought didn't have the satisfaction he'd expected.

Carter was still watching him. He hitched his eyebrows at her and
settled his ball cap more comfortably, made an *after you* gesture.

"Sir," she said. "Daniel's not armed. Neither am I."

"Aware of that, Captain."

"You're putting unarmed team members in front?"

"Let's put it this way, I'd rather be watching over you," he said.
"Nothing personal, Carter. We'll reverse when we get closer to the
camp."

"Sir, if you'd give me a handgun…"

"No."

Silence. Wind whipped sand at them, but neither of them blinked.
Jack slid on his dark sunglasses.

"Move out, Captain," he said. "That's an order."

She shifted her weight fluidly, with animal grace, and stalked away, moving after Daniel.

He let out a slow breath and limped after.

They were attacked, by Jack's calculation, just thirty minutes later. It happened fast – a hoarse yell, a blizzard of rocks being hurled, and Daniel went down to his knees, stunned. Carter darted forward and grabbed his shoulders, dragging him behind a broken, headless statue. Jack saw a bright red bloom of blood on Daniel's face and felt a surge of pure fury, mostly at himself.

"Sir!" Carter yelled. He ignored the screaming protest of his ankle and surged to a run, hearing Teal'c's boots pounding behind, and slid feet-first into cover next to Carter. He had the MP5 up and searching targets in seconds. He felt a tug at his waist and knew Carter had drawn his handgun, but he was past arguing about that.

Teal'c's staff weapon fired, blasting chunks of rock into the air, and Jack heard panicked screams and running feet. He added a rattling blast from the MP5, sighted on fleeing black-robed attackers, and held fire.

Something hit him in the back and bit cold and sharp; he slammed forward against the cold marble and started to turn but Carter was faster, twisting like a cat and emptying the clip of the M9 with surgical precision.

A body thumped down behind them.

"Sir," she said, alarmed, and he felt her hands on his back. "Spear. Doesn't look deep, I think the vest stopped it. Hold on."

He choked back a groan as she yanked it free and held up a bronze-tipped pole with about a quarter inch of red at the tip for his inspection. Her fingers probed the wound with merciless efficiency.

"Flesh wound," she said. "The vest slowed it down, the ribs stopped it – "

"Yeah, I'm blessed," he said breathlessly. "Daniel?"

"I'm here." Daniel was trying to get up; Jack pushed him down and glanced into his eyes. He looked dazed, and there was a jagged cut pouring blood down the side of his face.

"Carter. Check him out."

She holstered the pistol and did the follow-my-finger thing, probed his head wound and pronounced that it was a good thing he'd been wearing the boonie hat.

The street was quiet again. Teal'c came jogging up, looking concerned.

"The kids?" Jack asked.

"They fled during the attack," Teal'c said. "I have been unable to locate them. We should move. This area is not defensible."

Jack tried sitting up and found that the hole in his back wasn't as bad as he'd feared; he winced when he turned, but it was do-able. The body lying behind him had a neat grouping in the chest, and whoever the guy was, he'd been wielding one of those bronze knives.

Old blood on his hands.

"I thought you said you were okay during the day," he said to Carter, and nodded down at the body.

She looked startled. "I am, sir."

"He wasn't."

They contemplated that in silence, and then Daniel reached over and folded back cloth to reveal the man's silver mesh collar, and the stone in the center.

It was black. Coal black.

Daniel's was one quarter. Carter's was one half. Teal'c's, so far as Jack could tell, was still pure white, and he knew his was, too – how he knew that, he couldn't have said, but it felt true.

"Well," Daniel said, breaking the silence, "At least we know what we have to look forward to." He sounded shaky, and not a little spooked.

The dead man's mouth was caked with blood.

Carter, after a pause, held out the M9 to Jack.

"Keep it," he said soberly. "You were right, Captain. Teal'c. Give her back the MP5." He handed back Daniel's pistol and knife as well, or tried to; Daniel shook his head. "Take them."

"I'd rather not."

"Wasn't asking your preferences. Don't worry, I'll collect them before dark."

Daniel holstered the weapons, avoiding his eyes.

There was a slight, metallic *click* from the body, and the collar slithered loose in two parts on either side of the dead man's neck.

Daniel pulled it off, frowning, and they all watched as the black stone swirled and turned pure white. Daniel stowed it in a pocket on his vest.

"You keeping that?" Jack asked. Daniel nodded. "Why?"

"I don't know."

"But...?"

"Seems like a good thing to do."

No arguing with that. Jack watched him as he got to his feet – still a little shaky, but not bad – and covered his concern by reverting to standard Jack O'Neill operating procedure. "We're burning daylight. Teal'c – "

"Sir!" Carter's blurted shout. Jack whirled and braced into firing position; he was fast, but Daniel went from wounded archaeologist to fastest gunslinger in the West at warp speed, pulling the M9 in a blur.

And, thank God, didn't fire, as a child darted from cover and raced across open ground. Girl or boy, tough to tell – small, long-haired, dressed in a grimy ragged sack. Skinny little stick legs smeared with dirt. Carter bounded after, scooped up the kid under one arm and brought him-her-it back over, struggling like a wild animal.

"God, she's starving," Daniel murmured, and holstered his M9 as if he'd forgotten he'd even drawn it. Jack didn't move out of firing position, focused not on the kid but at the deserted ground beyond. "Sam, put her down."

That was difficult; the kid was feral, trying to bite and scratch and kick with every ounce of strength in that forty-pound-or-so frame. Sam finally crushed her in a bear hug from behind and held her still as Daniel pushed the girl's grimy chin up enough to get a look at her collar.

"It's white," he said, and leaned back on his heels to exchange a slightly sickened look with Jack. "She must be eight or nine, Jack, but she's – "

Malnourished. Belly swollen, limbs like sticks, face barely more than a skull. Without prompting, Daniel dug in his pack and found a candy bar – trust Daniel to consider Butterfingers a mission essential – and unwrapped it. It was shattered into fragments; he picked the largest one and held it out.

"Careful," Sam warned. Sure enough, the girl snapped at his fingers. Daniel avoided the teeth and pitched the candy into her open mouth; surprised, the kid nearly spit it out, then sucked on the sugary taste, chewed and swallowed.

"More?" Daniel asked. She didn't move, just stared at him. "Open." He showed her by opening his mouth and tossing a bit of candy in.

After a few long seconds, her pale lips parted. Pitch. Chew. Swallow. Like feeding a baby bird. He'd never thought of Daniel as especially good with kids, but there was something warm and gentle in him that the kid responded to, even while her whole body shuddered with a desire to run.

Or maybe it was just that she liked Butterfingers.

When the wrapper was empty, she whispered, "More?"

Daniel paused in the act of crumpling the slick paper and glanced up at Jack, then back at her. "A little later," he promised. "You'll get sick. Are you thirsty?"

She nodded, hesitantly. Daniel got out the canteen. Carter loosened her hold to let the girl reach for the water, and she took it, swallowing greedily, until Daniel tugged it free.

And then she bolted, twisting free and running like a deer over piles of rubble. Carter swore and started after, but Jack called out a countermand. He was relieved to see Carter obey.

"God," Daniel said, as he fastened the canteen tight again. "Are there more like that? Surviving out here?"

"Or not," Jack said grimly. "She seemed to know where she was going."

They moved out in the same direction. Jack kept his sights high, scanning the piles of rubble and what rooftops and walls were still standing; the next street had a row of nearly intact buildings, doors gaping empty and columns cracked but still upright.

Daniel pointed out a flash of skin, the flutter of a robe. "She's ahead of us."

"Heading for that building," Teal'c said. It wasn't much different from the others, except that it had a fully intact roof.

"Temple?" Jack asked.

"Doubt it. Maybe a civic building, something secular. We must be getting close to the center of town." Daniel's eyes were glazed; his head wound must have been hurting him, because he didn't look all that fascinated. "It's the first one we've seen with a door…"

The girl broke cover and darted up the steps, dirty feet flying, to batter on that door with both fists.

It swung open, and she flashed inside.

More people came out. Tattered and ragged and ill-kept, most of them, but not bloody. There were six of them… seven… ten. Women and children. Mostly children.

They stared silently down at SG-1, and SG-1 stared back.

An old man stepped forward, carrying himself with dignity despite the straggly state of his white beard and oily hair, and inclined his head to them slowly.

"If you're looking for a way out," he said, "you might as well stop, friends. Ahead lies death."

"Ah… hi," Daniel said, and moved forward a couple of steps. "How do you know that?"

"Because I've been there," the man said, and raised snowy white brows. "To the temple. That's where you're going, yes? To the goddess? To seek her favor? Might as well seek the favor of the crows, or the mercy of the wolf. There is no rescue there. My name is Laonides. You are strange to us… come you from Delphi?"

Daniel took two more steps forward, then stopped when Jack made a gesture. "Actually, we came through the Stargate from Chalcis."

"Star… gate?"

"Chappa'ai," Teal'c supplied. He'd shifted his staff weapon to vertical, making it look like nothing more offensive than a particularly big, clumsy walking stick.

"Ah!" The man's face lit up, then smoothed out again. "Yes. The Chappa'ai. So we came here as well. I am from Delphi, where the Oracle lives. But – I have been to Chalcis, and you seem – different."

"We're peaceful travelers," Daniel said. "From a distant planet called Earth. This is Jack – Sam – Teal'c. I'm Daniel."

Laonides bowed with great, slow dignity. The others clustered around him bowed too. "We are pleased to see you." Then he focused on their collars, lingering on Daniel's and Sam's. "I grieve that you cannot stay with us long. The moon calls for you. It will not be safe. But please, come inside. Share what little we have."

He made a grand gesture. Jack exchanged a look with his team, each in turn; Daniel looked eager, Carter doubtful, Teal'c guarded. He nodded and looked at the rank of steps marching up to the shelter.

Stairs. Why'd it have to be stairs? Haven't these people ever heard of handicapped access?

He set his teeth and began the limping process. Unexpectedly, he felt an arm under his shoulder, and looked over to see that Carter was taking part of his weight. She avoided looking back at him.

"People will talk," he murmured, and saw her lips quirk, just a little. "Ow."

"Save your breath, sir."

"For screaming?"

Somehow, he made it to the top without passing out. Laonides bowed again, and up close, his eyes were sharp and very clear. No fool, this guy.

"Accept rest and comfort," he said. "There's little enough of that here, we offer what the gods allow."

Something – maybe respect for his elders – kept Jack from spouting off some flippant remark about the gods and what kind of acrobatics they could get up to with themselves; Laonides' people backed up into the shelter of the columns, then filed into a broad open doorway. The door looked battered and cratered, but sturdy. It wasn't contemporary with the rest of the ruin, and looked hand-crafted, even down to the rough metal hinges.

It slammed with finality after Teal'c entered, and all of them, even Daniel, shifted body language from polite to alert. But no ambush was in the works, just two thin girls who'd swung the door shut, and dropped three heavy metal bolts in place to keep the place secure.

Jack turned his attention from the door to the room. It was big, heavily scarred by black starburst impacts, and the marble floor was cracked and uneven.

It was a camp. Tents made from stitched black robes, or patches of other fabrics that must have been personal tunics; most looked threadbare. A few enterprising souls had built some stone walls out of small blocks, cordoning off sections of the room. Lots of kids; it hit him full force when he saw them standing together, watching. The oldest was about twelve, the youngest no more than a toddler, dirty fingers jammed in her mouth. Like third world kids from every black ops mission he'd ever regretted, kids without a future, kids destined to starve or be hunted or just die of utter disinterest.

The women ranged in age from matrons to barely-legal, all thin and gaunt. If any of them had once been pretty, it had been scoured off of them by bruises, stress and hunger.

"Please," Laonides was saying, gesturing them to a section of the room near a small, well-ventilated fire. No chairs, of course. No blankets, either. No pillows. The place was no better than the poorest refugee camp, and Jack frankly couldn't imagine what it was they ate, if they managed to eat at all. Water trickled painfully out of a broken fountain beyond the end of the hall, and was being collected in some small chipped jugs.

Jack eased himself down to a sitting position, disguised a pained hiss as a sigh, and held out his chilled hands to the warmth. Where were they getting the wood? They must have been scavenging for days to find the supply piled in the corner, and it was still pitifully small.

Laonides was waving a young girl forward, the prettiest of the bunch, relatively speaking; she carried a shallow bowl with her. It looked like it was full of a thick paste, kind of like oatmeal, only the color of prunes. Smelled rancid. She knelt in front of SG-1 and offered it up to Jack with a fixed, frightened smile. He looked at Daniel.

"We probably, ah, should accept," Daniel said as he sat cross-legged on the floor. "They're just trying to be welcoming."

He reached for the bowl to scoop some out. Jack caught his hand and put it back in his lap. He leaned over to Carter and whispered orders. She dug in the pack and took out five MREs, began ripping them open and separating them into components. "Very generous offer," he told Laonides. "Actually, let us pay you for your hospitality. Be our pleasure."

"There is no need…" The old man's voice trailed off as he saw what Carter was doing, and he actually licked his lips before he could control himself. "Food is scarce, it is true. There were storehouses in the city, but they have been emptied over the years by survivors."

"Survivors?" Daniel asked. He picked up a packet of peanut butter and held it out to a thin young boy, who snatched it and turned it over greedily in his fingers, searching for its secrets. Daniel showed him how to tear it open. There was a general indrawn breath as the rich smell of Peter Pan hit the air. Teal'c offered an oatmeal cookie bar, which the shy girl who took it carefully divided into four parts to share with others.

This was going to break his heart, Jack thought, and handed over Mexican Rice to a middle-aged woman with a face like a skull. She looked dazed, unable to imagine what she held in her hands. He pantomimed eating. Laonides held up a sharp hand when the others surged forward and sternly supervised the distribution of the riches; he accepted a small portion of Pork Chow Mein. The effort they took to savor it was painful.

"I'm sorry," the old man finally said, once he'd licked the last drops of sauce from the container and carefully put it aside. "You asked a question. Yes, there are survivors. Some of us live, after the Hunt. We find shelter. Form camps. Defend ourselves as we may, with the help of the gods. I have survived four Hunts."

He said it as if it was like climbing Everest with a broken leg.

"What's the record?" Jack asked.

Laonides blinked. "After I survive this one? Five."

A sense of humor, yet. "And the rest...?"

"Most survived once. Not twice. Some..." His eyes shifted uneasily away, then back. "Some choose not to try."

Like the two lying on the marble floor in the corner, presumably, who hadn't come to the fire or reached for the food. Both women, looked like, although they were so thin it was hard to tell. They were turned away from the fire.

"Have you seen a couple of kids – teenagers?" Jack asked. "Brother and sister. They were with us last night, got separated this morning."

"No," Laonides said. "No others have come to us for days. But our scavenging parties will look for them. If they are alone, they will not survive for long."

"Thanks."

"Scavenging parties?" Daniel asked.

Laonides beamed and put his hands on the shoulders of two of the nearest kids. One was the girl they'd followed. "The children are quick enough to stay out of sight. They do well."

"You send your *kids*?" Jack asked. He couldn't keep the chill out of his voice, and didn't want to.

"The women are too clumsy, I am too old." Laonides shrugged. "We have little choice, my friends. All must contribute, or die."

Daniel said, "Do the kids fight, too?"

"No. We do not fight. You do not know the strength of those the goddess rules."

"Oh, got a fair idea." Jack pointed at the black starbursts on the walls, looked over at Teal'c. "Staff blasts?" Teal'c nodded. "So your Artemis, she's got an army, right? Armed with weapons like the one my friend carries?"

Laonides said nothing. His eyes stayed narrow. After a few seconds he tried another smile, but this time Jack could see the calculation behind it. "You have great weapons, it is true. We do not. Therefore, we do not fight."

"Not the way we do," Jack agreed. "But you stay alive."

"We hide."

"You welcome strangers at the door."

"Strangers may become friends and allies."

"And fighting can take all kinds of forms, right? Like hunting. Like scavenging. Like ambush. And these kids, they really work for you, right? Lots of folks out there not quite ready to knife a kid in the guts. Yet." No answer. Jack made sure his hand stayed comfortably on his MP5. "So, you asked us in not because you're so damn friendly, but you thought maybe you could take us down. Get, oh, some nice shiny weapons? Maybe some clothes, some fresh supplies? Don't blame you." Jack reached out, took the bowl from the girl who still knelt next to him. She looked shocked. He sniffed the contents and met Laonides' stare. "Yummy. How fast does it do the job?"

Silence. You could have heard a pin drop. Daniel shifted and frowned, clearly mystified, but Laonides was tracking things perfectly.

The old man reached out, took the bowl from him, and handed it back to the girl. "Put it away," he said to her. "Be very careful."

"Jack?" Daniel asked. "What's going on?"

"These nice folks are pretty non-violent. That doesn't mean they're not survivors, Daniel," Jack said. "So what was it? Ground glass? Arsenic?"

Laonides shrugged and reached for a small patchwork bag that lay near the fire. In it, shiny green leaves that looked like holly.

"It grows wild here," he said. "The desperate eat it, when they can stand the hunger no longer. It kills within moments. I am sorry, but as you said, we are not warriors. These – they are the helpless. I do what I have to do to keep them living. Sometimes that means killing those who are stronger."

Daniel was just figuring out how close a call he'd had; Jack saw the color drain out of his face, then surge back. *Object lesson, Danny boy. Not everybody's your friend.*

And then Daniel looked down at the remains of the impromptu feast spread out before them, the hungry faces, and methodically tore open another MRE package and began offering what he had to the kids.

There were times, Jack thought, when he was genuinely proud to know this man.

Laonides was shaken. He watched Daniel silently distribute food, watched his people take it, even the girl who'd brought the poison, and said, "What will you do to us?"

"Actually, not a damn thing," Jack said. "Just passing through. This goddess, she lives in the temple, right? Up on the hill at the center?"

"The Acropolis, yes. But if you go to her, you will die, or worse."

"Worse?" Daniel paused, breaking up crackers. A child dared to steal one from his hands; he smiled with absentminded kindness. "Worse than death?"

Laonides' face was a mask behind the beard. "We don't speak of it."

"Hey. You do now," Jack said.

The whole group stayed still, waiting, and then Laonides let out a great, gusty sigh. "I will tell you what I know," he said. "I think it is more than anyone who lives, outside of the Acropolis. But it is little enough to help you. Some who go to the goddess are sacrificed on her altars, this I have seen; the smoke rises up black to heaven. Some... some are slain by her guards. Some are taken to *become* her guards, and when they are taken, they change. Even those we know... they are no longer themselves. It is the same with the mooncollars. Once the change begins, it cannot be stopped."

He extended one grubby finger to point at Carter's collar. She reached up to touch it, startled, and looked grim. "I almost forgot," she said. "It's bad, right?"

"With the moon comes madness," Laonides said, almost gently. "You forget yourself already, yes? At night, the moon calls you? And sometimes in the day?"

She nodded. Daniel, unreadable, didn't move.

"Tonight, the moon will take you far. You will kill, and forget who you are. I have seen fathers kill their sons, wives their husbands; I have seen terrible things." He turned that look on Daniel. "*You* still have the mind to resist. It will be the worse for you, that you will run and kill and know what you do. Better you die now."

"No," Jack said flatly. "Not gonna happen. We'll tie them up if we have to. No killing on either side."

"Do you not think it has been tried, my friend? Lovers pledging faith, parents swearing protection for their children? I bound my son, during my first Hunt, to save him. He is not with me now." Laonides looked severe and sad. "Either they will kill, or they will be taken by other hunters, as will you. You can only save yourself, out there. No one else."

He took a branch out of the patchwork bag, shiny green leaves gleaming in the firelight, and dropped it on the marble in front of Carter.

"Take it," he said to her. "When you wake tomorrow with the blood of friends in your mouth, you will thank me for what comfort the gods allow."

CHAPTER 8 – NIGHTFALL
σούρουπο

Much as he wanted to, Jack couldn't hate the old guy. Sure, he'd tried to poison them; sure, he was foisting off suicide pills on Carter and Daniel with gay abandon. But there was a kind of dignity to it that was tough to argue with. Daniel had palmed some of the leaves and baggied them – when he'd seen Jack looking, he'd sworn it was for analysis later, back at the SGC. And Jack had let him do it, and he wasn't really sure why. Maybe because he knew Daniel. He wouldn't have trusted himself with an easy out, in that situation, but Daniel had been through hell and back, not just once but at least twice, and suicide had never even occurred to him.

Carter… two days ago, Jack would have said that Carter could be trusted with anything up to and including the nuclear football and launch codes. Now… not so sure. She was quiet, watchful, looking at these skinny refugees with new awareness. She wasn't just the visiting Western missionary who could drop off powdered milk and cheese and run back to the Sheraton; she was in this thing, body and soul. One of them. One of the victims, maybe for the first time in her life. Jack was used to it, and he knew it came as no shock to Daniel and Teal'c, but Carter was having a real learning experience. And he was keeping an eye on the shiny green leaves, just in case.

Laonides was answering Daniel's question about Artemis. In true archaeologist fashion, he was asking after origins, history, the shape behind the shadows. Not that it was going to help them much, Jack strongly suspected, but that was Daniel – full disclosure. He listened with half his attention as he watched a woman across the room lying on the floor – a skeleton in rags – drag in one meaningless breath after another. No life left in those eyes. Just a fatalistic sense of waiting.

"The goddess Artemis feeds on slaughter," Laonides was saying. "Our deaths are meat and drink to her. Once she ruled this city in peace, so the legends say, but for a thousand years, she has consumed it, destroyed it, drained it of life. Our worlds, where the Chappa'ai reaches, feared to make war on her, and began to send sacrifices to appease her. So it has been. So it will continue. It allows our worlds, our people to live in peace."

Daniel was stung. "You can't – you can't just continue to placate her. She's killed thousands – "

"Hundreds of thousands," the old man agreed, unmoved. "And our sacrifices allow millions more to live. It is the duty we owe our families, our states and our worlds. Would you not do the same?"

"No," Jack said, and bit down on a cracker. "I'm all for duty and sacrifice, don't get me wrong. But the time comes to take the fight to the enemy, not just survive."

"She is a goddess." Laonides made an unfamiliar motion with his hands; some kind of shrug, Jack thought. "Goddesses do not die. Men die, and so will we all. But go to her temple, and you will die quickly, and to no purpose. Stay, friends. Stay and live for a time. You are not unpleasant, as company."

Yeah, like I'd bed down here, with you at my back. The old guy looked harmless and well-meaning, but the poison had been a dead – no pun intended – giveaway. He had a knife out for them, one that would come in the dark and in the back. They had too much he wanted.

Unexpectedly, it was Teal'c who spoke up. "I served a god for many years." His deep, booming voice echoed through the room with warmth and power, and everyone turned toward him. "I tell you that the gods can die, and they are not truly gods. You owe them no worship and no obedience. You must fight for your lives, if you would live free. This I have learned."

And Jack was genuinely proud to know him, too. That little speech had cost him. There was a solemn, respectful silence in the room afterward, and then Laonides inclined his head in acknowledgement. "But we are not fighters," he said. "We cannot do more than die, and you will need more than just you four to kill a god."

"You'd be surprised," Carter said, and gave him an urchin's smile that wiped out whatever lingering doubts they had about her half-black collar. "Unless you can suggest somebody, of course. We wouldn't turn down help."

"The Dark Company," one of the women murmured, keeping her

eyes down; Laonides sent her a quelling glance, but didn't speak. "Honored father, perhaps the Dark Company would speak with them."

"Perhaps." Laonides crossed his arms, sat back and frowned fiercely. "It is a dangerous thing to do, to approach them. I have done it only twice, and both times nearly paid with my life. Are you bold enough, friend Jack? To risk so much?"

"Who's the Dark Company?" Carter asked, and Jack pretty much knew the answer just from the look Laonides gave her. The look that lingered on the half-black collar at her throat. He remembered the first murder victim they'd seen, bleeding out his life and whispering the name.

Hunters. Had to be. The same dark, elusive shadows that had been tracking them, on and off, since the beginning.

Laonides shrugged. "Survivors, like me. By day, they cling to who they were, but by night they are a killing pack. They are fewer, these days. I do not think you will find help there, but they hate and fear the goddess, this much is true."

"Where do we find them?"

"Closer to the temple," he said. "There was a great theater, once. They shelter there by day. But they are strong. Be wary."

"Oh, I'm always wary." He locked eyes with Laonides, and knew his own expression was as hard and cold as any of those shattered marble statues. "Feed these people."

"Which...?"

"The ones you're letting die in the corners," he said, and tossed over another unopened MRE. Chicken Parmesan. Rice. Pound cake. "Get 'em ready to move."

"Move?" Laonides' expression slid toward a frown. "This is our only safe haven. Where should we – "

"Next time you see us, we're taking you to the Stargate. Chappa'ai. And you're going home to tell your folks that Artemis is out of business." Jack stood up, checked his watch, and nodded at the others, who quickly gathered up their stuff. "Get ready."

Laonides rose too, dignified despite the tattered robes, the ratty hair and beard. A survivor, no question about it; Jack recognized the strength, he'd seen it in the darkest holes of prison camps and battlefields. Strength wasn't always honorable. Sometimes the strong got strong on the blood of the weak.

The man reached out and grabbed his elbow, and Jack let him do it. "Don't promise such things," he said softly. "Don't raise our hopes. Disappointment is a fatal thing, here."

"*I'm* telling you you're going home," Jack repeated. "You decide what you want to believe."

He slid on his sunglasses, armored up, and glanced at Carter. She nodded.

"Six hours left before sunset," he said. "Let's get as far as we can."

The air outside was still, dry and oppressive.

Daniel fell in behind Jack, watching the uneven lurch of his friend's shoulders. Jack's ankle had started out bad, gotten better and was on the downhill slide to worse again, but he knew better than to suggest that Jack take a rest. They didn't have time, and there wasn't anything that felt safe anymore. They needed answers, and they needed to get out of here before things... got worse.

The collar at Daniel's throat felt warm – not blood-warm, warmer than that. As if something electronic was at work inside of it. He didn't feel different, but he wasn't sure he'd know if anything changed; Sam had been caught by surprise, after all. Maybe he wouldn't notice a thing until he took the knife out of Jack's belt and slashed it across –

Disturbingly, it was way too vivid. Blood on pale dust. Jack's face turning to whitewash, draining of life.

Daniel swallowed, felt his Adam's apple constricted by the collar, and found something else to look at than Jack's knife, Jack's sidearm. *I shouldn't be armed anymore,* he thought, and remembered that Sam was armed too, and Sam had saved their lives back there in the ambush. Conditioning. Maybe the collar only worked during the daytime when you let yourself think too much.

He was too close on Jack's heels, and recognized it when Jack looked around with a harassed expression. Behind the sunglasses, his face was drawn and tired. *Jack can survive anything.* He'd known that since Abydos, since seeing the man tap into some unimaginably deep core of strength to stand up against Ra the first time, against

Apophis the second. Daniel, on the other hand... Jack might think of him as brave, but it wasn't bravery, it was blindness. He just didn't understand when to step back, most of the time. All his life, he'd had to defend himself by simply being more stubborn than anybody who attacked him, either physically or intellectually; he hadn't known when to back down with Ra, and it had killed him. Sheer luck that he'd been revived by Ra's sarcophagus; sheer luck that he hadn't managed to get himself killed with Apophis, after flinging himself in the line of fire too many times.

He had to admit, dying didn't hold much terror for him. Living seemed infinitely more intimidating.

"Daniel," Jack snapped, and he realized he was crowding him again. He dropped back, into a cold middle distance. Teal'c was behind him, bringing up the rear; Sam was pacing along in front, demonstrating a loose animal grace that was like her usual stride, but more immediate and less controlled. As if she'd forgotten to pay attention to her body, and what it was doing now was what it was made to do.

It was – *admit it, Daniel* – mesmerizing. He pulled his gaze away from her, back to the ruins around them. He'd given up trying to collect artifacts; he'd never be able to carry any more, and the batteries were dead in the cameras. Even his note pages were filled. A city of wonders, of amazing things, and it was just scrolling by as he tramped through it, heading for another fight.

If he needed more proof that he wasn't a soldier, this was it; he wanted to stop, run his hands over the intricate, delicate carving on a cracked plinth, or get on his knees and dig a gold-filigreed, half-rotten timber out of the rubble. Then again, if he needed more reason to hate the Goa'uld – not likely – all he had to do was look around him. This had been beautiful, once. Humans had made this out of their sweat and dreams, and a Goa'uld had taken it away for nothing but her own bloodthirsty satisfaction.

What if it's Sha're? What if, when I face Artemis, she's looking at me out of my wife's eyes?

He hadn't shown the picture to Laonides; he wasn't sure if that meant he'd just forgotten, or if he hadn't wanted to know the answer. If the Goa'uld possessing Sha're was named Artemis... no, impossible.

Artemis had been haunting this place for a thousand years, according to Laonides. Of course, he'd only survived four Hunts, which by Daniel's calculations must have been about fourteen months...

"Dammit, Daniel, quit walking on my heels," Jack snapped irritably, and Daniel blinked and realized that he'd been drifting again. "Go up with Carter."

Daniel stepped around him and jogged up to pull even with Sam, who shot him a sideways look and wiped dust from her face. She was drinking from her canteen, and offered it to him; he took it and rinsed his mouth. Brackish, tepid, delicious. He was too used to the water on Abydos to complain about the quality.

"You okay?" she asked him. He nodded. Her blonde hair was sweaty at the ends, sticking to her forehead and cheeks, and she still had that faint flush in her cheeks, like fever. "Good. Talk to me. I keep wanting to – " She took another swig and fastened the canteen back in place. "Pull ahead."

Run, she meant. Lope like a tiger through these dusty streets, looking for signs of life. Daniel felt a headache dig in dull claws behind his eyes, and took off his glasses for a minute, rubbing the bridge of his nose. "I keep crowding Jack," he admitted, and checked his watch. "Still three hours until sunset."

She didn't acknowledge that at all. She kept moving her eyes restlessly, looking from one hollowed-out doorway to another, not as if she was nervous but as if she was looking for something. Walking close, he could feel the burning-wire tension coming off of her. She was working hard at this, at being *Sam*.

"Is it my fault?" she asked suddenly, and he saw her hands go tight and tense around the weapon hanging from its sling. "The colonel, Teal'c – why aren't they affected? Why me? Why *you*? Why are we so much worse?"

He didn't answer immediately, because the same questions had been running through his head all day, in various shades of guilt and denial. He'd come up with a dozen explanations, none of them satisfactory; there was just no way to know. Maybe it was some innate ruthlessness. Maybe it was some buried experience, coming out. Maybe it was nothing but blind luck. From the violence with which it boiled out of her, Sam had been thinking about it much harder, and with much worse results. "Sam… it's going to be okay."

She sucked in a sudden breath that spooked him, and he looked around to see if there was anything about to pop up and kill them. Nothing. She had a blank sheen of tears in her eyes, before she blinked them away. Fast.

"What is it?" he asked, very quietly.

"You sound… God. How can you sound like that, like you're not having these *thoughts*? These *feelings*?"

"What kind of…" But he knew. He'd had that vision, nearly erotic in its intensity, of the knife, the blood. He'd been watching her move and admiring her predatory grace. "I don't know. How do I sound?"

"Like you don't want to kill people. Like you forgive me for wanting to." She let out a long breath. "Three hours left. Laonides said that tonight I was going to…"

"Forget what he said. Sam, you can do this. You can hold on. I know you can."

Her smile came, bitter and twisted. "Yeah? You barely know me, Daniel. Until yesterday you couldn't even decide whether to call me *Captain* or *Doctor*." She attempted a smile, and failed miserably. "If I lose it… you'll stop me, right? Don't let me hurt anybody. No matter what you have to do."

It probably wasn't the time to mention that she had advanced hand-to-hand training, military experience, and the best he'd managed was to shoot just straight enough to pass the minimum marksmanship score for the M9.

"It's a deal," he said. "If you'll do the same for me."

"You didn't answer my question. Is it me? Is this happening to me first because I'm – " She made a gesture with one hand, frustrated and vague. "Wrong, somehow?"

"No! No, Sam…" He glanced back. Jack and Teal'c were still out of earshot, he thought. Jack was having to limp faster to keep up with their accelerating pace, but he was doing it, teeth gritted, face set like stone. "I think it's random." He didn't, really, but there was no point in making her believe anything else. "If it were some kind of measure of violence, why not Teal'c? He's fought all his life. And Jack, God knows Jack's got plenty of experience at it. Why wouldn't it make them the hunters? Wouldn't they be better at it than the two of us?"

She was listening, however unwillingly. "So maybe it goes against type?"

"Or maybe it just pulls on what we're afraid of," he said. "Teal'c and Jack might be just as afraid of being prey as we are of being…"

"Predators."

"Exactly."

She hesitated, then said, "Are you? Afraid?"

Some part of him wasn't afraid at all. He'd fought before, when pushed to it, but he'd never gone looking for it. Maybe that had been self-preservation; he'd always been the new kid, the strange kid, the unwanted kid. He'd learned to take beatings, but never to give them. It was a darkly, liquidly seductive feeling, knowing that he was going to change that… and that he had no choice in the matter.

"Yes," he lied. "But you're going to look out for me, right, doctor?"

She gave him a fragile shadow of a smile. "Right, doctor."

They stopped for a rest about thirty minutes further on, in the shade of a massive half-destroyed portico. More bodies inside, mostly skeletal. No collars, again. Teal'c – who had more energy than any of them – scouted the rubble piles, then came back to crouch next to Sam. Like her, he didn't let his eyes stop searching for long.

"Captain Carter," Teal'c said. "I must take your weapons now."

"No," she said. Not aggressively, but there wasn't any room for discussion about it, either. She had her head down, examining her MP5 and wiping away dust; when Teal'c just sat, unmoving, she looked up and focused those wide blue eyes on him. Daniel felt the impact from two feet away, but Teal'c didn't flinch.

"I do not wish to fight you," he said, with unexpected gentleness. "Whether you wish to fight me is a thing you must decide for yourself."

Sam flinched, blinked, and looked away.

"I too have felt the heat of battle. It is a seductive thing. Jaffa are trained to resist, because we must follow the orders of our masters without question," Teal'c continued. "There are meditative techniques. Tonight, I will teach you."

"Tonight, I probably won't be able to listen," she said. "But if I am… I'll try, Teal'c." And she reached out and put a hand on the man's massive arm. Daniel was struck by how delicate she was, next to the Jaffa; even with both hands, she probably couldn't have spanned his bicep. "Thank you."

It might have been a trick of the shadows, but Daniel could have sworn he saw something like a smile on Teal'c's normally impassive face. "If you wish to thank me, you can surrender your weapon. Otherwise, I must explain to O'Neill why I have not been able to comply with his order."

"Can't have that," she said, and eased the nylon strap over her head. In Teal'c's hands, the MP5 looked like a particularly deadly toy. "Everything, right?" At his nod, she gave over the M9 and knife as well.

And then Teal'c's eyes met Daniel's.

No, that thing inside of him said, that alien thing that was so much a part of him it was almost like the obscene invasion of a Goa'uld. *Don't let him take it. You need it. What if Sam turns on you?*

What if she does? he argued with it reasonably. *What am I going to do? Shoot her? Cut her heart out?* Both things held vivid, almost sensual images. He shied away, revolted, and before he could think too much yanked the pistol from his belt and handed it over. Teal'c made it disappear as efficiently as a stage magician. Once the knife left his hands, Daniel felt a surge of relief so strong it was almost sickening. *Have to use your hands now,* the thing in him said, grinning, and *that* had images, too, strong ones, dark ones.

He didn't let himself look at Sam at all. He remembered Laonides saying that the hunters preyed on each other, too. *If she turns her back on me…*

But she wouldn't. Captain Samantha Carter, even under alien influence, was much too smart for that.

"Yo," a shadow said, and Daniel squinted up to see Jack's face haloed by cold blue afternoon light. "Up and at 'em. Let's move. I want to find these Dark Company guys before Werewolf Hour."

"Not funny," Daniel sighed.

"Yeah." Jack studied him, then offered him a hand up. Daniel shook his head and managed a smooth, athletic sort of grace coming up – easier than he'd expected, actually. His legs felt steady, and his body centered and running a little hot…

… a little hot, like Sam's.

Oh, God.

Jack was still looking at him, those dark eyes sharp and knowing.

"Tell me," Daniel said, and pointed at his collar.

Jack jerked his chin once. "Coming up on half full. Been rising all afternoon."

He took off his glasses and dug the heels of his hands into his eyesockets until he saw multicolored stars and rockets. Jack looked so tired. It was indecent to feel so damn *good*.

This shouldn't happen.

"Daniel," Jack said, and he felt the man's hand fall on his shoulder. Couldn't control the flinch. "We're gonna get through this."

"I know." He carefully put his glasses back on again. "I know, Jack."

"You good to go?"

From Jack, that was as good as a three-minute speech, followed by a hug. Daniel gave him a faint, wintry smile – best he could manage, or had since Sha're had been taken away – and left the shelter of the portico to step out into the late-leaning sun.

Jack grabbed his shoulder and yanked him back, off balance, stumbling, a second before an arrow – *an arrow* – hissed past him to shatter on a conveniently-placed piece of fallen roof.

"Cover!" Jack yelled, and bodily shoved Daniel toward some. "Carter! Down!"

He and Teal'c weren't dropping, though. They were armed and deadly and scanning the ruined buildings facing across from them.

Jack held his fire, even when another volley of arrows cut the air, arched, and fell short. One slid to a stop at his feet.

"Jack?" Daniel asked urgently. Jack shook his head.

"They want to see what kind of firepower we've got. Otherwise they'd have hit us already."

Chess. It had surprised Daniel, how good a player Jack was, but he supposed it shouldn't have; you didn't reach the exalted rank of Colonel without having an advanced grasp of tactics. It was on the tip of his tongue to demand his gun back. *Or the knife,* the thing inside whispered. *Yes. The knife.*

He broke out into a cold, trembling sweat as he watched dark shadows separate themselves from the buildings opposite and step out into the clear daylight.

They wore black tunics – the thick long robes of the tribute sacrifices cut into rough knee-length chitons, tied with rags. A kind of uniform. At least ten, that Daniel could see immediately, all men. They were armed with the familiar bronze daggers, a few with battered swords and spears, and two with homemade bows. The arrows were fire-hardened, carefully shaped sticks.

"Declare yourself!" one of them yelled. He was young, blond, and either hadn't been here long or wasn't genetically prone to beards. Daniel's stubble was thicker after only – *God*, had it only been two days? "What world?"

"Earth," Jack said. "Hi. Wanna quit trying to impress us?"

The men exchanged looks, and the two archers lowered their weapons. They kept arrows on the strings, Daniel noticed, and he was pretty sure that they could aim and fire in about the same time it would take Jack to let loose with the MP5.

"The boy spoke of you," the blond said, and took a couple of steps forward. "He said you were friends to him and the girl."

"The boy – ah. Pylades." Jack's expression eased, just a little. "He's okay?"

"We let him pass our ranks. I tried to tell him, but he would not listen." The blond shrugged. "Most abandon their loved ones, when the moon takes them. He was different. The girl – he was determined she would live, even at the cost of his life."

"Where'd he go?"

"To the Temple." The man held out his hand and turned it over, a gesture like pouring something out onto the ground. "A waste. I told him the goddess would slaughter them, but he paid no mind. His sister had a vision, he said. She is a seer."

"You let them go."

"She is a seer. Should I argue with the gods?" He jerked his chin at Jack. "I am called Eseios. I lead the Dark Company."

Daniel stood up, slowly, and saw that Sam was coming out of cover too. Teal'c stayed where he was, statue-still, with his staff weapon raised to fire.

Every one of the men in the black chitons had a fully black stone in their silver collars. Not one of them had bloody hands.

"Two of you may stay," Eseios said, and pointed at Daniel and Sam. "Two must go. It is not safe for you here, past night. This is our hunting ground."

Jack walked down the steps to stand face to face with the man – he was taller, Eseios broader and more muscular.

"We're going to the temple," Jack said. "We're going to take down the Jaffa, find Artemis and kick her snake-infested ass. Want to help?"

Eseios blinked at him, and for a second he looked very young. They all did. Daniel remembered Skaara and the boys on Abydos, training grimly on the Earth weapons to be ready to kill. These young men hadn't even been given that choice.

"You think to destroy a god?" Eseios asked doubtfully.

"Wouldn't be the first time," Jack said. "And if you ask me, looks like this one really needs killing."

Eseios looked at him for a long time, then turned on one callused heel and walked away. When Jack didn't follow, he stopped and made a firm gesture.

"No offense, but we've been offered as much local hospitality as we can stand," Jack said. "Let's talk out here."

"*Out here* is not safe for you," Eseios said. "Unless you think that your death will accomplish this god-slaying; and I warn you, I have seen a great many men die. *She* lives yet."

He kept walking. Jack looked at Teal'c. Teal'c gave a little, nearly imperceptible shake of his head.

Jack said, "What the hell," and led them after Eseios.

The Dark Company – a dramatic name for a bunch of ragged, scruffy post-adolescents – took them through a twisting maze of alleys, shattered houses, down into a tunnel lined with brick, tall enough to stand in. Sewers, Daniel thought. He recognized the construction, although it was more advanced than that of ancient Greece; the arches were more Roman in origin. They came out into a kind of underground wheelhouse, round, with a number of entrances like spokes radiating from a central hub. In the center was a bubbling cistern.

"Fresh water," Eseios said, and indicated it. "Drink and wash."

Jack tasted it first, then nodded; they gathered around and scooped up cool, fresh mouthfuls, and Daniel splashed grit from his face and hair. Eseios and his band watched them, then nodded to one of the radiating tunnels. "That way," he said. "Safer."

The tunnels looked the same – mud-colored bricks, tightly sealed. There was a sound of trickling water, and the air felt stale and humid.

They'd only gone about fifty feet down the tunnel when Daniel caught the sound of voices, and looked across at Sam; the glitter of her eyes told him she'd caught it, too. Jack and Teal'c hadn't, yet. The Dark Company was massed in behind them, following close, and there was a sense of heat to them, shimmering invisibly. A kind of magnetic energy Daniel felt himself drawn to.

"Voices, O'Neill," Teal'c said, after another thirty seconds of walking.

"I hear 'em."

We heard them first, Daniel thought. It meant his senses were sharpening. He could smell things more clearly now, see better in the dark. *Werewolf Hour.* Jack had been only a little ironic.

Up ahead, there was a shine of orange, flickering light. Torches? It glittered on slick, moist, well-trampled mud, and the voices were clearer. Men, women, children. Daniel flashed back to the memory of the children in Laonides' dirty temple, their bellies bulging with emptiness, their eyes blank and hungry. *Not again.*

Eseios, leading them, turned the corner, with Jack and Teal'c behind him, Sam next and Daniel last.

Daniel felt hands fasten over his shoulders, and one covered his mouth before he could do more than suck in a startled breath, and then he was gone, lifted off his feet and carried off. He caught a confused glimpse of the same thing being done to Sam, and felt a rush of fury and despair. *Ambush.* They had walked right into it.

"Quiet," a whisper said near his ear, and the hands holding him squeezed tighter in emphasis. "If you want to live, *quiet.*"

There wasn't anything he could do about it.

The men carrying him turned a corner, and he lost sight of Jack and Teal'c altogether.

Damn, these guys were good.

Eseios had given absolutely no signs; he'd been relaxed and open, leading the way. Jack had been wary, but wariness wasn't enough; maybe the pain and lack of sleep had compromised him, or maybe it was the collar, sucking away his strength and purpose.

When they'd turned the corner and seen the people crowded into the big room, talking or sitting casually together, Jack had turned back to glance at Daniel and Carter, and found nobody back there except the bearded, grim faces of Eseios's not-very-merry men. Eseios had said from behind them, "Surrender your weapons."

Knives and swords were out, but that didn't matter. Teal'c *moved.*

Ought to have him teach me that, Jack thought in the second he had to watch Teal'c convert his energy weapon into a blunt-ended staff and sweep it masterfully through the ranks of the Dark Company, sending men flying. Teal'c didn't stop, even as he was completing that move, flowing into something else… Jack lost track, because he swung around, grabbed Eseios and fired two deafening rounds into the ceiling, then put the MP5 to the kid's head.

"Call them off!" he yelled. Eseios didn't struggle; he felt stiff and muscular in Jack's hold. "Dammit! I'll kill you!"

"No you won't," Eseios said. "I have your friends."

"And I'll go find them *over your dead body.*"

He didn't expect to be hit from behind, because after all, the enemies were in front of him, but suddenly there was weight on his back and somebody was screaming in his ear, and the weight was unmistakably female. He staggered. Eseios flowed smoothly out of his grip, turned and with a blindingly fast motion ripped the MP5 out of his hands, reversed it and smashed it with brutal but precise force into Jack's face.

He went down, the woman under him, and rolled off of her to probe at the stunning ache in his cheekbone. Not broken, but damn close.

The woman – very young, only a couple of years older than Iphigenia – glared at him and bounced up to wrap her arms around Eseios, who was still holding the MP5 like a blunt instrument. She was a pretty thing, golden-haired, with a sharp tilt to her chin that made her look like somebody with an opinion and the mind to speak it.

Eseios's attention was focused on Jack with a predator's intensity, but some part of his mind was on the girl, too; his hand kept smoothing over her hair, her shoulders, her back.

His collar was all black, hers pure white.

"My wife," he introduced her. "Briseis. Stay down, friend. We mean you no harm."

Teal'c was still fighting, but they were bringing him down by sheer force of numbers. Some of them looked like they were having a pretty good time – hell, for that matter, so did Teal'c. As Jack watched, one of them finally hit Teal'c in the bend of the knees and sent him crashing down to the floor, and then piled on to keep him down. Somebody produced rope.

"Yeah, I can see that," Jack said, sharp with sarcasm, and probed his nearly-broken cheekbone again. "What the hell is this?"

"Safety," Eseios said somberly. "You will need it, come sunset."

He motioned to his wife, who stepped forward and took Jack's knife out of its sheath, then, doubtfully, the M9 pistol.

"Have you other weapons?" she asked.

"No."

"You lie."

"Search me."

Eseios waved his wife off and did, carefully; he came up with Jack's hideout boot knife, puzzled over the radio in his vest and finally decided it wasn't dangerous. The thick GDO device on Jack's wrist held his attention, too, and he finally took it off.

"Need that," Jack said tersely.

"I will keep it safe." Eseios looked up at the ceiling, as if studying the sky. "We haven't much time."

He squatted down next to Jack – Teal'c was dragged over and deposited at his side – and Briseis followed suit, along with five or six of the other Dark Company goons. The others in this big room – more like a cell, Jack saw now, every exit securely barred – kept to themselves, but nobody looked particularly frightened. They'd seen this happen before.

"You would stand no chance out there at night," Eseios said, and jerked his chin at the outside world. "Only hunters stand a chance, and many of them will not survive the night. You – you would be nothing but meat."

"So what's this?" Jack shot back. "Protective custody?"

"We save those we can."

"Why?"

Eseios's eyes turned dark. "Perhaps you are not the only one who hopes to be a godslayer."

Jack understood that look; he'd seen it in the mirror, seen it on Daniel's face as he'd watched Apophis laying possessive hands on his wife. Seen it on Teal'c's face in that dungeon on Chulak as he made the decision to betray his god-king.

Pure, uncomplicated hate.

"I want my people back," Jack said. "Now."

"I don't put wolves among the sheep. Your two will stay with us tonight."

"We'll tie them up. Keep them out of trouble."

"Useless," Eseios countered. "The influence of the goddess gets stronger, the closer you come to the temple. When the moon takes them, they will rip their own flesh to free themselves. You can't stop it. Let them run."

"*No.*"

Briseis, the wife, said, "I watched my brother die, fighting the moon. He had fits, in the end. If he'd run, if he'd obeyed the call, he might have lived. Let them go, if you care for them. In the morning, they will return to you. As Eseios returns to me."

"My people aren't killers."

The two of them sent him identical, pitying looks. "We are all killers," Briseis said, not unkindly. "When you wear the dark moon of Artemis, you can be nothing else. Even those of us without it are capable of killing if we must. As are you, yes?"

Eseios signaled his men, and they all stood with that strange, athletic grace Jack had seen in Carter, was starting to see in Daniel. Eseios bent to kiss his wife.

"We go," he said. "I will look after your friends. See that you look after my wife with the same care."

Briseis laughed. "He well knows I can look after myself."

Discretion was definitely the better part of valor, with Eseios holding the firepower and Teal'c trussed up hand and foot; Jack sat up, wincing at the additional damage inventory, and began working at the knots holding his wrists.

At the far end of the room, Eseios and his guys clanged shut a heavy barred door and fastened it with some kind of flat key – Eseios kissed it and tossed it effortlessly to Briseis, who caught it with the same grace. She slipped it into the neck of her chiton – was that right? Couldn't ask Daniel – where the fabric was held in a criss-cross pattern with strips of fabric. Probably wrong to notice that she wasn't wearing a bra, so Jack decided not to. Notice.

"You keep the key?" he asked her.

Her bright brown eyes sparkled. "If you think to take it and run, you'd be a fool," she said. "Look around you. My husband and his Company have saved almost a hundred thus far, and they fight every morning to stay true to their purpose. Most of them have loved ones here. That helps. But at night… not even I can go out with any security, and Eseios would cut his own throat before harming me, in daylight."

She said it with the calm certainty of a woman in love. Jack didn't doubt her; he'd seen it in the other man's expression when they were together. Last time he'd seen something like that, it had been on Daniel's face as he held Sha're in his arms.

This was bound to end just about as badly.

"Look," he said, and succeeded at freeing Teal'c's hands; the Jaffa quickly sat up to finish the job on his feet. "Not that I'm not grateful for all this tender care, but I'm going to have that key, one way or the other."

She raised her eyes from him to stare at someone standing behind him. Jack felt the cold prickle of a knife at the back of his neck.

"You say…?" she asked patiently.

"But not right now," he finished, and then she was all smiles.

"Then come and meet my friends."

No telling how far away they were from Jack and Teal'c; Daniel had lost track somewhere in the twists and turns. He supposed that was deliberate. Somebody had covered his eyes with a tattered rag, at some point, and turned him around in circles to make him dizzy and disoriented. By the time they'd removed the blindfold, he'd been completely lost. No way to figure out which way was back.

At least Sam was with him... although, at the moment, that didn't seem necessarily to be a plus.

"You can't keep us here!" Sam snarled. Daniel winced at the ferocity of it, but he understood it; he felt the same furious energy screaming through his veins. Fighting wasn't just a good idea, it was an imperative. Evidently, the men holding them knew that; they weren't taking any chances, and he hadn't sensed a single opening to exploit. Not that he could, of course. But Sam hadn't been able to break free, either. "Let go or I swear to God I'll – "

"Kill us?" The blond, Eseios, stepped around the men holding Sam and considered her for a few seconds with dark, hooded eyes. He looked older now, watchful, tense with control. Like Sam, like Daniel himself, he was starting to feel the tidal pull of the moon. "Are you so dangerous, do you think?" He reached out and put one finger on Sam's moonstone, which was occluded to three-quarters dark. "You have a road to go before you're ready for that, I think."

"Let *go!*" She twisted furiously, fluidly, but didn't succeed in breaking free. "What did you do with Colonel O'Neill and Teal'c?"

"Your companions are safe, with the others." Eseios leaned toward her, looking directly into her eyes. "Safe from *us*. So they will remain. Now, you need to give your attention to what will happen to *you*. It is very easy to die, tonight."

Daniel felt a hot wave crest over him, and said in a low, dangerous voice, "Probably easy for you, too."

The man's dark eyes flicked toward him. "Always," he agreed. "Dying is the simplest thing in this world – what are you called?"

"Daniel."

"Daniel," Eseios repeated slowly. "You have the wolf in you. You know this?"

"Leave him alone," Sam snapped. "You were talking to me."

"I don't need your protection, Sam."

"The hell you don't!"

And suddenly their anger was directed at each other, sparking and bright as a cutting edge; if he'd been free of the hands holding him,

Daniel knew he would've been going for her, and her for him. Fists pounding flesh, breaking bones, blood...

He sucked himself back from the abyss and saw Eseios watching them with that dark, unsurprised stare.

"You see?" he asked, and quirked pale eyebrows up and down. "So easy. The goddess will use that against you, be warned. The Company has learned to be stronger than such things. So must you." He put his hand on the pommel of the dagger thrust through his rag belt, and then deliberately took it away. "Sunset is coming, and *she* will hunt tonight. If you can remember nothing, remember this: do not go to her. She will call, but you must stay with us. There is strength in a pack."

"And what will *you* be doing?" Sam flung at him. Eseios chuckled. So did some of the men surrounding them.

"Hunting," he said. "Hunting *her*."

There was a low, menacing growl of agreement. Sam looked over at Daniel, who felt a frown grooving in his forehead.

"Now that we have weapons, we may succeed." Eseios said, and held up Jack's MP5 in one hand, strap dangling. "Show me how this works."

"No." Sam's response was clipped, curt and immediate.

"If you don't, I will try anyway, and I may kill you." Eseios looked at the weapon closely, decided the open muzzle must face out, and aimed it straight at Sam. He was holding it wrong, but his hand was dangerously close to the trigger mechanism. "So?"

"Don't," Daniel said.

"Shut up, Daniel!"

Eseios was reading the weapon like a blind man reads Braille, fingertips sliding over the bumps and protrusions. The selector switch – Daniel couldn't remember. Was that safe position? Or firing? Eseios worked it, then put it back carefully the way it had been.

He slowly found his way back to the trigger.

"You want our help," Daniel said, watching those hands get closer to the right answer. "Don't you?"

"I don't require it."

"But you'd *like* our help. Even if we show you how to use those weapons, they're complicated. Are you going to learn everything that quickly? What about training? Are you going to remember that in the moonlight?"

Eseios didn't look away from Sam, who was glaring at him like a rabid animal. *Daring* him to shoot her.

"*Eseios.*" Daniel put extra urgency into it, and got a glance. "We're not going to tell you how to use them. But if you give them back to us, we can fight for you. Right, Sam?" No answer. Her breath was coming faster. "Sam? Captain?" *Doctor* probably wouldn't get him anywhere, just now.

"Yes," she said. "We'll fight."

Eseios frowned. "Against the armies of the gods."

She smiled, with teeth. "It's what we do."

Eseios moved forward and pressed the muzzle against her throat. "Then you'd better be good at it."

He took the nylon strap of the weapon and slung it over Sam's head, let the MP5 hang heavy across her chest, then jammed the M9 into Daniel's hip holster the wrong way around. He looked up at the blank bricked ceiling again. Daniel checked his watch.

Time, or very close to it.

"When do we feel…" It was an academic question, asked in a dry, academic way, but he broke off when he realized nobody was listening to him. Not even Sam, who had her head tilted back as well, staring at nothing.

They were all doing it.

Maybe while they're doing that, I can get back to Jack and Teal'c, make sure they're okay…

A cold sensation, like a very concentrated wind, prickled the skin on the top of his head, and he couldn't help it, he looked up. The cold spread down, moving over him with slow surety, and after the first few seconds he closed his eyes to feel it more intensely. It was like… like…

Like nothing he could even put a name to. Every nerve shivered with interest, every tiny hair on his body trembled to attention.

He heard Sam let out a breath. A slow lover's sigh.

His heartbeat began to pick up speed and thud hollow as a drum. He remembered nights on Abydos, firelight and moonlight sharp enough to cut, Skaara's moonshine and the rhythm of drums as the women danced… as Sha're danced, eyes shining and secret under the veil…

He heard her voice whisper, *Run, Dan'yel,* and he didn't question it. It was only an excuse to do what his blood and bone ached to do, and he heard the others moving around him, smelled the warm odor of flesh and blood and sweat.

His fingers brushed cloth. He opened his eyes as he gripped Samantha Carter's wrist, and for a second they looked at each other, into each other.

Then she pulled free and loped after Eseios and the Dark Company, and he ran with her.

Hunting.

CHAPTER 9 – HUNTER
κυνηγός

"I do not think this is wise, O'Neill," Teal'c said.

"You know what? Probably right. And yet." Jack closed his eyes and worked the thin strip of metal farther into the lock on the gate. "Not going to let Carter and Daniel run around out there alone."

Teal'c, leaning on the wall next to him, was facing out at the room where the others, including Briseis, were sitting and talking. Quite the tea party these people had going; Jack knew denial when he smelled it, and the place reeked with it. They were having dinner. Seemed like – not too surprisingly – the Dark Company folks had more supplies than Laonides' little starving band five or six neighborhoods away. *Spoils of war.* Eseios and friends were out there right now, hunting down more victims to donate to the cause.

Not with my people, they're not. Plus, even though he didn't *think* Eseios and his group could figure out the MP5s and M9s in time to do much damage with them, especially impaired by moon-crazy aggression, he'd brought advanced weapons into this thing. Whoever ended up on the wrong end of them was his doing.

And he was worried – *really* worried – that when he found Daniel and Carter, there might not be a whole lot of choices left. For any of them.

He felt something catch in the lock, and concentrated on turning it. The flexible strip bent rather than levered. *Dammit.*

"O'Neill," Teal'c warned, and Jack turned with the lockpick back in his pocket and a welcoming, if ironic, smile on his lips.

Briseis had come calling. She was frowning at him.

"What are you doing?" she asked.

"Examining the fine craftsmanship." Jack reached out and rattled the bars. "Good work. And hey, I know prisons."

"It is not a prison," she said. "It is safety. You should know this. Have you not seen it? Seen the dead outside?"

"Trust me, it's a prison. Only difference is that instead of locking up the violent offenders, you're locking up the victims. I'm thinking cows in a pen. The cows may think it's for their protection, but hey, we all love a good steak."

She looked mystified, decided to ignore his words and went back to something she understood. "Eseios made the bars. He was a blacksmith, on Delphi."

"Are you not from Delphi, as well?" Teal'c asked.

"No. I was born on Sikyon. I came here with my father." Briseis looked away, but her voice stayed strong and steady. "When he – became violent, Eseios saved me. That was three Hunts ago. Since then, he has built this protection for us, and in the days he and the other members of his Company forage. They use what the gods have granted to find more food, weapons, anything we can use. And they protect us."

Sounded like Eseios was a heck of a guy, except that he ran around killing people in the moonlight. *Like Carter. Like Daniel.* "You know a guy named Laonides?"

That got her sharp attention, and a frown. "How do you know of him?"

"Spent the afternoon at his place."

Her eyes went wide. "Then you are fortunate indeed to live to tell it. There is a creature on my home world – an insect that lives in a hole, baits a trap and eats what falls into its web from ambush. Do you know this?"

"Trap door spider. Yeah, got 'em back home, too."

"This is Laonides. He baits his trap with starving children, and preys on those who pity them. He poisons his visitors and steals from the dead." She shuddered, and Jack saw the gooseflesh coming up on her arms. "He came here twice, trying to treat with us. To trade food for women."

That didn't make any sense. "Food? He didn't have any food."

"Of course he does. He hoards it for himself and his favorites, starves the rest. He can always find helpless orphans, so he told my husband. He takes them in, feeds them just enough to keep them alive, and sends them out to forage for him and lead back victims. He loses one or two children a month, at least. It is of no importance to him. They are tools, nothing more." She rubbed her bare arms with her hands to drive away the chill. "He is an evil old man, Laonides. Eseios would have killed him, but I couldn't bear it. There is enough killing here. More than enough."

"Can't agree more," Jack said, and took a step toward her. She instantly backed away. "Briseis. Look, I think you're doing the best you can, but this can't last. You know that. Eseios said it before – the hunters turn on each other. He's maintaining control for now, but for how long?" He got an unwilling nod in return. "We need to go after the source. End this once and for all."

"Kill the goddess," she said. "Yes. I heard you say as much, but you don't know what it would take. Do you not think the Dark Company has tried? There were nearly fifty strong, the last time Eseios took them to war against her; barely twenty returned. No. The best we can do is make a life for ourselves, at as little cost as is possible."

"We have a saying back home; blessed are the peacemakers. Only problem is, a situation like this, the peacemakers get their asses *killed*. I'm sorry, Briseis, but you're wrong. Eseios is right. Fighting means life. Otherwise, all you're doing is compromising with death."

She was silent, considering him.

"If you unlock this gate for me, my friend and I will go. And we won't come back until Artemis is dead and you're free to make a life for yourself, or go home."

"Home," she echoed softly. "I hardly remember what home is."

"Got to be better than this, right? Living in a cage half the time? Having a husband who has to wash the blood away before he comes to you?"

She looked past him at the locked bars, and said, "You don't know what waits for you, or you would not ask this. And I would be a fool – worse, a murderer – if I agreed. No. Wait the night, my friends. Wait for morning, and speak with Eseios."

"My people may not have that long."

"That is the will of the gods, not yours." She turned to go. Jack reached out and grabbed her arm; it was chilled and still textured with gooseflesh.

"Briseis. You want to bring your kid into this world? With a father who'll hold him by day and kill him by night?"

She turned, lips parted, eyes gone wide and blind. "How – "

"Good guess." He glanced down at her slightly swollen stomach. "Laonides told us he's the guy with the best track record on the planet – he's stayed alive for four Hunts. What is that, a year? Maybe two? What kind of odds does that give a baby?"

She twisted free, furious and blushing; probably some kind of cultural taboo about feeling up pregnant women. Daniel would have known. *Dammit. Daniel's out there. Carter, too.* And the moon was up.

"Talk to Eseios," she gritted out. "*In the morning.*"

He could have grabbed her, taken the key, but she had three burly guys standing by with knives and frankly, he didn't want to do it. She was small and fragile and brave, and no matter how it came out, he couldn't do it without hurting her.

They watched her walk away, and then Jack turned to Teal'c and said, "Watch my back." The Jaffa nodded and settled himself again to face the room, and Jack went to work on the door.

For all the good it did him.

The lockpick broke with a sharp, cold sound about an hour later, and the pieces tinkled down to the stone floor. *Crap.* At least he hadn't jammed the lock. Jack got down at eye level to peer inside, but even his penlight didn't give him much of a view, considering it was all black iron.

He settled on his heels and rubbed his eyes. Damn, he was tired, and his ankle hurt, and all he could think about was that half his team was out there in the dark, running around killing because a Goa'uld thought it was fun. Daniel would never forgive himself. Carter –

The thought crashed off the rails, because when Jack's eyes adjusted again, he saw somebody standing in the shadows of the tunnel, about fifteen feet away from the iron bars. Not moving.

"Carter?" he whispered, because it was the last name he'd been thinking. No response. "Daniel?"

The figure moved slowly forward, feet stumbling in the thin mud of the tunnel floor. When it moved into the flickering curtain of torchlight, it was wearing a torn pale tunic and one sandal, and it was definitely not anyone from SG-1.

Other than that, it was tough to tell. His face was a mask of blood, his tunic stained with it. He held one arm close to his body, and there was something not quite right about his leg, either.

"Pylades," Teal'c said, and the kid's face clicked into focus for Jack. "Where is your sister?"

The boy lunged forward – or fell forward – and grabbed for the bars; even that didn't help him stay upright. He slid slowly down, still gripping the iron, and leaned his forehead against them. His eyelids flickered and for a second Jack thought he was going out, but he seemed to pull himself back by main strength.

"Iphigenia," Pylades said. His voice sounded as raw as his wounds. "They took her. They have her."

"They who?" Jack reached through the bars to shake the kid's shoulder. "Pylades! Who took her?" He was mortally afraid it was Carter. Daniel. The girl wouldn't stand a chance.

Pylades didn't speak, but he touched his fingertips to his forehead and drew a circle.

"Jaffa," Teal'c said definitely. "Artemis's Jaffa have taken the girl. O'Neill, if Eseios and his men are hunting – "

"Yeah, they'll smell his blood a mile away. Dammit. Briseis!" Jack yelled the name back over his shoulder and kept his hand on Pylades' shoulder. "Get that key over here, *now*!"

She came, sandals slapping the pavement at a run, and drew at least a dozen people behind her. Some of them were her personal bodyguards, Jack saw; one or two of them had daggers out, the better to poke you with, Colonel O'Neill.

He pointed to Pylades, bleeding and wounded on the outside of the bars. "Unless you want a ringside seat for the dismemberment…?"

She realized immediately what he was talking about, and he saw something terrible pass over her face in a wave. Maybe it *had* happened before. Maybe they'd had to sit in here and watch someone die out there, within an arm's length of safety.

"I can't," she said. "They're out, and they're hunting. Remember Laonides and his starving children? He is not the only one capable of baiting a trap, stranger. They could be waiting for us to open the gate."

"If we're going to be locked up together, might as well call me

Jack," he said. "Look, you've got two choices, and I thought you said there'd been enough killing. What's it gonna be? Watch him die out there, or take a chance to save his life?"

She looked hard at Pylades, then at Jack's face. Teal'c's.

Then pushed past Jack to fish the heavy black key out of the bodice of her dress and jam it into the lock. The metal turned with a thick *clank*, and the shriek the bars made coming open must have alerted every hungry hunter citywide; Jack darted out, grabbed Pylades under the arms and dragged him through the open gate.

"Hurry," Briseis gasped. Teal'c moved Pylades's half-bare feet out of the way, and then, as she started to the swing the gate shut again, caught the iron in one big hand and stopped it cold. "What are you doing? Let go! You'll kill us all!" She tried, uselessly, to push it closed.

He looked to Jack. "Captain Carter and Daniel Jackson should not be alone."

"Shut the gate!" Briseis shouted, furious, and struck at him with her fist. It had about as much effect as a butterfly hitting a brick wall. He didn't even look at her.

Jack got up, stepped through the gap to the other side, and nodded to Teal'c to shut the gate. The Jaffa followed him outside and slammed it closed; Briseis lunged and turned the key to fasten the lock, then stepped back to stare at them.

"You're mad," she said, and the key went back down the neck of her dress. "You'll be torn to pieces."

"Thanks for the vote of confidence," Jack said. "Take care of the kid. I'll want to talk to him in the morning."

"Jack!" Her voice echoed after him, and he glanced back to see Briseis pressed against the bars, peering after them as he and Teal'c walked back the way Pylades had come. "Be careful. Your friends will not know you now."

"They'll know me," he said. "And I'm tough to kill."

Blood had so many scents.

Old, dried blood, days or weeks gone; that had a slightly crisp odor, like burned leaves. Hours-old, tacky blood was like souring fruit. But *fresh* – fresh had an aroma like burning pennies, hot and silky in the back of his nose. Daniel breathed it down and felt the seduction of it spread through his body, urging him to run. The blood was in drops, spatters, uneven and lurching through the street; someone wounded had come this way, and recently.

The thick trappings he wore made him feel trapped and clumsy; he ripped at the slick black fabric of the vest until he found the zipper and shed it like a skin, then stripped away the shirt underneath. The thin fabric beneath was acceptable, even damp with sweat as it was; he kept it. The trousers and boots were too much trouble to shed. He bent down to drag his fingers through a fresh red drop on the stone of the street.

In the white blind moonlight, Sam's pale hair and bared arms gleamed. She crouched next to him and fingered the stain as well, then smelled the blood and tasted it. He tasted it too, savoring the thick half-bitter tang of it.

She laughed, and some part of his brain said *this is crazy, we can't be doing this,* but then she was running, and he was chasing, and the blood glowed like beacons leading them on. Running released ecstasy into his veins and made him breathe faster, deeper. The blood-smell grew stronger, along with the taint of metal and oil and sweat. He knew that smell, although he couldn't have said why.

It's your own smell. Humans. Earth.

Sam's smell, flavored with something extra, made him run faster. He wasn't sure if he was chasing the prey, or Sam… either one would do, here in the moonlight. Blood and flesh and hunger…

He lurched to a halt as he rounded a corner. Sam was nowhere in sight, but someone else was. A tall woman, dressed in a short white chiton that swirled in a wind he couldn't feel. Dark hair and dark eyes, and eyes that pulsed whiter than the moon as she smiled at him.

Something in him screamed *no, run, get away,* but then she was extending her hand and touching his sweating hair, running her cool silver fingers down his cheek, and he realized that she was wearing a hand device, like Ra and Apophis.

A Goa'uld hand device.

"Another stranger," she said, and tilted his chin up to look at him. "Pretty." Her hand traveled down to stroke over the moonstone collar. "And receptive. Something in you calls to me, you know."

He had never wanted to kill more in his life. The urge to rip, tear, *destroy* was overwhelming, and if he'd had the chance…

But he didn't. The hand device was glowing an anticipatory orange.

"You look like my wife," he said.

"Do I?" That smile, that terrible smile. "How lucky for her. And you."

She bent forward and kissed him, and he could taste something on him like poison, like madness. Something stirred behind those lips that wasn't a tongue.

"Do you want to serve me, pretty stranger?"

"No."

She pushed him away. His foot caught a loose stone and he fell, breathless, back on the rubble-strewn pavement. Her sandaled feet walked slowly toward him as he crawled back, and then she leaped on him, crouched over him, and threaded her fingers in his hair to drag him back upright.

He gagged on the kiss, but something inside of him couldn't deny her; she tasted like blood and violence and he wanted that, wanted it so badly it was like starvation.

She's doing this to me. That couldn't stop it, just made it more sickening that he let it happen, let her hands move over him with jealous, greedy excitement.

That he touched her in return.

When he opened his eyes, she was Sha're. Sha're's abundant curly hair, veiling them both. Sha're's dark, challenging stare. That odd glint of humor, as if she found everything he did funny, and wonderfully entrancing. He felt a kind of drugged, sluggish wonder. A need to accept it, to believe the miracle…

"I am here," she whispered to him. "You see? I can be here for you, Dan'yel. If only you will let me."

She released her painful hold on his hair and let him drop back flat. His hand was next to the M9, still backward in its holster. His fingertips brushed it but it felt cold, alien, part of another life…

And he clearly heard Sha're – not this Goa'uld copy, but *Sha're*, real and immediate as the sweat on his skin – whisper, *now, do it now, don't let her take you away from me.*

As Apophis had taken Sha're, with Teal'c looking on. Taken her screaming, fighting to hang on… fighting to come back to him.

He fumbled the pistol out.

"You're not my wife," he gasped, and fired blind.

The sound of the shot was muffled but still deafening, and the smell of her was wiped out by the hot burn of cordite. The shell ejected and burned as it struck his throat; he yelled and fired again, two more times, and the weight on him, the weight that looked like Sha're but wasn't, moved away.

He was blinded by orange pulses of light, and when he blinked them away he saw that Artemis was herself again, standing, not a spot of blood on her white tunic. Her eyes were wide and dark and furious. *No, no, I couldn't have missed, I couldn't have…!* But he wasn't even sure now if he had fired at all. Maybe that was a dream, maybe it was all a dream… nothing was clear now, except the wrenching agony pounding behind his eyes. His forehead felt charred.

"You will be punished for that! Run for me, little fool," she spat. "I will have your blood *hot* as I drink it!"

He scrambled to his feet, and ran.

She wasn't alone, he saw; dark shapes in the moonlight, loping after him, and no matter how fast he ran they closed the distance. Moonlight glinted on armor. *Jaffa.* A staff weapon blew the night open and exploded a pile of rubble to his right; he used Jack O'Neill strategy and darted toward the explosion, not away. The smoke would cover him, and they'd expect him to dodge away…

Sure enough, more staff blasts destroyed columns to his left. A tottering building rumbled and collapsed in a thick, choking blanket of dust; he used the cover and kept running.

Jack…

He was alone. Nobody was coming to help him this time.

Carter paused, frozen, by the alien sound of weapons fire in the night. She'd paused to taste blood again; she knew the prey was close, probably hiding, but her attention was caught by the noise behind.

Daniel. Less a name than an image, a feeling, a sense of connection. He'd been behind her. No sign of him now.

Carter rose, looking back, and saw fires burning. Someone was running, many chasing; she felt her blood catch and burn with the desire to join the hunt.

But the fresh blood was better. More immediate.

She slowly padded forward. The heavy, ugly metal around her neck felt awkward, but she kept her hands on it, holding it steady. It would serve, she knew. Not as good as the knife, not as sure, but it would bring down prey for the kill.

She heard a dry rattle of rocks ahead, and froze to crouch in the shadows. Wind brought the smell of sweat, metal, oil... male.

She raised the MP5 to her shoulder and flowed forward, keeping to shadows.

He stepped out into the full fierce glow of the moon, and she went motionless again. Did he sense her? Would he run? Anticipation of it caught in her throat...

No. He didn't sense her. She could take him, take him with such ease and speed, crippling him first, then closing with the knife, to rip and tear the flesh from his bones.

He moved on, limping awkwardly. *Now. Now. NOW!* It beat wildly in her temples, but somehow she held on, trembling, sweaty, poised on the knife-edge of violence with the taste of terror and blood thick in her mouth.

And then she saw the child.

It crept out of the shadows in his wake, a ragged shadow with a moon-white stone in its collar marking it as prey. The sight of it made her blood boil in her veins.

The child was following her quarry for comfort and protection. One of Laonides's starving, hollow orphans, sent out to gather food. Lost in the dark. The boy was rank with fear, sweet-hot with despair, and she breathed in his scent and felt saliva fill her mouth and the *hunger* was like nothing she'd ever known.

She let the MP5 slide out of her hands to hang heavy on the strap around her neck, drew her knife, and glided forward to take the prey.

It saw her and screamed, high and thin, and scrambled backwards for the shadows. She grabbed it by one thin, dirty leg and pulled the boy into the cold glow of moonlight, and brought the knife down, screaming out her victory –

-- and her wrist was caught by another, larger hand.

"No!" the man roared, and threw her back, off-balance. The prey-child scrabbled to hands and knees and darted away, into the shadows. She tried to follow. The man lurched into her path to block her. "No! Captain Carter!"

She fell back a step, startled by the name, the face, the sudden flash of sanity that vanished in the next cold stroke of moonlight. He'd knocked her knife away, but she still had the metal weapon around her neck, and hands that knew how to use it. They closed around the MP5 and aimed, and she knew just how it would look when she fired, how his blood would mist the cold pale air. How his death would smell, blood mixed with terror and burning powders.

He could see his death coming. He *had* to see it coming. Now he would run, and the hunt would begin...

He didn't run. "*Carter*," he said raggedly. "Put it down. Don't do this."

She understood him, and felt her muscles trembling with a desire to obey, but the heat surged through her again at the thought of pulling the trigger, seeing his blood spill hot on the stones.

"*Captain*. Put down the weapon. That's an order."

Can't, she wanted to whisper, and almost did, but moonlight locked her in silence. Something kept shifting inside of her, trying to escape. Part of her that screamed in horror at what she'd tried to do, and still wanted to do.

"Captain, I'm not going to tell you again, lower the damn – "

She saw someone lunge at his unprotected back. A knife glinted.

She instantly shifted aim and fired a rattling burst.

O'Neill dropped, rolled, and came up with his own weapon pointed at her.

Behind him, a black-robed attacker swayed and collapsed with the knife still in his hand.

She couldn't get her breath. She wanted to keep firing, turn her commanding officer into bleeding dead meat, and it took everything in her to toss the MP5 down on the street and sink to her knees, hands locked behind her head in a position of utter surrender.

Run, the moonlight urged her. The burning in her turned toxic. *Run! The hunt is leaving you behind!*

She had a sudden vivid image of Daniel, bleeding, running and dodging, of something terrible behind him.

Even the hunters are the hunted.

"Help," she gasped, and knew she was crying. She tasted blood from a bitten lip. "Daniel. In trouble. Help him – "

She didn't know Colonel O'Neill's face could look like that, so bitter and tired and cold.

"Teal'c's on it," he said. "Stay down, Carter."

"Can't." She was shaking all over with the pain, the need, the *burn*. "Help."

He came, limping, and painfully went down on his good knee. "How?"

"Tie me – "

"Need to be able to move. We're not safe, Carter."

"Can't – "

"You will." His eyes held hers, merciless and utterly cold. "You *will*. That's an order."

She wailed inside, wordlessly. The moonlight burned like acid, and her shudders got worse. She felt a small, tortured moan work its way free, and felt her eyes flood again with helpless, raging tears.

Help me.

He was helping her.

He wasn't running.

Teal'c did not dream, but he remembered with a vividness he suspected most humans could not achieve. *Nobody remembers pain,* Jack O'Neill had told him a week before. *We just remember that we had pain. That's how we cope with it.*

Such was not the Jaffa way. His memory of pain was exact and exquisite, as was his memory of everything else. He could recreate, with perfect detail, how it had felt when he had taken a staff burn to the side. He could remember how it had felt to watch Apophis slaughter his brothers for a defeat in battle, though they had retreated with honor and protected him with their blood.

He could remember, with precision, the hallucination that he had experienced two nights ago, of running in the moonlight with predators on his heels.

Tonight, it was coming true, except in one critical regard: he felt no panic, no shame, and he was not helpless. O'Neill had given him that, by example and steady, ironic endurance. So long as O'Neill endured, he would be himself. He knew the tricks of the Goa'uld, and rejected them with the same conscious, bitter anger that he had felt in the dungeon on Chulak, watching his men advance to slaughter another group of victims on the world of a false and faithless god.

I can save these people! O'Neill had shouted, and he had recognized in him someone worthy of his trust.

Tonight he had said, *Go after Daniel,* and in his dark, wounded eyes had been the same burning purpose. *I'll take Carter.* Even though Carter was the more dangerous, even though O'Neill was wounded. Even though O'Neill was not prepared to kill.

And Teal'c had obeyed, because he believed.

He ran, lungs filling and emptying with fast, regular breaths, and felt his muscles stretch in welcome to the challenge. The streets were stark-lit with white moonfall, black shadows, but he sensed others watching. Following. He was not concerned with the Dark Company; their spears and arrows could be dodged, or blocked.

The Jaffa ahead were a different matter.

Daniel Jackson was running with all his strength, all his heart, but Jaffa were bred and trained to endure, and these were honed by service to a merciless god with a thirst for death. Teal'c was gaining, but ahead he knew that the man would be tiring and growing clumsy.

They had been running for nearly an hour, and even the endurance granted by the power of Artemis's collar could not keep a mere human at the level of a Jaffa much longer. Muscles would seize and rip, deprived of rest. If not, stressed bone would shatter, or ligaments break.

Or the tough fabric of his heart would tear itself apart.

Teal'c adjusted the balance of his hold on his staff weapon and increased his speed. The human uniform of the SGC he wore was lighter and more flexible than the Jaffa's armor; that worked in his favor.

He heard more explosions ahead, saw the raw orange bursts, and had a flickering glimpse of Daniel Jackson darting aside from the new attack. Slower now. Still running.

The false female god ran with her Jaffa, silver in moonlight. An easy target. Teal'c leaped up on the unsteady support of a marble block, aimed, and fired; at the last instant, his support shifted, and he missed, bringing down one of the Jaffa next to her. She whirled, and he saw the white flare of her eyes even at this distance.

"Jaffa, kree!" she shouted, and pointed at him. He jumped before her dogs could fire on him; the marble support burst into melted shrapnel behind him. He landed, sure-footed, and dodged into the maze of broken buildings.

His last glimpse of Daniel Jackson had shown him that the human was dodging to the right, down a street that dead-ended in a wall of rubble. A killing trap. Teal'c scaled marble steps that led to nothing but ruin, threw himself over, and rolled up fluidly to his feet, heading at an angle to Daniel Jackson's position.

Behind him, the Jaffa were in confusion, but some were breaking off to pursue him. He found high ground and fired, never staying for more than one fast shot; each burst took down a pursuer. He knew the weaknesses of the armor.

Artemis continued in her hunt, single-minded with fury.

Teal'c caught sight of two Jaffa ahead; as he sighted to fire, black-robed figures ghosted out of the shadows and set on them with knives and spears. One of the Jaffa went down. The other warrior won free, but Teal'c's shot caught him low, crippling him for the survivors among the hunters.

Cruel sport, this was. It sickened him, but he did not turn away from the need.

He threaded through the maze and found a two-story building still standing that faced down on the blind trap Daniel Jackson had fallen into; the ground floor was blocked with ruins, but the steps were still partly intact within. Teal'c vaulted the empty gap and threw himself up the crumbling, unsteady stairs; they collapsed when he was still two strides from the top. He rolled forward and clawed his way up as the support fell away, slid breathlessly on the gritty, groaning floor, and came up on his feet to lunge for the open, jagged window.

Daniel Jackson had reached the end of the street and found his way blocked. True to his nature, he had not given up. He was grimly attempting to scale the sheer cliff of rubble, but it shifted and shook him free in a hail of stones and dust.

As he fell, a thick stone column rumbled loose and slammed down over his legs. From his vantage point, Teal'c heard the sharp, agonized cry, and knew Daniel Jackson was finished running. He risked a look, and saw his friend face down, pinned by the column across the upper part of his legs.

Artemis rounded the far corner, surrounded by a pack of seven Jaffa marked on the forehead with her sigil – a simple circle. The dark moon. They advanced, staff weapons at the ready, but paused as she paced forward toward the downed man, taut with rage and purpose.

Daniel Jackson's face was blank and focused as he watched her come for him. He would die with dignity, Teal'c knew. He would never surrender his life without a fight, even if that fight was in his mind instead of his body.

As his wife had fought, so hard, to remain herself.

Teal'c had failed Sha're. He would *not* fail again.

He fired on Artemis, but one of her Jaffa threw himself in the path of the blast as she extended her hand and bathed Daniel Jackson's face in poisoned orange light. She seemed not to even note his attack, and her Jaffa closed on his position. Teal'c shifted aim and fired at the looming ruin behind them, choosing the spot with precision.

It shuddered, leaned, and fell, crushing all four beneath its thick marble rush. On the ground, Daniel flinched, covered his head, and then Artemis stood alone in the smoking street, and her eyes were full of madness and hatred.

Teal'c faced her, and for the first time, he raised his hand directly to a god. Something in him cried out, shuddered, tried to turn away.

She extended her hand toward him. "Betrayer!" she screamed. "I am your *god!*"

"No god of mine," he said, and fired into her just as her energy bolt hit him with stunning force, throwing him back into broken, empty darkness.

Daniel saw Teal'c fire and felt a surge of fury as he saw Artemis's attack hit, liquefying the stone wall. Teal'c disappeared, dead or thrown back, he couldn't tell.

And then he realized that Artemis had been hit.

She stood still, staring down as if she couldn't believe it was possible – Daniel couldn't believe it himself, until he saw the black smoking hole in her stomach, and blood began to stain her white gown. Spreading fast. Dripping down her bare legs. Artemis staggered, holding both hands to the terrible wound.

"Impossible," she murmured, and tried to take a step. Her leg collapsed. "Impossible…"

Her eyes fixed on Daniel, and he saw the feral glow of the hunter in them. Felt an answering bitter spark. *Die*, he thought. *Just die, you evil bitch.*

She gave him a smile that he knew would live in his nightmares and rolled up to her knees, then pressed shaking fingers to the controls on her hand device.

"You," she panted. "Your death I taste later, little hunter. We will have time."

Transport rings fell out of the sky, stacked, and she disappeared in a streak of blue light. When the rings left, there was nothing left except a pool of blood where she'd been, and the groan of shifting rubble from the building that had buried her Jaffa.

"Teal'c," Daniel whispered, and closed his eyes. "Oh God."

He sat up and began the hard, agonizing work of levering a stone pillar off of his trapped legs.

He passed out halfway through the process.

Okay, this is bad, Jack thought. Carter was watching him, with those blank eyes and huge pupils, and there was a fine, delicate vibration going through her body every five seconds or so. As if she was resonating to something Jack couldn't hear or feel.

"Carter?" he said, and kept his voice low and calm, as if talking to a wild animal about to spring. "Talk to me."

She didn't speak. They were in shadows again, sitting down; the moon was getting close to setting. Out in the darkness, they'd heard the firefight, but Jack couldn't leave her, and couldn't trust her at his back in any kind of a struggle.

So he sat, watching her, her watching him, both of them listening to the sound of their teammates fighting for their lives. The truth was he wouldn't have been able to get there with his ankle doing a good imitation of broken, and even if he had, it would have been over before he could have closed the distance.

And still, he hated himself for it.

"Daniel," Carter said. Just the one word, and then, slowly, as if sounding out a foreign language, "Teal'c."

"Yeah." He kept eye contact. He'd found out the hard way that it seemed to help her keep control. "Have to hope for the best."

"Help."

"Don't think we can, Captain."

She blinked, and he saw something change in her – not so much in her eyes, which were damn close to blind, but in her body language.

He felt something in that exposed, vulnerable place in the back of his neck, and risked a glance away from her.

They were surrounded. *Shit.*

Silent, black-robed figures. He hadn't heard a thing. They were that quiet, that fast, that deadly. He had both MP5s, but that wasn't going to help all that much. Too many bodies, too little time, and somebody was going to get to him.

Maybe Carter.

"Help," Carter repeated, and Jack saw one of the figures shift out of shadow into moonlight. He wished he could say it made him feel better to see it was Eseios, but the truth was none of this was making him feel better.

He brought the MP5 to fire position, steady on Eseios.

The man was carrying a Jaffa staff weapon, and there was blood splashed on his arms, his hands, his face. His eyes were as wide and dark as the black stone in his collar.

"Come," he said. He said it like Carter, as if the words no longer made sense to his mind and he had to consciously fit every sound together.

"Where?" Jack demanded.

If Eseios was capable of telling him, he didn't choose to; the figures still in the shadows seemed to melt away like ghosts. Eseios himself walked away, moving deceptively fast, and looked back over his shoulder at Jack with unmistakable irritation in his face.

"Come," he repeated, and slid down a small hill of rubble, out of sight.

Jack looked back at Carter, who had gotten to her feet without him noticing. She was vibrating again, but he didn't get a sense of imminent danger. Not that it necessarily would mean anything; she'd surprised him at every turn, so far. He'd probably still be thinking everything was a-okay when she stuck a dagger up his –

"Come," she said, and offered him a hand. He looked at it, then up at her face, and grabbed hold.

They moved pretty fast, with Carter's arm under his shoulders and his draped around her neck; awkward, but effective. The pain in his ankle had ratcheted up another notch – where was it now, eight? Getting close to the record – and he couldn't put more than half his weight on it, at best.

Not that she was letting him.

Whatever trail she was following, he couldn't spot it; apart from that one hallucinogenic vision of the Dark Company surrounding them, Jack saw no sign of them at all on the streets. No sound, either. It was suspiciously quiet. He couldn't check his watch, but the moon was sliding toward the horizon, so maybe the worst was over for the night. Carter's moonstone still showed a fraction of white, maybe an eighth of its surface.

Even making pretty good time, it took a couple of hours to close the distance to where they were heading, which seemed to be deeper into the city, toward the gleam of the Acropolis. It was close enough now to shine over the tops of the ruins, and Jack had an idea of how massive the thing was. Immense. Something on the scale of Ra's pyramid ship. *Man, Daniel will drool...*

If Daniel was still alive.

"Rest," he finally said, panting, and Carter stopped to let him slide down to a sitting position on some cracked stone steps. "How much farther?"

She crouched down, hands loose between her knees, and nodded down the street. Which didn't tell him much. He stretched out his cramping leg and swore softly at the pain. Whatever he'd managed to mess up in there was well and truly screwed; he was looking at a couple of weeks of rehab at the very least. Maybe surgical pins. Not like he didn't have some experience of that...

Carter grabbed him and hauled him back to his feet.

"Ah. Right. Moving on," he choked, and felt the world start to unravel at the edges when his weight came down wrong. Carter, either oblivious or not bothered by his moaning, dragged him forward. He managed to get going again, after a few drunken seconds, and focused hard. Weakness was *not* going to be rewarded.

Two more blocks, and then a sharp right turn, and then, suddenly, there were black robed Dark Company guys standing in the way. They parted to let the two of them through, and Jack saw Eseios crouched next to a fallen body, staff weapon held at ready position.

Defending it.

Jack sucked in a deep breath as he recognized Daniel, shoved free of Carter and hobbled forward without worrying about the pain. Pain was something you locked away, dealt with when you had to. Right now, he had other things to worry about.

He pressed his fingers to Daniel's cold, pale throat, and felt the rhythmic surge of a pulse. *Thank you.*

Eseios, who continued to hold the staff weapon like he was about to fight a small war, was glaring at the other hunters, including Carter. When he looked up, Jack saw why. Daniel was down, wounded; Jack was prey, pure and simple. Even Carter was looking tempted. The rest of the Dark Company... feral. Predatory. Ready to spring.

"Teal'c?" He yelled it. "Teal'c!"

"O'Neill."

The voice was weak, and came from somewhere off to his left. Nothing there but an impenetrable wall of rubble. Jack looked up and saw a bombed-out shell of a building with half its outer wall slagged into volcanic glass...

... and Teal'c. Burned, bloody, but aiming his staff weapon down at the hunters surrounding him and Daniel.

"You okay?" Jack asked. Teal'c nodded. "Can you get down here? I need you to help me with Daniel."

"A moment."

It was longer than that, and the Teal'c who finally dropped down out of that broken jagged window didn't look like the same Jaffa he knew. He looked slow, clumsy, and just two steps behind Jack in the injury race. He limped over, and Jack got a good close look at his face. Blistered. His shoulder was bleeding freely from a deep gash.

"Your version of okay looks worse than mine," Jack told him.

"My symbiote will heal me. I have had more serious injuries."

"Let's hope he has, too." Jack pointed down at Daniel. "Help me get this thing off him." He grabbed one end of the column and heaved; Teal'c barely broke a sweat, lifting the other and flinging it aside. Jack hissed in agony when he had to go down on one knee to field-check Daniel for injuries. "He's out. I don't think his legs are broken. Can you carry him?"

Teal'c shook his head.

"Yeah, me neither." Jack looked at the hunters, checked his watch, and said, "We wait for morning. Got a deck of cards?"

Before dawn, Daniel started to stir. By that time, Teal'c was already improving. The blisters had receded to an uncomfortable-looking texture, and the wound on his shoulder had stopped bleeding entirely. Daniel had woken from time to time to murmur Sha're's name and phrases that Jack assumed might have been Abydonian, but for all he knew might have been in one of the twenty-something other languages the archaeologist spoke.

If Teal'c understood any of it, he didn't let on.

When Daniel did come out of it, it was abrupt, as if somebody had flipped a switch. He sat straight up and went berserk, yelling in – again, a guess – Abydonian; Jack held on and talked to him until he felt some of the tension easing away. "You're okay, Daniel," Jack finally said, and let go.

Daniel sat up slowly, feeling his head as if trying to press the pain out. "Jack..." He twisted to give him a wordless look, then turned to Teal'c. "Teal'c, I thought you were – "

"I am fine, Daniel Jackson. I am relieved to find you are well."

"Don't know if this qualifies as *well*..." Daniel pressed his forehead and looked nauseated. "Artemis. Sha're was – "

He stopped talking and leaned forward to hide his face in his hands. Jack moved to sit next to him, between him and Eseios, and the other hunters who were still prowling the perimeter.

"Oh God, Jack," Daniel whispered. "*God*." He sounded shaken. Dangerously shaken. "Where's Sam – "

"She's fine. She's right there." Jack indicated her with a jerk of his chin; she was sitting against a wall, hands on her knees, watching them. Still had the predator's shine in her eyes, but it was fading. "Talk to me, Daniel."

That got nothing but silence. Daniel sat, head in his hands, as the dark spun into day, and the pale blue sun rose in half-hearted glory over the horizon.

And then Eseios put his bloodied hand on Jack's shoulder and said, in an utterly exhausted voice, "My men will help you now."

CHAPTER 10 – NEMESIS
Νέμεση

It took half the morning to get back to the Dark Company's camp. When they arrived, it looked like a completely different place. Eseios led them into the big, open area that Jack guessed had once been a theater, and it was full of people with a purpose – armed men patrolling the entrances, women and children cooking and washing clothes and sewing together rags for tents or cloaks or blankets. A living, breathing settlement.

Some people looked hungry, but nobody was starving.

"My wife unlocks the cage at dawn," he said, when he saw the question on Jack's face. "We come home to this. It is – helpful."

"Eseios!" Briseis came running, then slowed when she saw him. The joy in her face flickered when she saw the blood on him, then turned determinedly back on full shine. "You are safe, husband."

"We lost six," he said. He sounded exhausted, and sank down on a camp stool that looked as if it had seen better days as a pile of scraps. It creaked, but held his weight. "I – I tried not to – I will speak with their women. Larides had a son…"

"Later," she said, and touched his hair with gentle fingers, then turned away to snap out an order for water. Someone lugged in three full pails. Eseios washed his hands and face clean, then cleared the way for the next man who needed to wash away the night, the hunger, the blood. Some spit and rinsed rust from their mouths.

SG-1 watched, silent but still together. And none of them, Jack reflected, was having to wash murder away.

Not yet.

Briseis turned back to them, frowning, and said, "The boy who came last night, Pylades. He wanted to talk with you. Will you…?"

"Yeah," Jack said, and sighed. "Guess we'll go to him." His ankle reported it had a problem with this plan. He told it, for the forty-fifth time this morning, to shut the hell up and follow orders.

Surprisingly, Briseis shook her head. "He is as bad as you and your friends. I have not been able to keep him resting," she said. "I will get him. Stay." She shoved a pail of water into Jack's hands. "Drink."

It was clean and fresh, out of the underground cistern; he drank until the water felt heavy and glassy in his stomach, then passed it to Carter. She shared with Teal'c and Daniel first, then took two mouthfuls and splashed handfuls over her sweaty face. As she mopped the moisture from her skin she looked a little better. Maybe. Daniel concentrated on wiping his mouth but – Jack watched carefully – it wasn't to get rid of the taste of blood. Apparently.

This was going to be one hell of a debrief, if they ever managed to make it home.

"Jack!"

It was the kid, Pylades, coming fast but still supported by Briseis. He was bandaged, and one arm was strapped securely down. His face was thick and purple with bruises, one eye swollen nearly shut.

"Hey, kid." Jack offered his hand, and Pylades gripped it with furious strength, then sank down to a sitting position on the sandy ground. Briseis lingered, frowning at all of them as if she was tempted to put them in some kind of traction, and finally went to speak with her husband. "You look better."

Pylades shook that aside. "I was lucky," he said. "You – the four of you – I did not believe you, before. But now I think you can do anything. You survived – and the goddess was hunting you – "

"The goddess has a great big hole in her gut," Jack said grimly. Daniel had told them that much, somewhere between all of the Abydonian speech. "Whether or not it will kill her is anybody's guess."

"Kill...?" Pylades shook his head. "She can't die. So Iphigenia told me. The goddess wears many forms. One body dies, another – "

"That's true, Jack, she could have transferred to another host," Daniel said. "Though God, I hope not. Was there a sarcophagus?" Pylades looked blank. "You went to the temple, right?"

"Her guards found us. They took us there," he said. "The goddess – the goddess weighed our hearts and found me unworthy. She gave me to her guards and said I was to be sacrificed." Jack saw the panic surface in his face for a few seconds, and then the kid locked it down. "I won free, but I couldn't get to Iphigenia. I came here for help."

Daniel wasn't about to be shaken from his question. "Did you see a box, longer than a man – gold – big enough for a coffin – tomb...?"

Pylades frowned. "I saw something. It might have been an altar – gold, and there were strange symbols on it. There was a moon above it, a black moon on a field of stars. Gods witness, I don't know – they took me to the back – I tried to get to my sister – "

Jack's turn to get him off the subject. "How many people in the temple? Counting the Jaffa?"

"I don't know. Not many. It – it feels like a place of burial. Many – " His face was sickly white. "Many dead. The smell – but there are guards, still. I don't think you can defeat them alone, I think, even with your weapons. *She* has weapons, too. Terrible..."

He had a burn on his forehead. Jack knew what kind of weapon did *that*; he'd seen its effects on Daniel, first-hand.

The kid had tried to protect his sister. No question about that.

Pylades' Adam's apple bobbed as he struggled for control. There were tears in his eyes. Jack waited, and saw Daniel look away, study-ing something in the distance. Teal'c was impassive, but then, when wasn't he? Only Carter reached out to the boy, and put her hand on his shoulder.

It steadied him, mainly (Jack suspected) because he didn't want to look weak in front of a woman. Even a woman with automatic weapons.

"We'll get her back," Carter said, and Jack shot her a sharp, frown-ing look. He didn't like promises like that, with all kinds of hairpin turns and impossible odds. *Try* to get her back, that was better.

But Pylades was already taking it for granted. "Thank you," he said, and sighed. "She's so young... the goddess recognized her as a Seer. I do not think she will hurt her."

Yeah, Jack thought cynically. *She's the soul of reason, old Artie.*

"She leaves her lair at night." Eseios still had that night-preda-tor stealth; he'd slipped up unnoticed. Briseis was beside him, hands clasped over the barely-visible swell of her baby. "Most of her guards go with her as well. This we know. During my second Hunt, I sent white-collars to observe the temple during nightfall and report the movements of anyone inside. Those left inside number less than half those who are there in the day."

"Anything else?" Jack asked.

"Most of the Acropolis is a tomb," he said softly. "Her victims multiply and cry to heaven. She lives in only a few central rooms, we think. And she has gone mad."

"Ya think?... So we hit her hard, after dark. She's away doing the crazy thing, we get the control crystal to the DHD..."

"No," Daniel said. "Jack... "

"Daniel, it's a decent plan. We get inside, ransack the place, find what we need. If Snake-girl comes home, well, great. One less Goa'uld in the universe."

"*Jack.*"

He met his eyes, harassed. "*Daniel?*"

The man took in a deep, unsteady breath. "Night is after dark. Sam and I... we can't be counted on to help. Just the opposite, actually. I think she could use us against you."

"I would go," Pylades spoke up instantly.

"Yeah, big help, kid." Jack's mind was racing, reading the message in Daniel's averted eyes, Carter's blank, empty expression. They'd lost themselves, last night, in a way Jack couldn't begin to understand. It was like Goa'uld possession, only the next day you remembered everything, knew what you'd done... worse than playing house with a snake, wasn't it? Because at least the host probably wouldn't know what was happening, what its body was being forced to do. For Sha're's sake, for Skaara's, he hoped that was true. "Okay, you and Carter stay here..."

"No." Eseios sounded definite about it. "If you tie them, they will die – my men will slaughter them, I can't stop that. Let them run. Let them hunt."

"Tie them and put them in the cage."

"No!" Briseis snapped that out, furious. "I tell you, I saw it happen once. We tied a young boy, tied him *well*, and for all that he broke free in the night, he slaughtered a dozen before we could bring him down – would you pen innocent children in a cage with these two? *Could* you?"

"That won't happen," Daniel said softly. "We're not going in the cage. And we're not going to hunt."

"Daniel, maybe that's the best choice. In the morning you'll be ..."

"Fine? The same? No. We won't."

"Daniel's right, sir," Carter said. "I'm not going through it again. You don't know, Colonel. *You don't know.*"

Her eyes were haunted. He looked away from them, saw Daniel with the identical expression, and raised his hands helplessly. "Right. Can't leave you, can't tie you up, can't *lock* you up, can't kill you…"

"What?" Daniel had an odd look on his face.

"I was going to say, without being brought up on charges…"

"No. Back up. *Can't kill us…*"

Oh, he wasn't going to like this. Wasn't going to like it at all. "Daniel…"

"I have an idea."

"No, you have a *stupid* idea. I know, because I've seen that look before, and I'm not going to – "

"No, you're right, it's not even an idea, it's sort of a plan. I have a plan." Daniel looked surprisingly smug about it. "Want to hear it?"

"No."

"Jack?"

"If it involves what I think it does…"

"That's exactly what it involves."

"Then no. Don't want to hear it." He leveled a finger at Daniel. "*Ever.*"

"What the hell are you two talking about?" Carter asked, mystified.

"We're having a strategic discussion."

"About what?"

"Daniel, *don't say it…*"

"Dying," Daniel said.

He'd told him not to say it.

It couldn't properly be called a plan, really. A plan had simple, executable steps, and some kind of desirable outcome.

This had a half-assed wild logic to it, but it couldn't be called a *plan*, and there was *no way* Jack O'Neill was going to risk everything on speculation as to what an eighteen-year-old kid from a provincial Greek planet had seen in a dark room, when he was scared half to death.

"It was a *sarcophagus*," Daniel insisted.

"You don't know that. In fact, Daniel, there is no way you can know it, so stop trying to convince me. If you were a superhero, your special power would be to leap logic with a single bound…"

"Jack, this Goa'uld has been on this planet for a thousand years. Of course she has a sarcophagus! If she'd just been looking for a new host – " Daniel looked briefly, horribly sick. "Then I was lying there waiting. It would have been easy. I think she went back for her sarcophagus."

As logical leaps went, it was – once Jack looked back on it – not as much of a superheroic bound as it had looked on the far side.

"Fine. *Maybe* she has a sarcophagus. Even if she does, we're talk-ing way too many ifs, Daniel." One finger up. "First of all, you com-mit suicide, which frankly just stinks as plans go, I don't care how you dress it up…"

"The collars come off after death. We know that. We've seen it." Daniel had that stubborn look. The one Jack dreaded. "And if the collars come off, she can't control us, and we can be assets instead of liabilities."

"Oh, yeah, sure. *If* you're not too dead to revive. If the sarcopha-gus even works, provided it's even there." He resumed the count. Two fingers up. "Let's continue to examine this brilliant plan. Sec-ond, we have to actually get into this place without, oh, inconve-niently *dying*." Three fingers. "I don't need a third. This plan *sucks*." He dropped the first and third fingers.

Daniel's brows pulled together in a fiercely focused frown. "Got a better one?"

"Yeah. Kill 'em all."

"Jack, this will *work*."

"What is it about killing them all that doesn't work? If Eseios and his buddies will step up – "

"Which they won't," Daniel countered. "I know from experience, they can't be counted on, not for this. If you try to plan on *them,* you'll end up fighting *everybody*."

Carter leaned forward. "Sir," she said, and caught his eyes. Hers burned with earnestness. "I think Daniel's right. And I think you have to trust us, and we have to trust you."

"This isn't *about* trust! I'm not letting you just – " Jack couldn't even say it. Couldn't even believe they were having this conversation. He tossed a rock angrily across the compound, watched the puff of dust it skimmed off of the open ground, and limped away. Daniel let him. When Jack looked back, SG-1 was calmly unpacking MREs and doing the usual compare-and-trade to try to get the combination they most liked. Pretending it was just another normal day, and butter wouldn't melt in their mouths.

He swallowed a curse that would have shamed a Marine drill sergeant, and walked over to where Pylades was sitting, talking quietly with Briseis. They both fell silent at his approach, shading their eyes to look up at him.

"Show me what you saw up there," Jack said, and sat. "Draw it."

The kid enthusiastically began going through it, step by painful step, describing everything in each room so thoroughly that Jack felt as if Pylades might be some long-lost relation to oh, say, Daniel. "I don't need to know the color of the walls," Jack interrupted. "Just the entrances, exits, who's in the rooms. Right? Tactical information."

Pylades drew a floor plan in the dirt with a stick that had probably once been part of something expensive – it had flecks of gold leaf still clinging to one end. Every room seemed to have at least two exits, some as many as three or four. A nightmare, so far as either attack or defense went. Too many angles, too many places to hide.

The only good news was that Artemis, bug-eyed crazy that she was, seemed to haunt the front part of the structure. Throne room, second room in. Some kind of temple with an altar – or sarcophagus – and that black moon symbol, behind it. Past that – Pylades just described an open area.

"What's there?" Jack asked. Pylades didn't look at him.

"Sacrifices," he said. "We go soon, right? To get my sister."

"Yeah. Soon. Okay, what's here?"

"I don't know. I didn't go so far."

"Here?"

So it went, one question after another, drawing out the details a little bit at a time. Not that it helped. Pylades didn't have a strategist's eye; he couldn't say exactly how many Jaffa there were on the steps, how many in the first room, how many in the big throne room. None in the temple proper, or so he said, but of course that might change depending on the Goa'uld's moods, phases of the moon, whatever.

A big shadow fell over them. This time, Jack shaded his eyes and squinted up.

"Teal'c," he said. "Join us. I'm getting a tour of the local sights. You know, up the hill."

Teal'c squatted down, and Jack ran him through it, point by point. Pylades watched in fascination. Maybe the kid had a grasp of tactics, after all. "Again?" Jack asked.

"I have it," Teal'c said. Just like that. One fast run-through, and he'd remember every detail. That was the way his mind worked. Jack had never shown him anything more than once, except weird little cultural details that Teal'c thought were plain stupid and not worth storage space. "We should rest while we can, and leave before twilight. Eseios has said his men will escort us to the base of the hill, then go before night falls."

"Big of him," Jack grunted. "Considering we're fighting his war."

"It is not easy to discard one's gods. Especially those who walk among you."

"You did."

"I took a hundred years," Teal'c replied. "And when I turned against Apophis, I still did not strike at him directly, only at my own kind. Do not judge them harshly. They are doing what they can."

"Yeah. Killing each other instead of the enemy."

Teal'c set it aside. "Will you speak with Daniel Jackson about his plan?"

"His plan bites, Teal'c, so no."

"It has tactical advantages none of the other approaches – "

"I said no." Jack kept it hard, cold and abrupt. "First of all, we have to fight just as hard, but carry dead weight along with us. Second... shit. I don't even need to count it out. Just no."

Teal'c said nothing. He stood and walked back to the fire where Daniel and Carter were finishing up their meal. They were swapping oatmeal bars for cookies, looked like.

"It's a bad plan," Jack told Pylades, who hadn't actually spoken. "Why?"

"Because it is. Why doesn't anybody believe me?"

He stood up, dusted himself off, and limped back over to the rest of the team. When Daniel tried to talk to him, he gave him a dangerous look and dug into his Smoky Beef Frankfurters, and dared anybody to bring up the damn plan.

Carter speculated about the construction of the theater. After a silent period of monologue, Daniel joined in, and the science talk flowed back and forth, leaving Jack to brood.

Jack bedded down with his hat over his eyes for a one-hour nap, leaving precise, instructions with Teal'c about when he expected to be woken. Daniel waited until Jack was breathing heavily before he walked over to Briseis and Eseios's patchwork tent. Pylades was with them. Crouching down, Daniel looked at the diagram that Pylades had drawn – the wind had already blotted out most of it – and then up at Eseios.

"You know what I want," he said. "Can you help?"

"Your friend will not be pleased if I do."

"Yeah, well, he's grouchy. He'll feel better once it works."

"Do you believe it will? Work?" Briseis sipped at a cup of water. The cup wasn't glass, Daniel noticed; he doubted anything glass had survived around here. This was crude pottery, fired over low heat. They'd made it themselves. In a lot of ways, these people reminded him of Abydos, of his people. His adopted people.

And in a certain light, Briseis reminded him of Sha're.

"I wouldn't volunteer for it if I didn't."

"Really." Her voice sounded flat and disbelieving. "I have seen this before, Daniel. Some can't accept what we are now. What we've become."

"I don't accept it because… because I haven't become it, not yet. Look, I'm sorry, but this is our choice, right? We just need a little help."

She exchanged a look with Eseios, who frowned and shook his head, jaw set and hard. "I've lost enough. Six men last night. These – they speak of killing the gods, and yesterday I believed that could happen, but today… today there are six who say it can't, from Hades. No."

"Husband – "

"I won't ask it."

"Some might go of their own choice, if it meant an end to this. You know it."

"I *will not ask*."

Briseis stared at him, then nodded and put the cup aside. She stood and walked away, graceful and composed in the cool afternoon light. She stopped a white-collared man, smiled, and murmured something to him with a hand on his arm. Eseios watched her with angry eyes, muttered something behind his hand and bit into a chunk of rough-baked bread.

"Your fault," he said finally, to Daniel. "Until you came, we knew the order of things. We were making a life for ourselves. You – you and your friends, you made the goddess angry. We'll all pay the price in blood."

Aggression and anger came with the collar. Daniel knew that, and he fought hard to choke back his instinct to fling back words in kind. Words, and then fists, and then more.

Blood, in the end.

"You aren't living," Daniel said. "You're existing. You can't give up, not while there's still hope."

Eseios spat out a pebble from his mouthful of food. "Tell it to the dead."

Teal'c woke Jack up exactly on time. Carter and Daniel were already packed up and ready, their weapons in Teal'c's possession. Jack checked the angle of the sun, the distance to the base of the hill, and signaled to Eseios that they were ready to go.

They had an escort of nine men and three women, all dressed in black Dark Company robes. As they walked out, the rest of the men, women and children stood in rows, watching them. Some spoke, some didn't; some invoked the gods, which more or less creeped Jack out, given the obvious.

Eseios didn't say anything to him at all. He was pissed off, and he set a deliberately fast pace up the hill. Jack sighed, set his coping mechanism a notch higher, and started reciting lines from *The Simpsons* in his head as he followed the Dark Company up the hill.

"Jack," Daniel said.

"What?"

Daniel nodded to the horizon. The sun was dipping low, the edge just starting to flirt with disaster. "Soon."

"Yeah. Yo! Dark Company! Little speed!"

"Um, with that ankle, I don't know if that's such a good – "

"Good, bad, it's still an order. Pick it up, Daniel."

Not that it was a problem for SG-1's two Children of the Wolf, who practically loped as night approached. Teal'c stayed with him as Carter and Daniel pulled steadily farther and farther ahead.

They made the overgrown trees just below the Acropolis when the sun was a semicircle, sliced by the horizon.

"Right," Jack said as Eseios stalked back, looking way too good at it. "Thanks. Better get out."

"We'll hunt the lower part of the city tonight," Eseios said. He nodded his men permission to go down the hill; they'd been holding back, because as they left it was a full sprint, all of them moving as a unit.

As a pack.

Eseios, the alpha male, looked into his eyes and said, "It is a good plan. You should listen to him."

And before Jack could advise him where to stick it, he was gone down the hill with the rest of them.

Only... not *all* of them.

Daniel and Carter were standing off to the side, which was fine; he had the zip cuffs, he'd tie them and move out fast... but there were two strong-looking guys in black robes still hanging around, and that was *not* fine.

He recognized these guys. Personal bodyguards, from the cell. Belonged to Briseis, or at least were loyal to her.

Their collars were white.

"Daniel...?" He made it a dangerous sort of question. Daniel didn't look up. He was going through the pockets of his tac vest – they'd scavenged both vests and Carter's BDU shirt on the way back from the night's adventures – and was producing artifacts, folded notes, leftover digital tapes... "Okay. What the hell are you looking for?"

"A baggie... ah. Here." He pulled it out and opened it, then sniffed the contents. Must not have liked the results, because he pulled the bag quickly away and held it at his side with a grimace of distaste.

"You two," Jack said, rounding on the two bodyguards. "You got names?"

"Menelaos," one said. Copper-haired, rangy looking.

"Philemon." Dark, olive skin, rippling with scars. Warrior's eyes. He was almost Teal'c's size.

"Menelaos, Philemon, sorry, been a mistake. You guys take off."

They didn't move. Daniel said, "They're here for me and Sam, Jack."

Which set him off like a Roman candle, and dammit, he didn't care. "*No!* We're not doing this, Daniel!"

Daniel reached into the baggie and pulled out a handful of shiny green leaves with sharp points, like holly. He counted out half and put them in Carter's open palm. "Sorry. I don't know the dosage. It's probably pretty potent – "

Jack growled and came at him.

He never even saw Daniel move, just felt the blow that lifted him off his feet and threw him ten feet across the ground to slam hard into the ground. Saw stars. Coughed and rolled on his side, and felt Teal'c's strength levering him back up.

Daniel was staring at him. Daniel with a black stone in his collar and that fey and feral expression on his face.

Carter, too.

The sun was setting.

"Don't do that again," Daniel said softly. "This is hard, you know. I don't want to hurt you."

"Then don't." Jack pulled free of Teal'c's grip and limped forward. "Just don't."

"Jack, Artemis isn't just controlling us by dividing us into hunters and prey." His voice was coming faster, rougher, driven by urgency. "*Christ*, don't you understand? She can *make us believe.* She can do anything, once she's close to us. I saw it. I felt it. Didn't you? Don't you understand this? *You need us free.*"

He was begging him for an answer. Jack, throat tight, thought back to that second night in the ruins, that moonlight-splashed courtyard, Artemis's fingers digging in to the soft flesh under his chin. *You will be punished enough, before I am done with you.* She'd made him helpless out there. She'd made Teal'c blind and deaf.

"*You can't save us,*" Daniel said. "And she can't control us once these collars are off. And that's something she can't foresee. It's the only advantage you'll have."

"Ah God..." He couldn't breathe. Couldn't do this. "No."

"Jack."

"No."

And then Carter, who hadn't spoken at all, said, "Sir, please. I can't – I can't let her do this to me. I'd rather be dead, even if you can't bring me back. Last night – last night I tried to murder a child." Her voice wavered, then went rock steady. "I'd rather be dead, and you would, too, in my place."

He could have stopped them. He had the guns. All had he had to do was bark out an order and back it up with a bluff, shoot to wound, not to kill...

Daniel undid all that by saying, in a very quiet voice, "We trust you, Jack. We wouldn't be doing this if we didn't believe you could make this work."

For one critical second, he didn't move, and that was enough.

Daniel let his breath out in a little sigh, closed his eyes, and put the handful of leaves in his mouth.

Jack lunged forward, making a sound that didn't even qualify as speech, but Teal'c held him back.

Daniel would have broken his neck, anyway.

Carter chewed her own mouthful. Daniel chewed and swallowed, forced a smile, and said, "Minty. Look, I don't know how long this will – " His face changed, and went blank and slack.

Oh God no.

Daniel went down. His knees just folded, and then he was down, looking shocked. Teal'c released Jack, and Jack got there seconds before the first convulsion hit; Carter collapsed too, caught in Teal'c's arms on the way, and Jack sent the Jaffa a silent agonized glance as she started seizing violently as well.

It went on forever, and Jack heard his breathing turn ragged and tortured as Daniel and Carter died, and died, and kept on dying. He'd seen a lot of men die, hell, he'd seen the man he was holding in his arms die once already, but that had been war, battle, a sudden shocking thing.

This was cold and deliberate and worse, so much worse.

And it was worse when it was finally over, and they were quiet.

For a hard, horrible second all Jack could think of with Daniel's limp warm weight in his arms was the name of his son, *Charlie, Charlie, Charlie,* chanted over and over inside his head in a keening wail.

He couldn't look at Daniel's dead face. He just sat, holding him, until he heard the soft metallic click of the collar coming open around his neck. It slithered off to thump down in the grass, and the stone swirled red, then white.

Jack carefully laid the body down and walked away to lean against a tree, shuddering, watching the night fall. Above them, the Acropolis glowed like a beacon.

"O'Neill," Teal'c said quietly from behind him. He had laid Carter – no, Carter's *corpse* – down next to Daniel. "Captain Carter – her collar has released."

Get it together, Colonel. It's up to you now.

He turned, fixed the two big men wearing the white collars with a look that made both of them – burly as they were – look nervous. "Pick them up," he said. "Anything happens to them, you'd better *hope* Artemis gets you before I do. Understand?"

They both nodded and moved off behind him. He heard rustling, grunts, the sounds of bodies being lifted into fireman's carries.

He waited, motionless, watching as something just slightly blacker than the sky floated up from some open area inside the Acropolis. Hawk wings opened, and it glided nearly silently over their heads, heading toward the city.

A Goa'uld glider. Artemis, on the hunt.

"Let's move," he said.

The place was incredible. Daniel would have been in some kind of religious frothing ecstasy. Jack, cold and furious and hard as steel, only cared about how many he had to kill, and what he was going to have to blow up.

Six Jaffa hanging out by the front door, for a start. If Pylades' information was right, SG-1 had to go through four rooms with more than two entrances in each one to get where they needed to go. No telling how many guards. Pylades hadn't been exact in the count.

Jack gestured sharply to Teal'c, breaking the targets into groupings. Teal'c nodded and raised his staff weapon.

Jack took in a deep breath, flicked the MP5 to fire position, and thought, *all you have to do is not miss.*

He wasn't in the mood to miss, actually.

Three brief bursts, full auto. Three Jaffa down with holes where their symbiotes used to be. Teal'c had taken out his targets with fast, accurate energy bolts.

They never got off a shot.

Surprise was blown; Jack pelted forward and attacked the steps. He ignored the pain. His ankle was so far down the list of things he cared about that even the pain was just another input, one to be marked off the list as not tactically useful. He could feel things ripping. Screw it. That was what infirmaries were for, when the bleeding was over.

He slid on the marble at the top of the steps, paused to put a round in one of the guards who was still weakly moving, and moved into the first room. Teal'c flowed in with him, silent as a shadow, unlike the three Jaffa who pounded noisily out of a side entrance at a dead run and threw themselves in the path of another combined burst of auto fire and plasma.

The statues and treasures in the room that Daniel would have found fascinating were just things to be negotiated around, or shoved out of his way. Behind Teal'c, Menelaos and Philemon were coming in, bearing their burdens. Jack could hear their fast, scared breathing.

Prey. Yeah. Prey on this, Artie.

"Left," he ordered Teal'c; they moved together, either side of the door. Teal'c took high, Jack low, and Teal'c was a half-second faster to fire at a Jaffa hiding behind a thick-muscled marble statue. It blew apart. The Jaffa behind it staggered out in the open, blinded, and Jack took him down. His mental map told him this was the reception room, where Pylades and Iphigenia had been separated. Pylades had been taken left, his sister right.

"Left," he said again. Another doorway. Jack turned to check their six and caught the golden glitter of enemies on their tail; he barked at Menelaos to duck and fired over his shoulder.

Over Carter's dead body.

Teal'c, facing the other way, was firing too. Getting it from both sides, *Goddammit, Daniel, I told you this wouldn't work,* but then suddenly it was quiet again, and Teal'c pronounced an all-clear.

One more room.

Big one. Lots of marble. Columns for days, and at the end, a throne fit for a goddess. Empty. No sign of any damn sarcophagus.

He saw a flicker at the corner of his eye, and instinctively ducked. Too many columns, too many places to hide – he came around again, and fired at two more Jaffa. A staff blast smoked the air beside him; another one boiled marble at his feet. Menelaos and Philemon ducked and covered; Jack went down on one knee and fired and missed, fired again and scored.

He tracked the last figure in the cluster and prepared to shoot, but Teal'c's staff weapon knocked across the barrel and sent it out of line. "No," Teal'c snapped. "It is the girl."

The girl... Iphigenia. Tiny, fragile Iphigenia, curled into a shaking ball at the foot of the throne, hands cradling her head, surrounded by the bodies of fallen Jaffa. She was wearing an expensive-looking white silk robe trimmed with gold, and had a gold diadem on her head. Handmaiden to the goddess. Pylades had been right about Artemis being interested in Seers.

"Iph," Jack called, and beckoned to her with one hand. "Come on. Hurry."

She raised a tear-streaked face, saw him and hid her face again, then took a second slow look.

"Come on!"

She got up and staggered toward them, flinching at the bloody bodies of the fallen Jaffa. She was swept up in a hug against Teal'c's body, and the little war party moved on for the exit in the back of the hall.

The temple, where Pylades said the altar was.

Iphigenia gave a shrill scream of panic when another guard darted from cover, and Teal'c turned his body to protect her as Jack fired.

The Jaffa went down with a crash and a groan. Maybe dead, maybe not; no time for worrying about it. Jack moved toward the dark gaping hole that led to the last room they were going to need.

It was empty, except for a huge black disc on the far wall, ringed in silver, and a shimmering field of stars. Holographic. They danced and flickered in a mesmerizing rhythm.

There was no sarcophagus.

Oh God. Jack felt the weight of it hit him in a way he hadn't allowed it to since he'd watched Daniel and Carter chew the leaves.

It was for nothing. All for *nothing.* There was no sarcophagus, no return, no miracle.

Teal'c shook Iphigenia by the shoulder – gently, but enough to get her attention. "Was there not a golden box in this room?"

She shook her head and averted her eyes. Terrified, Jack thought.

"Maybe an altar?" he put in. "Did they move it?"

"Nothing!" she said. "There was nothing!"

Jack stared at the empty room, only half listening. He closed his eyes and heard Daniel saying, *Christ, don't you understand? She can make us believe.*

He started walking toward what wasn't there, hand outstretched, and ten steps from the far wall that looked off into space, he banged hard into something that came as high as his chest. Ran his hands over empty air and felt raised carvings.

Relief washed over him in a hot, stinging flood, so strong it almost raised tears. "Teal'c." His voice sounded rough and rusty. "It's here. We just can't see it. Help me find a catch, should be on this side –"

Teal'c joined him, feeling his way along the invisible structure until there was a grating sound, more stone than metal, and the invisible scarab wings opened, and light sprang up white and real and solid from the center of exactly nothing.

Iphigenia pulled away and retreated to a corner.

He gestured to Menelaos and Philemon to put their burdens down, and watched as they lowered Daniel and Carter lifeless to the floor. *What if it only works once? What if I can't save them both?*

Not really a choice. "Carter first," he said, and motioned Menelaos forward. The man came, pale and scared to death; he and Jack lifted Carter's limp body and laid her in the empty capsule, hands folded.

Not because she was female, but because she was a dead shot, and she knew what the damn missing DHD part looked like, and it was a command decision with cold, hard parameters.

He didn't look at her face. It hadn't been a pretty death.

The wings grated shut, and the whole thing went invisible again. He paced, checking the exit, waiting for the other hobnailed sandal to drop. Artemis wouldn't be gone forever. Somebody would have gotten off a message, would have recalled the ship. It wouldn't be long now, unless Her Exalted Snakiness was too crazy to care anymore…

Come on, come on…

He realized someone was missing. *Crap.* The girl. Last he'd seen her, she'd been crammed in the corner, looking scared.

"Teal'c," he said. "Iphigenia. Where'd she go?"

Teal'c looked surprised, but then, he'd been staring at the sarcophagus, too. "I do not know, O'Neill. I did not see her leave."

"I'd better go find her."

He took two steps toward the exit, then spun around as the sarcophagus ground open.

Silence, except for the sound of his heart thudding faster in his chest. He held his breath until he saw a pale set of hands groping at the sides, and then Carter's blonde head as she sat up.

She looked around, dazed, and blinked at them. "Where – " And then she knew; he saw everything kick in. Fast, his Carter. She climbed out of the sarcophagus, steadied herself, and flashed him an unsteady smile.

"Nice to see you, Captain," he said, straight-faced when all he wanted to do was grin and whoop.

"Same here, sir," she said.

"Feeling okay?"

"Better than ever." If there was any lingering trauma, she had it well buried. "Can I have my weapons?"

He unslung the extra MP5 and tossed it to her. "Carter, you're with me. Teal'c, get Daniel in the oven. Philemon, Menelaos – " No clue what to do with them. "Scavenge some staff weapons. Shoot anything that comes in here, except us. Got it?"

They nodded. Philemon was handing over Daniel's body to Teal'c, who was cradling it with care. Daniel's head lolled limply, at an impossibly uncomfortable angle.

"All right, sir?" Carter asked him.

"Find me a DHD part, and I will be. Check your targets. We've got a civilian kid loose out here somewhere."

"Iphigenia?" she asked. He nodded. "Yes sir. You can count on me."

"Yeah. Getting that."

They hit the door together, heading for the rest of the temple.

It kept nagging at the back of Jack's brain, and in that little nervous spot of skin where his hair brushed his collar...

Why hadn't Artemis come back?

He and Carter conducted a methodical sweep, concentrating first on the Throne Room; they flushed out four more Jaffa, but there was no sign of Iphigenia. Carter got a minor burn on one arm, he got some cuts from flying shrapnel when a marble block exploded; they came up with nothing of any practical use. In a room to the other side, they found a locked door that resisted MP5 fire so effectively Jack figured it had to be made of naquadah. Carter, ever resourceful, retrieved a staff weapon its deceased owner wouldn't need and fired, over and over, until the lock melted into slag.

Beyond *that* door was something mind-boggling.

"My God," Carter breathed, staring.

"Yeah, nobody ever told them size doesn't matter," Jack said, but even sarcasm fell flat measured against the scale of the room. It went on – nearly literally – forever. Gigantic, echoing, full of glowing silver stands with stones set in the top. Some were gray – offline, Jack guessed; most were lit up at the base, with stones showing either black or white. As he watched one of the stones swirled from white to gray, and the light switched off and powered down.

"It's the control room." Carter motioned helplessly with the muzzle of the rifle. "All these collars... thousands. Tens of thousands."

So many people, literally being manipulated from here. The technology was staggering. *Evil*, but staggering.

He shook himself out of it and said, "Find the off switch."

"What if I can't?"

"Then make one, I don't care how you – Carter!" He caught sight of a Jaffa – a really stealthy Jaffa – easing into the room with a staff weapon already aimed. He fired, and Carter joined him as she whirled around; the Jaffa flew backward, out of the doorway. Jack lunged for the wall and took a slanted look outside – more coming. Five or six that he could see. "Go, Carter! Get it done!"

She didn't waste her breath on an acknowledgement; she ran for the most obvious suspect, a big silver platform with a board laid out in front of it. As soon as she stepped on it, alarms went off, screaming like banshees. She ignored them and started pushing buttons.

Jack engaged the Jaffa, counted for three and saw the rest head off in full retreat just as an explosion shook through him, blew him off balance, and he saw Carter go flying across the room.

The whole console was slagged. What indicators were left on it flared white-hot, and shut down.

And one by one, so did the control stands, switching off like miles of failing fluorescents. Jack scrambled over to where Carter was rolling over to her hands and knees, dazed and bleeding, and helped her up. She wiped her cut lip and grinned.

"Off switch," she said. "Made one. C-4."

"Put yourself in for an extra vacation day, Captain. Let's go."

She was staggering a little but hell, so was he; his ankle couldn't keep it up, not even with the constant pound of adrenaline. He was going to crash, and then burn, and then his *ashes* were going to ignite.

"Still need to find the DHD thing," he said. "Go, Carter. I'll take this way."

They split up, searching the room; he spotted something in a thick glass case that looked familiar.

An elegant Greek statue of a goddess with a diadem of stars on her head, one foot on a rock, one hand lifted toward the sky. He'd seen larger versions of it shattered in pieces all over the city, but in the ones he remembered, she'd been holding a golden orb.

This one was holding a thick blue crystal.

"Carter!" he yelled, and smashed the glass. No booby traps he could find; he didn't have time for dicking around being careful, and reached in to snatch it up. It felt warm. Best of all, it didn't go off in his hand like a grenade. "Think I've got it!"

She wasn't moving. She was standing in the corner, looking down at something.

"Carter?" He waggled his hand and the prize.

"Take a look," she said, and he limped over to her.

Dead body. Female. Dressed in a short white silk robe, tied off with a gold belt. Cross-laced golden sandals.

A big blackened hole in the guts, and the whole front of the tunic was tacky with blood. Sightless dark eyes stared up at the ceiling, and there was blood trickling out of her mouth, too.

"She didn't make it to the sarcophagus," Carter said, and reached down to press fingers to skin. "Sir, she's been dead a while. She's cold."

"No," he shot back grimly. "The *host* is dead. The *snake* is on the loose."

And he had a damn good idea where to find it.

It wasn't quite like the last time he'd come back from the dead.

Daniel gagged in air, felt his lungs expand and had the same compressed drowning feeling he remembered, but this was colder, longer and more chilling.

Also much more painful. *Definitely* worse than taking a staff blast to the chest. He sat up, coughing, trying not to gag on the sticky lingering taste of the leaves, and saw Teal'c standing there, smiling and extending a hand to him.

"Daniel Jackson," he said. "It is good to see you."

"Yeah, you too," he said, and looked around the room. Their two Dark Company guys standing near the door, clutching Jaffa staff weapons and looking nervous. Little Iphigenia, standing in the corner...

His eyes skipped past her, and then came back fast. Iphigenia. Pylades's pretty, fragile little sister, dressed in pale silk, with no collar around her neck.

Her eyes flared white.

"Teal'c!" he yelled, and pointed; the Jaffa whirled, but before he could shoot he staggered, fell to his knees, and went down. *Hard.* Eyes rolling back in his head. Daniel reached to grab him, and toppled out of the sarcophagus. Overbalanced and fell on the floor over

Teal'c's unmoving body.

The Jaffa was still breathing, but definitely out. What in the *hell*… the two Greeks by the door were falling, too. Collapsing on the floor.

A cold touch at the back of Daniel's neck made him flinch and twist over on his back. Iphigenia's eyes flared cold white, and when she raised her right hand he saw it was armored with a Goa'uld hand device. The stone flared hot gold, then flushed to orange.

"I waited," she said, and extended her palm out toward his forehead. "I waited for you to live again, so that you could *suffer* for defying me."

"What did you do to – "

"*I* command here. They see what I wish them to see, they live and die at my whim. As do *you*!"

"Not any more." Daniel inched his way backward until his shoulders hit the cold inscribed metal of the sarcophagus.

"I have more mooncollars," she said. "And you will serve. And you will *run*, dog, until I say you may be allowed to die." She lunged, pressed the stone of the hand device directly against his forehead. He felt the violent heat of it pulsing against skin and bone, and froze. "You cannot kill me. I am eternal. I was immortal before your kind crawled from slime."

His hand slid along Teal'c's side and bumped cold metal. A familiar angular shape.

The Beretta came into his hand as if he'd called it, and he pressed it hard against her stomach.

"You're nothing but a parasite," Daniel whispered, "inside of a teenage girl. Back off or I'll kill you."

Iphigenia's lips curved into a vicious smile. "Then try. I'll take you in her place, to give me life. Would that not please you? You could at last know what your lover knew, at the end of her sorry life. You could know the glory of what it means to be Goa'uld…"

She broke off with a sudden, startled gasp, and the glowing, twinkling starlights on the wall behind the sarcophagus flickered. An explosive rumble shuddered through the floor…

… and Daniel heard, in the silence after, the soft metallic sound of a collar coming open. Then another. And a third.

He saw fear blaze hot in her eyes.

Her fear turned to hatred, lightning-quick, and she ignited the hand device against his skull.

He screamed. Fire ripped through him, then acid-tipped needles, and he knew it was going to kill him this time, rip everything inside of him into bloody shreds. One second. Two. Three. A million years of pain.

And then it stopped, and he opened his eyes to see Iphigenia scrambling backwards as Teal'c lunged. His collar dropped free as he moved; she dodged him and ran around the sarcophagus, only to be blocked by the two Dark Company men, who were coming out of their stupor, too.

Iphigenia – no, *Artemis* – held out her hand threateningly, staring at them in rising panic. Three staff weapons leveling on her now, and Daniel rolled painfully to his feet and pointed the Beretta, too.

She had nowhere to run.

"You will go from this place," she said, clinging to some shreds of haughty dignity. "I will permit you to leave."

"Surrender or die," Teal'c said. "Choose."

The soft, pretty face convulsed in fury, and she shouted the words back in a voice so distorted Daniel had trouble understanding them. "No! No, I will *not!* *I rule this world!*"

Two more shadows loomed at the door, both bearing MP5s. Jack and Sam, looking out of breath. They took up firing positions with smooth precision, and Jack's gaze darted fast to Daniel. "Hey. You okay?"

"Okay," he said. It was about all he could manage. His head felt as if he'd been pounded with a mallet. He was sure his nose was bleeding. "Artemis – has Iphigenia."

"I figured," Jack said. His eyes were bitter and furious. "Breaking news, Artie. Your Jaffa are toast. You don't control these people anymore. You can thank Captain Carter here for that..."

"I will chase you, and it will be a daylight hunt such as this city has never seen, my Jaffa will run you down and I will strip the skin from your bodies while you scream... I will slaughter these rebellious helots and demand tribute! *I will rule here!*"

"Over my dead body," Jack said. "Go ahead. Try it."

She raised her hand, and Teal'c broke from cover, sliding on the slick marble floor feet first to slam into her knee-high from behind. She collapsed with a surprised squeak, and he rolled her over, on her face, and pinned her down with one huge hand on her back. She thrashed and screamed furiously, clawing at the floor, and Daniel moved to kneel at her side to pull the device off of her arm.

He handed it to Jack, who took it between a thumb and forefinger like a dead rat, turned, and tossed it to Sam. She examined it for a few seconds, then shoved it in a pocket of her vest.

"Iphigenia!" Daniel looked up to see Pylades in the doorway – bruised, leaning on the support of a confiscated staff weapon, backed by what looked like more of the Dark Company. "What are you doing? What have you done to my sister?"

Daniel slowly got to his feet and went to meet him. "I'm sorry," he said. "Artemis – Artemis took her. We were too late."

Pylades pushed past him and knelt down, stroking Artemis's brown hair; she was still struggling against Teal'c's hold, screaming like a wild thing. Harsh, keening screams of madness. "Hush, sister – Iphigenia – don't – it's all right, it will be all right now…" The boy looked pleadingly at Daniel, tears in his eyes. "Can the evil be cast out of her?"

"No," Daniel said, and hated himself for it. "I'm sorry. I wish I could say she'd be all right, but – she's been possessed by the goddess. Artemis. We don't know how to take it out again."

"No. No, my sister is *Iphigenia*, she is good and kind and gentle – she saw that we would live, she is a Seer, she *saw* it, this can't be true – "

Teal'c said, "She will live for as long as the Goa'uld within her wishes. But she will not be your sister."

"But I have to take her home! I promised I would take her home. My father – my father said I was to protect her – " His voice went thin and dry. "Protect her."

"You did." Jack put a hand on the boy's shoulder and squeezed. "You tried."

Artemis screamed and fought the floor, pinned in place by Teal'c's strength.

"Sir?" Carter asked. She was back at the door, facing out at an angle, watching their backs, but she risked wide-eyed glances toward them. "What are we going to do with her?"

Daniel made it a question. "Take her back... ?"

"Not taking *this* back to Earth, Daniel. She's too dangerous."

Pylades looked up. "She is my sister, I will take her home, we will care for her there –"

"Pylades, this isn't your sister. This is a Goa'uld – a god." Jack's face spasmed in dislike when he said it. "She'll kill anybody she gets her hands on. She may pretend to be your sister until she gets what she wants, but she'll kill and keep on killing, and sooner or later, you're going to have to deal with her as she is, not as you remember her."

"You mean you want to kill her."

Nobody seemed to want to answer that. Daniel realized the pistol was still in his sweaty hand. He slid it back into the holster and scrubbed his palm convulsively against his trouser leg.

Jack sighed. "Carter. Give her a shot, strongest thing you've got. See if you can knock her out."

Carter darted over, took out the medkit and selected from the color-coded array; she pressed the hypo against the girl's arm, and within a few seconds Artemis stopped screaming and writhing. She didn't stop talking, though. Her words came slow and deliberate, but they still came, promising death and destruction and tortures that Daniel had only read about in historical texts. Teal'c hauled her up and pinned her hands behind her. Artemis lolled her head drunkenly to one side, and under the maenad's veil of hair her eyes were glassy and sharp, Goa'uld.

And then they slowly slid closed, and she collapsed limp in Teal'c's arms.

"The Goa'uld will resist your drugs," Teal'c said. "There is not much time."

Daniel felt a lurch that might have been horror, might have been hope; the two were getting strangely mixed, here. "The sarcophagus," he blurted. "What if we put her in the sarcophagus? It's where Ra slept. Maybe..."

"Teal'c?" Jack interrupted. "Can she get out of it?"

"If the mechanism is disabled, she will not be able to open the device from the inside."

"And she'll sleep while she's inside, right?"

Teal'c studied the girl and didn't answer. Daniel felt cold crawl up his spine. *What if she stays awake? What if it's just one long, unending imprisonment in the dark...?*

Jack read him like a book. "Daniel," he said quietly. "It's this or..." Or a bullet, he meant.

Daniel closed his eyes and nodded.

Teal'c pressed the button to open the sarcophagus.

"Oh God," Daniel murmured. Artemis was whispering in slow but rising words. "She's waking up."

"I gave her enough to put down a horse, sir," Sam said. "Another dose – I don't know. It could kill her anyway."

Jack mutely shook his head, staring at the sarcophagus. The wings grated open.

Teal'c laid the girl's slender body down in the brightly lit interior.

"No!" Pylades lunged forward as the wings began to close. "No, you can't, she's alive, my sister is alive – the evil must come out of her! I can't just abandon her...!"

Jack grabbed him from behind and held him still.

Just before the wings closed, Artemis's eyes snapped open, and pulsed with Goa'uld fire, and she fastened a hating stare on Daniel.

She said, "If you would find your wife, look in the gardens. I have seen her there." An evil, malicious smile. It didn't belong on the face of a child.

He took a step back, shocked, and then the sarcophagus sealed over her.

Teal'c pressed buttons until they glowed a steady red. "It is locked, O'Neill."

Pylades put his hand on the living tomb of his sister, and wept.

Daniel turned, heading for the exit; he heard Jack call his name but ignored it. Sam held out a hand to stop him. He moved around her and hit the door at a run.

Dead Jaffa in the throne room, nothing moving. He kept going.

"Daniel!" Sam caught up with him and grabbed at his shoulder to yank him to a stop. "Where the hell are you going?"

"You heard. Sha're could be here – "

"No. Daniel, no."

He broke free and kept moving. Sam activated her radio; whatever Jack said, Daniel guessed the end of it was an order to stay on his trail and keep him from getting killed. He supposed there might still be Jaffa around. He didn't particularly care.

The next room held three living people, all dressed in black robes, wandering around looking stunned. Raw red marks on their necks where collars had been. Daniel paused next to a window and saw that there were torches out there in the dark, groups moving toward the Acropolis.

Coming to destroy their gods.

They ran into the Dark Company on the way. "Daniel!" It wasn't Sam's voice this time; he turned and was caught up in a bruising strongman's hug, and Eseios smacked him on the back hard enough to bruise a rib. "You live. And your friends?"

"So far," he agreed. The man was grinning. His people were behind him, or at least most of them; many were holding the hands of their wives, their children, their lovers. Briseis had come, too. She stepped forward to fold Daniel in a much gentler embrace.

"Artemis?" she asked.

"Won't be hurting you any more," Daniel said. "You're free. You can go home now."

"You see?" She smiled luminously at him. "Your plan was not stupid. I believed in you."

Eseios looked put out.

"No, it was stupid," Daniel said seriously. "It just worked… do you know where the gardens would be?"

"Gardens," Eseios repeated, and exchanged a look with one of his men. "Adaios went that way. He will show you. But Daniel – "

"Thanks." He extended his hand. Eseios took it and pulled him into another hug and back slap.

He followed the Dark Company soldier out of the room, Sam shadowing his heels. They went through several rooms, these looking abandoned; treasures in every one, but Daniel kept his eyes straight forward, on the back of his guide.

I have seen your wife in the garden. Artemis had pretended to be Sha're. She must have seen her…

The Dark Company soldier – Adaios? – stopped and turned to them. "I went no farther," he said. "You should not, either. This is a place the gods have deserted."

He walked away, and Daniel moved to the door. It was shut, but the handle moved smoothly in his hand...

The stench hit him first. He choked and covered his mouth and nose, and behind him he heard Sam do the same.

Garden. Maybe it had been a garden, once. All that grew here now were the dead, piles of them, stacks of decaying flesh and disarticulated bone.

"Oh God," Sam whispered, and grabbed his shoulder. "No, Daniel. *Stop.*"

I have seen your wife in the garden.

He turned and looked at her, and whatever was in his face, she let go. Her eyes glittered with tears for a second, and then she blinked and was Captain Carter again, cool and military and professional.

"All right," she said. "We'll look."

They weren't alone for long. Eseios came, and Briseis, and the Dark Company. Pylades, still pale with grief for his lost sister. A flood of people Daniel didn't know, and a few he recognized. Alsiros, still stained with old blood, trembling and pale. Two others from that doomed Sikyon group. Each took Sha're's picture in hand and looked at it, then murmured prayers and moved away to look into the dead faces. Cries echoed through the still-beautiful marble of the building, as friends or lovers or family found their lost ones.

"Let me see," a rough voice said, and Daniel looked up, numbed, to see an old man standing in front of him, hand extended. He studied Sha're's picture for a moment, then showed it to the women and children gathered around him. At least twenty of them. He'd brought his whole refugee camp, at least those enough strong to walk.

"Laonides," he said.

"Daniel. Like me, you are a survivor." Laonides looked pleased with himself. He gestured for the children clustered nearby to look at the corpses; Daniel felt a surge of misery, and reached out to grab him by the robe.

"*No.* Take them out of here."

"These children? They have seen worse."

"I don't care." Daniel focused on the man's eyes. "You're a survivor. If you want to survive five minutes more, you'll take them away from here. *Right now.*"

Laonides studied him, face settling into a frown, and nodded. He clapped his hands and told them to leave the garden, and the women and children hurried to obey him. Eseios was watching. He and Laonides exchanged a flat look that sparked like crossed swords.

"Still the hunter, aren't you?" Laonides said to Daniel. "Artemis chose better than any of us like to admit."

"My friend told you to get out." Eseios walked toward him. "Bring your women and children to my camp at dawn."

"And if I don't?"

"Then Daniel is right: you won't survive this Hunt." He showed teeth. "And I *am* a hunter, old man. Black stone or no. Make no mistake about it."

Laonides bowed slightly, and walked away. He stopped to look at a corpse with dark hair near the bottom of a pile of bodies, moved her hair and shrugged.

"One woman is very like another," he said, and looked at Daniel directly. "Call her gone, boy, and move on. You can't spend your life staring at the dead."

Sam's hand on his shoulder was all that kept him from going for Laonides' throat, but then the gray misery closed in again, and there were bodies to move.

Sha're wasn't there.

He didn't find her.

"How many?" Jack asked, as Carter took a weary seat next to him at the campfire. She'd scrubbed with disinfectant soap, both skin and clothes, and looked clean but exhausted. She propped her chin on raised knees and folded arms.

"Six hundred eighty-nine," she said. "But it's not over. They're finding bodies in half the Acropolis. Some date back several hundred years, according to Daniel. Pylades was right: this place was a tomb. It's appalling."

He hated to ask it, but... "No sign of Sha're, right?"

"None." Carter fluffed her damp hair absently. "I don't think he really expected there to be, but… "

"Had to try."

"Yes sir."

He handed her an MRE. "Country Captain Chicken," he said. "Your favorite."

She managed a wan smile, ate about three mouthfuls and yawned. Dawn was on the way, coming fast, and Jack felt the drag, too. Even Teal'c had settled down into some kind of zen yoga thing.

Daniel was still walking, out there in the darkness. Jack got up and went looking.

He found him standing on an outcropping of stone, surrounded by thin, whispery pines; overhead, the moon floated huge and white and – for once – innocent. The ruins of the Great City spread out from the base of the hill in broken concentric circles.

"Hey," Jack ventured. He wasn't sure the younger man even heard him. "Getting late."

Daniel nodded. He looked exhausted. "This place. It was beautiful once, don't you think?"

"Whatever. Get some sleep."

"Why? We're going back tomorrow. I'll sleep when I'm home." Daniel's lips tightened. "When I'm lying down on clean sheets, anyway."

"Yeah… about that, listen, how's the house-hunting going? I'm only asking because I think General Hammond wants those VIP quarters back, or he's going to start charging nightly rates. Call it the SGC Hilton."

"Don't."

Jack leaned against a convenient pine trunk. "Don't what?"

Daniel shook his head. "Don't patronize me."

Right. Jack crossed his arms and studied the toes of his boots. "Fine. She wasn't here. She was never here."

"I know that."

"We saved these people." No answer. "We can send them home." Nothing. "Daniel… "

"Pylades wants us to take a message back," Daniel said. "He's not going home. He's staying here to guard his sister. Eseios and Briseis aren't going, either. They think they can rebuild something. I think they're afraid their families wouldn't be too happy about a marriage made in hell, and apparently there's a real problem with intermarrying between planets. They're not the only ones... Jack, what if the tribute planets don't believe us? What if they keep sending people?"

"Then I think Eseios and Pylades will send them right back, with a nice little note. It'll change. Things change."

"Do they?" Daniel's glasses caught moonlight. "Maybe. That's something to hope for, anyway."

They stood together in silence for a while, and then Daniel said, "How's the ankle?"

"Miserable. Thanks for asking. Hurts like hell."

"You should be sitting down."

"And yet, tramping around in the dark after you." Jack debated it, and then he decided to go ahead and say it. "Laonides is a total bastard, but he's right about one thing. You can't look for Sha're in every face you see, living or dead. You know that, right?"

Daniel sucked in a deep, wounded breath, then let it out in a cloud of silver.

"Come. Sit, if you're not going to sleep." Jack led the way at a slow, exhausted hobble. "I've got cookies."

"What kind?"

"Chocolate chip."

"Okay." Daniel took one last look at the moonlight, and followed.

On the way back to the Stargate the next day, they had an escort of more than a hundred. It kept growing as they moved through the city; Eseios picked up an irritating habit of yelling out an exaggerated account of their battles to draw people out of hiding.

There were fallen collars all over the streets. Somebody had even tried to burn a pile of them, to no effect; Jack thought it was a pretty good idea. Maybe staff blasts would melt the things.

They found Artemis's black-painted Death Glider landed in a pile of rubble, a couple of miles down the road; the hatch was open, and one dead Jaffa lay nearby. Decoy. She'd known they were coming to the Acropolis that night. They'd been lucky, Jack realized; lucky she was crazy, and that Daniel was even crazier.

It was, strangely, a much shorter march from that point on. "Down-hill," Jack observed. He was feeling pretty good, since he'd finally allowed Carter to hit him with a fat dose of painkillers. The ankle-throb had subsided to an occasional, dreamy pulse.

"That, and we've got a construction crew," Daniel pointed out; the crowd had surged ahead of them, moving stones, clearing streets of rubble. Eseios worked as construction boss, cheerfully tossing out instructions and orders, adding his muscle-bound strength to moving the larger obstructions. "Kind of nice, to see them working together."

It wouldn't last, Jack thought, but he kept it to himself. Brotherly love and cooperation never did. Still, if Eseios could forge some kind of community out of this, some kind of purpose... maybe it wouldn't ever be the Great City again, but it'd be a pretty okay one.

Midday arrived with picnics in the streets. People met, talked, exchanged memories of home. They were separating into tribes already, Jack noticed – drawn by common backgrounds. Well, he couldn't judge them. He sat with his own tribe, all uniformed in olive drab, and finished up the last of the rations.

By the time they made the Stargate it had moved from picnic to parade to street festival, with singing and clapping and dancing; kids yelled and waved rags and chased each other around, if they had the strength. Even the thinnest looked just a little healthier.

And the sun seemed to shine harder, just for a while.

Carter dropped the control crystal into the DHD and made some adjustments, then conferred with Daniel for a few minutes. They started with the 'gate address for Sikyon.

It took the rest of the afternoon, and well into the evening, to get everyone moved out who was planning to go.

By full dark, they were standing with a hundred or so, including Briseis and Eseios and most of the Dark Company.

"Moonrise," Briseis said, watching it happen. "I will be able to tell my baby stories of a time it was not beautiful, to see it come."

"Wait a while on the storytelling," Jack advised. "And keep an eye on the sarcophagus."

"It will not open," she promised. "We will see to that. And I think her brother will come to accept it, in time."

Eseios handed over something from a bag at his side… Jack made out the metal shape in the dim light, and the Velcro fastenings.

"Ah. Was going to ask about that," he said, and slid the GDO on his wrist, cinching it tight. "Take care of these people."

"Take care of yours," Eseios said, and offered his hand. Jack gripped it. "I will see you again, Jack O'Neill."

Daniel went to the DHD and started to enter the coordinates back to the SGC. Jack stopped him with an outstretched hand.

"What?"

"We're not going home," he said. "One more thing to do."

"Okay… ?"

He motioned Eseios over, and asked for a favor.

When the wormhole opened, it opened to Chalcis.

The airport looked absolutely the same: full of chattering travelers, government worker bees, dark-tunic security. Jack clumped down the steps to the first security tunic he saw, grabbed it by a bunched handful of cloth, and said, "Acton. Get him. *Now.*"

"Jack – " Daniel was watching him anxiously, with a frown grooved deep. Carter wasn't second-guessing him, but he saw the doubt in her eyes, too. Lots of civilians here. Lots of collaterals to be damaged.

The security man, eyes wide, ran to somebody who must have been a superior, who dispatched a courier. Jack led SG-1 to the shade of the bar, thumped his MP5 down on the table, and sat down with a sigh. Painkillers were a fond memory. In fact, he was just about down to zero on every level, including patience.

"Jack, what are we doing here?" Daniel asked. "Shouldn't we get back, report to General Hammond…?"

"Sure," Jack agreed, and held up a hand to snap fingers at the bartender. "Only we don't need to go home to do that."

"We don't?"

Jack keyed his tac vest radio. "SG-2, this is SG-1, over." No response. "Sierra Golf Two Niner, this is Sierra Golf One Niner, respond."

And then the radio blurted static, and Major Dave Dixon's voice came back, clipped and warm with relief. "Sierra Golf One Niner, this is Sierra Golf Two Niner, and pardon my French, Jack, but where the *hell* have you been?"

"Oh, here and there, Dix. We're hanging at the airport. Join us."

"On our way."

Jack clicked off. His team was staring at him in varying degrees of surprise and confusion.

"SOP," he said. "Backup plan, remember? SG-2's been looking for us."

"How did you know they'd still be here?" Carter asked. "A search and rescue mission should have already determined we were gone, nothing to rescue..."

"It's Dixon," Jack shrugged. "He's a digger. No matter what kind of story Acton cooked up, Dixon would have smelled a rat."

"But he's acting against orders!"

"It's *Dixon*. And he owes me a couple, Captain."

She shook her head. The bartender, who was looking scared to death, finally ventured over and dropped off four glasses at the table. Daniel picked his up and turned it in his fingers, then sipped at the contents.

So did Teal'c, who put it back down. "There is alcohol," he said.

"Damn right," Jack said, and looked up at the sound of booted feet running outside. "Yo! Dixon!"

"Colonel." Major Dixon pushed in and shook his hand, then nodded to each of them in turn. He was a big man, with sharp dark eyes and an off-kilter smile. "Knew you'd be back, sir."

"Major, your orders were to report back to the SGC..." Jack checked his watch. "Sixteen hours ago, by my count."

"Technical difficulties, sir. With the Stargate."

"That would be the Stargate they're currently sending people through right now, out there in the airport...?"

"It's an intermittent problem, sir. Our dialing coordinates don't seem to want to sync up properly." Dixon's bright eyes stayed steady. "Sorry to say it, sir, but you guys look like crap."

"Must look better than we feel... did you talk to a snaky little bastard named Acton? Big head cheese guy? About so tall, gray hair...?"

Dixon's geek – Baldwin? Balinsky? – cleared his throat and said,

"I did, sir. He claimed that you stayed for a couple of days, parted on good terms, and decided to visit one of the other worlds in the Confederacy. He claimed not to know which one. We spent a couple of days traveling around looking before we came back here." He nodded at Daniel. "Dr. Jackson."

"Dr. Balinsky."

"Isn't this place amazing?… You saw the Acropolis? I mean, what a thrill! It's just…" Balinsky had the light of a true convert. Daniel's answering stare was darker. Quieter.

"Yes," he said. "It's amazing. And I've seen… a couple of them now."

When Balinsky opened his mouth to ask details, Dixon cut him off. "Where'd you go, sir, if you don't mind my asking?"

"Debrief later. I need a favor."

"Anything, Colonel."

Jack smiled, and explained things.

Half an hour later, they heard the sound of tramping footsteps. Acton must have taken the express chariot from the city, or he'd been close; he and his cronies appeared in the doorway, and Acton's expression wiped completely blank at the sight of SG-1 sitting at the table, sipping tropical drinks with SG-2.

Dixon slammed down his drink with the ease of a man who'd been in plenty of saloons, and SG-2 moved into position, surrounding Acton's bodyguards.

"Hey there," Jack said. He stood up, and SG-1 came with him as a unit. "Got something to show you. Let's take a little walk, Acton."

"I do not understand your language – " Acton began coldly, and then realized he did. Dixon looked confused. He and Balinsky exchanged a look. "You have learned to speak well, stranger."

"Actually not. But whatever." Jack grabbed hold of his shoulder and steered him out of the bar. "I'd like you to pay a little diplomatic visit. And then I'm going to want you to drop around to Mycenae and Delphi and Sikyon, and get *them* to pay a little diplomatic visit."

Acton was still trying to pretend he had the upper hand as they emerged in the bright sunlight. Daniel darted ahead with Teal'c and Carter behind him, more or less gently moved the airport employee doing the dialing out of the way, and entered coordinates. The wormhole activated, belched, settled.

"Diplomatic visit?" Acton said slowly. "To… your world? I am not prepared…"

"No need. You're not going to my world. Oh, and you won't need any food, or any water, or any clothes." Jack walked him up the steps with an arm around his shoulders. All of the warmth dropped out of his voice, and his hand on Acton's shoulder blade gripped hard enough to bruise. "You know, kind of like the way you sent all of those *other* people through here to die. You're going where you sent *us*. Have a nice trip."

"No – " Acton must have known; his eyes were wide and horror-stricken. "No! You cannot do this! She demands tribute, we have sent it – I was not chosen! What do you want of me?"

Jack just smiled, and said, "Say hi to your goddess for me."

And then he put a boot in Acton's ass and sent him flailing through the wormhole. When he turned back, SG-2 was facing out, MP5s aimed at the security guys, who were standing with spears half-raised and looking worried.

"No problem," he assured them. "Fact-finding mission. He'll be back."

The gate collapsed in a flicker of blue.

"Well, sir, that was sure fun," Dixon said. "Can we go home now? Because I'm overdue picking up the kid from camp."

He sounded casual, but Dave Dixon was anything but. Jack nodded to Daniel, who entered – *finally* – the coordinates for home, and hit the red ball to activate the cycle.

He sent the GDO code, motioned to Dix to send his as well, just in case, and they took a short trip through a long, long wormhole.

Infirmary.

Doc Warner – who wasn't as bad as most of the doctors Jack had encountered, in his years of service – had prescribed him bed rest for two days, and painkillers that Jack had decided, after all, to do without. He read magazines. Made hand puppets out of spare socks. Kind of enjoyed watching his bruises fade.

When he woke up on the second day, he found Daniel sitting next to him, reading a book that looked like it was written in Greek.

"Hey," Jack said, and cleared his throat. "Reading anything good?"

"*Iphigenia in Tauris*," Daniel said. "Euripides."

"So, reading anything good... Never mind. How's Carter? Teal'c?"

"Sam had some kind of allergic reaction to the drinks back on Chalcis," Daniel said, and his eyebrows went up. *Way* up. "Ah, delayed reaction. Didn't really hit her until we were in the debrief."

"Is she – "

"She's fine. Embarrassed, that's all." Jack made a *come on, give* gesture. "She climbed up on the table."

"You're kidding. And?"

"Well..." Daniel drew the word out to four syllables. "I really don't think I should say."

Jack was enchanted. "Oh, now you *know* you have to say."

"Jack."

"C'mon, Daniel, a little starved for entertainment here... give. What happened?"

In typical Daniel fashion, he backed up and steered around the question. "Teal'c got her down, brought her to Doc Warner, and he gave her some kind of test. Turned out that she had a specific reaction to some kind of fruit in the drink. He gave her a shot, she was fine."

"Carter did something embarrassing, and I *slept through it?*"

"Apparently."

"Please *God* tell me you're kidding."

"Would I do that?" Daniel had the innocent look down pat. When he got like that, there was no way to tell truth from fiction. Jack glared at him and made a mental note to check with Teal'c. And Carter. She could run, no way could she hide.

"Anything else?" Jack asked.

"General Hammond agreed to send a shipment through to Pylades and Eseios. Food, medical supplies, clothing, blankets – refugee supplies. Dixon and SG-2 took it through. Apparently, Eseios already has rebuilding plans. Quite an operation, so they say." Daniel put the book aside and rubbed his hands together. "I made it very clear that what Sam and I did, taking the poison... it wasn't by your order, Jack."

Jack sat up, swung his legs over the side of the bed, and stood up, testing his ankle. Warner had put it into a huge, clumsy black boot, pumped up with air; he felt like the Michelin Man. At least it matched the BDUs.

"Yeah, been meaning to say something about that," he said without meeting Daniel's eyes. "If you *ever* pull that crap again – "

Daniel didn't answer, or at least, not directly. "Dr. Warner wants us to talk to some kind of psychologist."

"Screw that."

"When I said *wants us to*, it was really more of an order."

"Not doing it." This wasn't the kind of thing that he could talk about, except with... with his team. "How about the four of us and a pitcher of beer instead?"

Daniel's eyebrows went up and stayed there. "I'll give it a try."

Jack jerked a thumb at the phone on the wall. "Call Teal'c and Carter."

It took more like three pitchers, but eventually the talking started. And it didn't stop.

Author's note

Some elements of this story are taken from Euripides' brilliant play *Iphigenia in Tauris*, which Daniel is reading in the infirmary. References to the team's visit to P3X-595, and to Captain Carter's removal of… something… can be found in the *Stargate: SG1* episode "Emancipation."

Anything screwed up in the course of this story is entirely the fault of the author, as she had excellent references, assistance, and genuine military types to tell her when she was in danger of going wrong. Not to mention outstanding editorial help.

Thanks for stepping through the Stargate with me.

Julie Fortune

STARGÅTE
SG·1

ALL NEW MISSIONS
ALL NEW ADVENTURES

VISIT OUR WEBSITE
WWW.STARGATENOVELS.COM
FOR MORE INFORMATION

STARGATE SG-1: A MATTER OF HONOR

by Sally Malcolm

COMING SOON!

The whispered conversation of his friends was the only noise in the vast chamber as Jack stalked through the forest of pillars, searching for a way out that didn't involve a return trip through last year's Halloween special. *Clutching white fingers in the dark, coming out of nowhere...* How the hell had they managed to creep up on him like that? No sound. Not a single sound.

He shivered; the place gave him the creeps. The whole damn city stank of decay and something worse. There was evil here. Not just the ancient evil of the palace's creator, but something else. A sense of dread that was all too alive.

Keeping his P90 raised, he turned a slow three-sixty as he walked. Shadows streamed out from the pillars, wide and slovenly in the diffuse light cast by the gaudy ceiling. But there was nothing there, no monsters hiding in the darkness. No ghosts.

He glanced up at the mosaic that was so enthralling Daniel. The face of the god wasn't familiar; it didn't wear the neat, trimmed beard of an urban sophisticate or possess the flat, dead eyes of a psychopath. Jack looked away and banished the thought – memory was a distraction. The danger was here, not in the past. His throat still burned from the fingers of the man – creature – who'd attacked him on the stairs. He had no desire to run into Skinny Legs and his creeping compadres again.

He checked his watch – six minutes left. It wasn't nearly long enough for Carter to get what she needed, but he was too antsy to lurk in this maze of shadows longer than absolutely--

A scuffing sound behind him yanked his heart up into his throat. Spinning around, finger on trigger, he scanned the shadows and pillars. He didn't breathe, straining to hear over the hammering in his chest.

Nothing.

Damn it! The shadows were deep here, back towards the wall of the chamber, dark and deep. Tension ran across his skin, crawling up onto his scalp as he backed slowly away from the ghost of a sound. Head towards the light, towards the guys, towards--

Fingers brushed his shoulder. He jerked around so hard he almost lost his balance. Only twenty years in the field kept him from firing. A figure, half lost in darkness, stood before him. *Baal! Shit.*

Fear clouded his eyes, suffocated him.

Baal!

His hands shook, his voice was dry and useless. But he stood his ground and faced the nightmare that had haunted him ever since he'd--

Wait...

Sluggishly, reason clawed through the panic. Baal hiding alone in shadows? No Jaffa? Baal dressed in Kinahhi robes? Like lightening in slow-motion, realization struck. *It's not him.*

"Get out where I can see you," Jack rasped, "or I'll put a bullet in your head."

The figure moved, tall and slender, but not him. Not *him*. And not white like the creatures who'd attacked them on the stairs. It was a man, and as he emerged from the shadows Jack's breath caught in surprise. "Quadesh? What the hell--"

The Kinahhi councilor raised a narrow finger to his lips and whispered. "No one can know I am here, Colonel O'Neill. My life depends upon it."

Still sick with receding panic Jack lowered his voice, but not his weapon, and said, "You've got thirty seconds before I start yelling. You've been following us. Why?"

A hint of a smile wavered across the man's face. "You did not really think you could evade our security so easily, Colonel?" When Jack didn't respond, Quadesh simply shrugged and added, "I hid your escape from my superiors. Had I not done so, you would all now be in custody. Or worse."

"And you did that because...?"

"Because I believe I can trust you, Colonel. And I think you may already suspect that all is not well here on Kinahhi."

"We got an inkling," Jack admitted, still staring at the man over the barrel of his gun. He didn't feel like lowering it. "Why don't you keep talking?"

Quadesh paused, as if marshalling an inner strength. At length he appeared to make a decision, both hands twisting around a slim metal tube he clutched like a talisman. "Although the Security Council talks of dissenters, Colonel, there is no real dissent on Kinahhi. No freedom of thought or expression. The *sheh'fet* sees to that – anyone harboring seditious thoughts simply disappears."

A sickeningly familiar scenario. "Disappears where?"

Quadesh stilled, hands tightening around the slim tube. "Here, Colonel. They are brought here."

Holy crap. His mind raced back to the creatures, hungry and violent, on the stairs. "What happens to them?"

"I do not know. But none return. I suspect they are killed."

He was probably right, it was the MO of every tin-pot dictator he'd ever encountered. Tortured, dehumanized. Then murdered. Was that who they'd encountered on the stairs? Escapees? Inmates? He lowered his weapon, slightly. "Why are you telling me this?"

Stepping forward, Quadesh's voice dropped. "So that you can tell your people. Stop them from signing the treaty with Kinahhi and instead help us to gain our freedom!"

Us? An image flashed into Jack's mind; the woman cradling her lost child, drowning in grief. "You one of them?" he demanded coldly. "Do you plant bombs? Kill kids?"

Quadesh's face paled. "No! No, you misunderstand Colonel. I have never--" Closer still, his amber eyes were full of fear. "This is the first time I have dared to act against the Security Council. I am not a murderer, Colonel O'Neill. I swear to you." And then, hastily, he held out the narrow tube he'd been clutching. "Please, take this as a gesture of my goodwill."

Reluctant to let go of his weapon, Jack studied the tube suspiciously. "What is it?"

"What you need," Quadesh insisted, a hint of a smile returning. "It is why you have come here, Colonel."

Jack raised his eyes. "And why have we come here?"

"You wish to rescue your friends from a planet trapped within the event horizon of a black hole." The hand proffering the metal cylinder began to tremble. "You wish to understand our gravitational technology."

And how the hell did he know all that? "Says who?"

Quadesh bit lightly on his lower lip, eyes shifting as if considering his options. And then his narrow shoulders lifted in an apologetic shrug. "Your Ambassador."

"Crawford?"

The Councilor nodded. "He told Councilor Damaris that he'd overheard you talking with Major Carter."

That night when he couldn't sleep, out in the courtyard. "The rat-bastard!"

"It is all here," Quadesh promised. "All the schematics held in the Kinahhi database – a copy, of course. They will not know it is missing and it is more than your Major Carter will glean here." He glanced over his shoulder, pushing the tube towards him. "I must go before I am missed. Please, Colonel, consider my plea."

His lips suddenly dry, Jack stared at the tube. Dare he take it? Could he live with himself if he did? The Security Council had already refused to trade the technology, so taking the schematics was tantamount to stealing from a would-be ally. It went against everything he stood for, everything he'd fought for when he'd brought down Maybourne's rogue NID agents who'd been doing the exact same thing.

And Kinsey! If he got wind of this it would be the end of Colonel Jack O'Neill. And if Jack went down, he had no illusions about the rest of SG-1. Kinsey was after their blood.

But none of that changed the fact that Henry Boyd and his team were still out there, still lingering in terror on the point of death. Or that this was probably their best chance of getting home... *And nobody gets left behind.*

Letting go of his gun, he reached out and let his fingers close slowly over the cool metal tube. A glimmer of satisfaction passed through Quadesh's eyes as he stepped backward.

"Thank you, Colonel." He bowed, hands pressed over his heart. "The people of Kinahhi thank you."

Jack said nothing; he hadn't done it for the people of Kinahhi and he didn't deserve their thanks. "I need a way out," he said by way of a reply. "Not the stairs."

Quadesh nodded and pointed a slender finger towards a thick pillar standing at the far end of the chamber. "In there is a conveyor. It will take you to the surface."

Jack gave a curt nod. "I take it we won't be discussing this again?"

"We will not," Quadesh agreed. "I just pray that I was not seen leaving the city." Then, with a short, nervous nod he turned and hurried into the shadows. Jack watched as he touched something on the mosaic surface of a pillar and a door slid silently open. Quadesh looked back once and gave a half-hearted gesture of farewell before he stepped inside and disappeared.

In the silence that followed, Jack hefted the slim tube in his hand. It was light, weighed almost nothing. And yet it was heavy with danger, possibility and risk.

Coming Soon!
Available from www.stargatenovels.com
Register at the website for email
updates and special offers

TRIAL BY FIRE

By Sabine C. Bauer
Price: £5.99
ISBN: 0-9547343-0-0

Trial by Fire, **the first in the new series of Stargate SG-1 novels**, follows the team as they embark on a mission to Tyros, an ancient society teetering on the brink of war.

A pious people, the Tyreans are devoted to the Canaanite deity, Meleq. When their spiritual leader is savagely murdered during a mission of peace, they beg SG-1 for help against their sworn enemies, the Phrygians.

Initially reluctant to get involved, the team has no choice when Colonel Jack O'Neill is abducted. O'Neill soon discovers his only hope of escape is to join the ruthless Phrygians – if he can survive their barbaric initiation rite.

As Major Samantha Carter, Dr Daniel Jackson and Teal'c race to his rescue, they find themselves embroiled in a war of shifting allegiances, where truth has many shades and nothing is as it seems.

And, unbeknownst to them all, an old enemy is hiding in the shadows…

Get the first book in the new Stargate SG-1 series by going to www.stargatenovels.com or order it directly from the publishers by sending a cheque or money order (currency: GB Pounds made payable to "Fandemonium") to: Stargate Novels, Fandemonium Books, PO Box 795A, Surbiton KT5 8YB, United Kingdom.

<u>Price</u>
UK orders: £7.30 (£5.99 + £1.31 P&P)
South Africa, Australia and New Zealand orders: £8.70 (£5.99 + £2.71 P&P). Not available outside these territories.

Or check your local bookshop – available on special order if they are out of stock.